Last Rites

Charles Beagley

First published 2018

Publishing Partner: Accentia Design
www.accentia.com.au

Prepared for publication by: Accentia Design
Cover artwork, typesetting : Michelle Hessing
Cover design: Charles Beagley & Michelle Hessing

A Cataloguing-in-Publication record is available from the
National Library of Australia.

ISBN: 978-0-6482776-1-3 (Paperback)
ISBN: 978-0-6482776-0-6 (ePub)

In special memory of

Charles Beagley
18 June 1936 - 25 April 2018

You wrote a lifetime of stories, secretly woven with snippets
from your own childhood adventures and growing up in
England - memories and moments of your life.

You achieved something most people only ever dream of.
Your love of storytelling and writing live on in
the pages of the books we created together.
Thank you for trusting me to join you on the journey
– even though it was all too brief, you gave me something
I'd thought I'd lost... purpose.

MICHELLE HESSING

AUTHOR'S NOTE

Following the completion of 'Carter's Boys' Inspector Jack Hammond continues to plague me. I thought I had put this wily old bird to rest, but it seems he has other ideas. He still lurks there in the back of my mind, digging into issues that do not concern him; prompting me to imagine how he would handle a situation. Such visitations, according to psychics, are a sign of a restless spirit.

Someone who just will not cross over.

I took great pains to resolve Jack Hammond's unsatisfactory end. After the fiasco of his last case, I awarded him a commendation, and promoted him so that he could retire on a Superintendent's salary. Unfortunately, in retirement, I left him to the mercy of his wife Marjory and a bunch of the most eccentric characters you could ever wish on anyone.

I suppose, if I was ever to achieve an undisturbed night's sleep again, I'll just have to resurrect him, and give him something interesting to occupy his restless spirit.

Such as two unresolved murders.

The trouble is, I have this awful feeling I am about to regret it.

LAST RITES

PROLOGUE

Reverend Peter Jay looked upon every day as a memorable one; serving the Lord in his capacity as the Vicar of a small community called Lower Cheedam. Yet today, October 10, 1985 would dominate his memory for some time to come. It marked the death of his favourite actor, Orson Welles and the last hours of a desperate man.

He had little recollection of his early morning fifty-five-minute drive across country, following an urgent phone call from the Warden of Hatchwood Maximum Security Prison. It was a comparatively new facility; unlike the granite and wrought-iron nineteenth century bastions he was familiar with when he visited 'Normal Villains': a guard's expression he was not familiar with.

The overwhelming abundance of tiled floors and gloss-painted walls compared it more to an animal compound than a human establishment. Its benign expanse bereft of any humanity; no more than an antiseptic warren for the outcasts of society.

Usually he visited the dangerously mental wing on a Thursday each week, spending most of his visiting period with a terminally ill inmate called Samuel Alluche. Although born in England, his accent led the Vicar to suspect Samuel's parents were originally from Normandy. His thoughts were preoccupied with the past months spent with this man, attempting to unravel his real life

1

experiences from the bizarre manifestations of a dying man.

The warden had a special reason for asking the reverend to call this morning. According to the prison doctor, Samuel had deteriorated overnight, and was not expected to last the day. During the lucid moments between his drug induced ramblings he apparently left particular instructions regarding his Last Rites.

Once passed through the numerous security gates and into the long corridor servicing the worst of the mentally disturbed inmates, the Vicar was not unduly surprised when he was re-directed from the hospital wing to the cell-block. Samuel Alluche had chosen to spend his last hours in the place he had come to know as home and felt secure in.

At the end of the cream and brown corridor he at last caught sight of the doctor talking to an orderly and guard outside Samuel's cell. They appeared concerned with the papers on a clipboard as the doctor looked up and saw him.

"Good morning Reverend," the young man in a short white jacket called out on seeing him approach, "good timing... by the looks of him he won't last long now," he continued in his unattached manner. Samuel was just old meat to him.

As the sullen guard walked back to his position the first thing that caught the Vicar's eye was a syringe on a chromium trolley beside Samuel's bed.

"Have you given him anything yet doctor," he questioned, concerned about his awareness of the circumstances, and the Last Rites ceremony he had to perform.

"No Reverend... just a painkiller. Although I hardly think it matters in his case."

The Vicar looked alarmed at his suggestion.

"Hardly matters! He's a human being, entitled to at least know what's happening to him when he dies. He needs the ability to make his peace with the Lord."

The doctor suddenly realised his lack of respect.

"I'm terribly sorry Reverend, I didn't think. I see so many of these cases end the same way," the doctor said, appearing genuinely repentant. "You'll find him quite lucid, he's been waiting for you," he continued, ushering the orderly out of the cell with his trolley. "I'll leave you to it; call out if you need anything."

The Vicar tried not to show his real feelings, not while he was wearing his collar. Instead he smiled politely and replied, "I will... thank you."

He waited until he was sure he had the privacy he needed for the Last Rites and turned to face Samuel in his own world for what appeared to be the last time. He was shocked by his appearance. After two years of listening to Samuel's disoriented tales, almost every week, he did not recognise the cadaverous frame.

Samuel's eyes were tightly closed, his jaw-line gripped in a fierce clench, either by the pain he was in or the onset of death. Then his expression relaxed; a mixed blessing he thought, and crossed himself as he watched and waited.

Looking at the pathetic figure that he no longer recognised, his thoughts pondered on Samuel's adamant claim that he was innocent of the murder he had been committed for; regardless of the overwhelming evidence to the contrary.

Perhaps his inability to comprehend the severity of the situation he was in, and his solicitor's lack of faith in concentrating on a plea of insanity, weighed heavily against him, forcing the judge to pass sentence before a trial by jury and committing him to a mental institution for further examination.

On recollection, the many hours they spent together going over his life amounted for little. The stories of his army career and subsequent glamorous civilian occupation jetting about wheeling and dealing had little substance, although at the time, sounded quite plausible. After all, by the time he was brought in front of the court, he was a mere shadow of his former self.

The Vicar was suddenly startled when Samuel's eyes sprang wide open, reminding him of the last seconds of a recent dying parishioner: full of vitality, as if the body was making a last attempt at survival before leaving this world.

"Reverend, I'm glad you could come," he said; if a little faint.

"Samuel, I thought you were asleep," the Vicar replied.

"I wouldn't be asleep on your visiting day Reverend."

Samuel stretched his arm down beside his thin body and fumbled amongst the folds of the blanket that was covering his legs, but was unable to find what he wanted, until the Vicar retrieved an old bible and pushed it towards his groping fingers. A smile crossed his unshaven face and he relaxed, rested his hand on the bible, taking satisfaction from its feel; like a child with a favourite toy.

His eyes had become sluggish again and rolled from side to side as he looked at the Vicar and said, "Hello Reverend... is it Thursday already?"

"Hello Samuel, do you remember the doctor being here a short while ago?" he asked him, hoping he would snap back into the reality of the moment. He needed to ask him about his faith, among other things.

"Oh yes, I remember. He told me I was dying... will it take long?" he replied nonchalantly. "I have so much to do today."

His matter-of-fact reaction to death surprised the Vicar; he almost felt Samuel was unaware of what it meant, and the Vicar had to find out what he really thought was going on, how he imagined death and if he was prepared to face his maker.

The Vicar took hold of the fragile hand holding the bible and lifted it above the covers and returned to the question Samuel asked. A question he was familiar with.

"I don't know Samuel, what do you think will happen?"

Samuel frowned in thought.

"Well I think someone will come for me. It won't be painful will it? I'm not good with pain you see," he said, looking into the Vicar's eyes for an answer.

"No it won't be painful Samuel, just like going to sleep."

"Only it was painful for the others, I wouldn't like that," he commented."

"Others?" the Vicar let out, surprised.

"Yes... the ones I sent upstairs."

The Vicar was sure he was getting confused again. "You mean the man you killed, the death you were committed for?"

"Oh no... I told you I didn't kill him... only the others." He was so adamant that there were others, the Vicar just had to find out.

"Perhaps you'd better tell me about them," he said, and reached into his small satchel for his note pad so that he could record everything Samuel said.

"There were quite a lot actually, I've lost count," he started, and then closed his eyes as if he was trying to remember. "But most were in the open."

"The open?" the Vicar questioned, more bewildered.

"Yes, Reverend, where they could be found, so God could take them upstairs. But there were two that I had to hide, so God doesn't know about them, and they keep haunting me." His eyes opened suddenly and he grabbed the Vicar's jacket, trying to pull him down closer.

"Careful, Samuel," the Vicar cried.

"You'll find them for me won't you, and say the words?"

"The words, Samuel?" the Vicar asked, totally confused.

"Yes... the ones you're waiting to say for me when I leave."

"You do realise I'm of the Anglican faith. Does that matter?"

"I don't know, Reverend; it won't stop me going upstairs will it?"

"No…of course it won't, but you do need to tell me if anything's on your conscience, like those others whoever they are."

"Didn't I?" he screwed up his face, appearing surprised in the oversight. "Well they must be the secret ones."

"What do you mean… secret?"

"The ones they told me I wasn't to tell anyone about."

"Who told you that?"

"They said I mustn't tell anyone."

"Samuel… if you want to go to the Lord with a clean conscience, you must tell me who the others are, and what this is all about. You said nothing during our talks, and if it was secret then I understand that, but that can't apply now."

"Maybe you're right," he paused. "Did you know I was a good shot?"

"No Samuel I didn't, you didn't say. But what has that to do with the others?"

"Well it was because I was a good shot, that they made me kill them."

"Kill who, Samuel… you're not making much sense."

"The other soldiers, Reverend… the other soldiers."

Samuel began to look impatient, his agitation was turning his face red and his shaking hands let the bible slip from his grasp. He fumbled amongst the folds of his bedding, like a blind man, until the Vicar put the bible back beneath his hands and reassurance crossed his face again.

"Sorry, Samuel, it's me, I didn't understand. You mean when you were fighting you had to kill other soldiers. That's all right. Well it isn't, but what I mean is, in war it's sometimes unavoidable; you have to kill to survive."

Samuel looked even more frustrated. Not so much with the Vicar but more with himself; not in control of his thoughts, unable to find his words.

"No that's not what I mean," he became agitated again and started thrashing his arms in the air, almost hitting the Vicar on the side of the face until he took hold of them and calmed him. "I mean the others, the ones specially picked for me."

A chill ran down the Vicar's back. What he was saying didn't appear to make any sense; although the madness of it sounded very real. "Samuel, are you telling me someone actually told you to kill those people?"

"Yes... the others."

"And how did you do this?"

"As I said, I was a good shot, so they made me a sniper. At first I just had to hide and pick off the infiltrators, whilst our men took on the main force. Then I was shipped out to a special unit and sent on missions, were I killed people not fighting us." The Vicar could now see the uneasiness of his conscience.

"How do you mean 'People not fighting'?"

"Some were in camps, others in towns or even driving on the road."

"I see," he was beginning to comprehend. "And the hidden ones?"

"Don't you want to hear how I did it?"

Peter realised he was about to embark on a vicious circle, and there was not enough time. "Never mind that now, just tell me what the difference is between the found ones and the hidden ones."

"Oh that's easy," he said, relaxing a little and searching again for his bible. "There were those I left for them to find. They would take them away to get rid of them but there were others I had to hide... so no one could find them."

"I'm even more confused now, Samuel... Samuel." He had closed his eyes, the Vicar thought for good. "Don't you leave me now, Samuel... not just yet?"

"I'm just tired, Reverend, that's all," he whispered.

"Good... I mean, good you haven't left me yet. You must explain if you want forgiveness when you enter the Lord's kingdom.

"What, Reverend?... oh yes, after leaving the army, I couldn't do anything else. I tried, then one of them found me again and asked me to do the same for him."

"Let me get this right, Samuel. After you left the army, someone actually found you and made you kill for him?" the Vicar was horrified at the thought.

Samuel seemed preoccupied with the bible, he tried to open it and found he didn't have the strength. He slumped back into a soporific state.

"Samuel?"

"I didn't kill this one, only the others, God has them now. But not the two I had to hide. You must find them and say the words over them."

Samuel suddenly became agitated again. He had become totally disorientated and had strayed completely off the path, returning to his original statement.

"He won't send me down there will he?"

"No, Samuel."

In the anxiety of the moment the Vicar could not appreciate the 'words' he kept referring to, and who were the others? "What words, where are they, Samuel?

"I'm too tired now, Reverend," he drawled and closed his eyes.

"Samuel, tell me where you hid them?"

Without opening his eyes, Samuel's hand searched again for the bible. With great difficulty he raised the thick volume barely off the bed as a gesture, and then it fell back again. The Vicar said nothing as he watched the arched back of Samuel's hand slowly relax. He could see the life ebbing from his body, and he placed his hand on his. He could feel a faint pulse, then nothing.

After alerting the guard to notify the doctor straight away, he returned to the cell and prepared to perform the 'Last Rites' on Samuel Alluche.

The doctor arrived, hardly paying any attention to the Vicar.

"He's gone hasn't he doctor?" the Vicar asked, already knowing the answer.

"Yes, as you would say, Reverend, he's gone to his maker. Was it peaceful?"

"He was so busy trying to tell me something; he just slipped away without knowing anything about it."

"And was he lucid enough to understand what you wanted?"

"He drifted in and out, but it was fine, I managed."

"I only asked because the cancer had reached his brain."

"He seemed to know what was about to happen."

Waiting for the doctor to complete his examination, the Vicar suddenly realised what he had been babbling about. The 'words' Samuel referred to were in fact 'The Last Rites', and somewhere two dead people were lying in a cold limbo.

'But where', he thought, 'and how on earth was he going to find them, and keep his word to this man'. The task seemed beyond his capability.

Reverend Peter Jay returned to Samuel Alluche when the doctor left the small cell; he crossed his hands over his chest and closed his eyelids. He knelt down beside the bunk, took the bible Samuel cherished in both hands and lowered his head.

"Dear Lord, please take this misguided man unto your bosom and have mercy on his soul. He was a confused man, with little intellect to know the difference between right and wrong, but as his last words are testament to him, he was fearful of your commandments. He confessed his sins and discharged his last responsibility."

CHAPTER 1

Following Superintendent Hammond's forced retirement in 1984 his wife Marjory was left a country cottage in a small sleepy village called Lower Cheedam, in Surrey, following her mother's death.

This country enclave was less than twenty miles from London's busy suburbs, nestled in the dewdrop of no-man's land, hanging from Guilford, bordered on one side by the road to Chichester and the other by the road to Worthing.

Several visits later, to sort out her mother's affairs, Marjory managed to persuade her husband that this was the place. Reminded him that he always said he would retire to the country before ending up behind a desk; how could he refuse.

The first time Jack visited Lower Cheedam he felt his wife was playing a joke on him, and that in fact they were entering one of those village film-lots. It was so typically like the idyllic country village he had seen many times before at the cinema; including the duck pond and the village green at its centre.

On entering the village the road immediately forked around the pond, servicing the local shops on either side. Each shop was no bigger than an average front room, and was soon discovered to be the meeting place for the local gossips, and like most village shops they were suspicious of strangers.

At the opposite junction, where the twin roads met, stood

a one-pump garage on the left with a 1920's tractor out front, and a seventy-year-old pub covered with geraniums on the right. No more than fifty feet separated this symbiotic relationship, where patrons of the pub found to be over the limit were forced to ring for a taxi from the garage opposite when the landlord confiscated their keys.

Further along the road, as the high street petered out on a steep incline, stood the typical square-towered Anglican Church, surrounded on three sides by a four hundred year old cemetery, and beyond that the start of the local Squire's Estate.

This immense tract of green pasture-land, extended from the north side of the bell tower, across a narrow meadow with scattered copses of hawthorn, then steeply climbed up the hill where the Hammond's cottage stood.

For the first month Jack spent most of his time getting used to the silence of his new environment: pottering around the massive garden, climbing over the old stile in the fence and walking across the small open paddock towards the adjoining plantation. Spending what seemed hours just enjoying the smell of the pines and sinking into the damp rotting leaves underfoot.

Marjory on the other hand, became a villager almost instantaneously; not an easy road for strangers. However, she was remembered fondly from her regular visits to her mother's cottage and that helped.

Although physically different from her mother, they both had the same corn coloured hair, soft green eyes and the most perfect complexion that Jack loved so much. In fact it was that and her good figure that first drew his attention.

It took no more than a week for her to be accepted as one of them, although she knew Jack's acceptance would take a little longer, at least until her plans for his introduction into village life were successful.

While joining the morning gossip she soon found out about the new Anglican Vicar, Reverend Peter Jay, who was also stamping his personality on the village. This Vicar had definite views on idle hands; as he would say, 'To be idle was to be ungodly', and vigorously set about organising the villagers.

He was a conscientious optimist, and found no mind too resolved that would not succumb to his gentle persuasion. Jack was soon to be drawn into this man's clutches when Marjory coerced him into accompanying her to the early Sunday morning church service. A cool breeze stirred the autumn leaves, the air was sharp and crisp, and Jack felt apprehensive.

Standing outside by the old Lichgate while she introduced him to the butcher, the baker and whoever else was of prominence in the village, he allowed his attention to be distracted by the large community board outside, decorated with a multitude of posters. It was covered with every conceivable educational class and recreational group activity held in the church hall: from amateur productions, woodworking, poetry, ironwork and many others, as well as a few commercial studies.

"See anything that interests you, Superintendent?" a croaky voice said from behind; not one of those nearby.

He turned, wondering who was referring to his old rank. It was the Vicar, evident by the short white vestment over his black suit and dog collar, standing alongside Marjory, who, for some reason, was flushed with excitement.

"This is, Reverend Peter Jay dear," she said, expectantly.

Jack hated sudden introductions, especially with enthusiastic clergymen.

He put on his best smile. "Reverend," Jack answered, holding out his hand. "It's nice to meet you at last. Marjory has told me all about your good works."

"You're so kind, Superintendent". He started in a raspy voice.

"Yes dear... we had a long chat about you, didn't we Vicar?" she said.

"That's right. I learnt all about your gripping exploits," he replied. "We must set aside some time to have a long chat," he continued with difficulty. "At the moment I must get started, although I don't know how I shall manage with this laryngitis". He forced a cough or two as he smiled at Marjory, "You wouldn't care to read for me would you, Superintendent?"

"Of course he would, Reverend," Marjory eagerly volunteered. Jack was just about to tactfully decline, his mouth still open. He glared at her, suspecting that this coincidence had been stealthily arranged.

"That's settled then, much obliged," and he was off with another cough and his vestment flowing behind, as the congregation began filing into the small church.

"What did you do that for?" Jack rebuked Marjory.

"Oh go on, Jack, it will be an excellent opportunity to introduce yourself to the village. Everyone who is everyone is here."

"And I suppose that stands for a lot? What if I don't want to be known to the entire village," he whispered into her ear from behind as they followed the others.

"It's better than being known as that old grouch of a retired policeman."

The Vicar started with a few words to his flock, explaining Jack Hammond's presence on the rostrum, indicating he would be standing in for him each time he required a lengthy reference to the scriptures; Jack silently shuddering at the thought.

The congregation's eyes turned to the large figure dominating the fine woodwork of the small, enclosed platform above them. He still had the presence of a policeman. His thick set physique, although less defined, was marred only by the extra weight he had put on in his later years; something else Marjory planned to change.

As he spoke, the congregation were drawn solely to his face; it was a strong face, the face that graced Sergeant Majors. At first he felt embarrassed, until he began to look upon the congregation as a gathering of blue uniformed Constables at the Academy, and the scriptures were in fact a reading of the police manual of conduct. After a while, he began to realise how much power he could wield from this small pulpit, turning his embarrassment into a sadistic enjoyment.

This first experience with the Vicar was not unlike any previous encounter with the clergy, and he took little interest in the man, other than to recognise his black presence below, and that annoying square of white plastic supporting his Adams apple.

Whilst waiting for his signals, Jack had the opportunity of studying this middle-aged ecclesiastic with so much control over his parishioners. An unassuming man, with a full head of black hair, apart from the receding inroads either side of his crown, displaying a sharp widow's peak and accentuated sideburns, making him look unfortunately quite devilish.

His hazel eyes were bright and sharp, constantly darting left and right as he sermonised, giving the impression that, should he pause and focus on you for one moment, you would be lost. While unassuming, he still had a theatrical way about him; his arms gesticulating in an arc of one hundred and eighty degrees as he preached in an evangelistic manner.

Following the unorthodox service, noticeable by the number of people rubbing their necks as they left, no doubt from their tennis-like attention to both the incumbent Vicar and Jack, performing their separate functions, the Vicar thanked Jack for his excellent contribution and the manner in which he read the scriptures.

Marjory held her head high as they followed the others, as

if today had been a triumph in her campaign to establish Jack within the community. The Vicar shook Jack's hand firmly, unable to finish his words with so many people congratulating him.

"I shall have to leave what I had to say until another time, Superintendent, my throat's getting worse, and your popularity is overwhelming. Thank you once again, and to you Mrs Hammond."

"Oh, Reverend please... it's Marjory," she said, noticeably under his spell.

"Of course, Marjory, many thanks," he said, and disappeared before she had a chance to say another word, back into the vestry.

Brushing a leaf from his shoulder that had fallen from an old chestnut spreading over the path from the church, Marjory snuggled into Jack's upper arm and he could feel her satisfied closeness. He had to admit, at that moment it felt good, and for the first time in a long while he felt part of something.

"Well, Jack, I'm very proud of you," she said, looking up at the face that showed little interest. "You made a good impression today, everyone was talking about you." He shuddered with anticipation. "You looked in command up in the pulpit."

"Did I?" he snapped. "I felt like a villain in the dock."

"Nonsense, you had them on the edge of their seats."

He stopped and turned to her.

"And you find that exciting?" he replied. "I find it frightening to say the least."

Marjory sighed, "Oh, Jack... when will you realise you're no longer a Superintendent of the Yard, and start settling into your new life in the village."

"I can't see my appearance winning any new friends."

She stroked the side of his face, "You'll be surprised what that determined jaw can do, dear. Although I do think you should do something with that moustache."

Jack raised his free arm and felt his pride beneath his nose and realised, like many other routines, he had forgotten his daily trim.

When they arrived at the small wooden gate in front of their cottage, he was too occupied trying to get it open, until Marjory calmly lifted it above the crooked paving and gently swung it away in front of him, to comment further. That simple action terrifyingly opened his mind to the future; he could see a never-ending expectation of mending gates and straightening paths.

The following day Jack was reclining on a rustic garden seat enjoying the early autumn sun, when the Vicar called to have that unfinished chat. Jack had fallen asleep and Marjory woke him with a start.

"Oh I am sorry, Superintendent," the Vicar's much improved voice rang out.

"Jack it's the Reverend, come for that chat," she added.

"Ah... Reverend... sorry, I must have dropped off, that is bad of me. Shows how old I'm getting," Jack said, regaining his composure.

"Say no more, Superintendent; I frequent that land myself on occasion," he said thoughtfully as he sat down beside him.

The Vicar sucked in the sharp morning air and undid his scarf and duffle-coat.

Marjory began to feel out of place and commented, "I'll brew up a pot of tea for you both." Then she left, knowing what the Vicar had in mind.

He turned to Jack, giving him that penetrating look he had seen earlier, "So... how are you settling in? Does our humble hamlet meet with your approval?"

"You've been speaking to Marjory," Jack answered.

"I've asked her the same question... yes," he replied protectively.

"To be honest with you, Reverend I'm not sure. Of course I find the village delightful, I always did when we visited Marjory's mother, and the countryside is beyond my limited ability of expression, but as to whether or not I personally can settle here as you say, after the big city, I'm not sure."

"Well… we'll have to see if we can find something to capture that mind of yours."

"And what sort of a mind would that be?"

"At a guess I'd say very astute. I wouldn't think you miss much."

"I have to warn you, Reverend," Jack started, looking equally as determined. "I don't take lightly to being persuaded to doing things against my will."

The Vicar could see he had met his match, not like the soporific folk in the village. "I never intimidate people, Superintendent, especially experts at the game like yourself, I merely try and show them how much more challenging life can be."

At that point Marjory returned with the hot drinks, perfectly timed of course, as if she had been eavesdropping. She laid the tray down on a small wooden table alongside, after Jack had brushed some leaves away.

At the same time he looked deeply into those scheming eyes. "No, Marjory, the Reverend hasn't broached the subject yet, I'll talk to you later dear… thank you."

She said nothing, knowing through experience when to remain silent, and returned back up the crushed granite path to the house.

The Vicar paused as he sipped his hot drink; vapour wafting away as a chilly breeze came up from the paddock. "I should have known better than to think I could approach a Superintendent of homicide in a diverse manner."

"I don't know, Reverend, why should you need to?"

"Because Marjory told me you were absolutely suspicious of people trying to draw you into anything you hadn't already full knowledge of; 'outright suspicious' was the term I think she used." He leant forward, helping himself to two lumps of sugar and began examining the plate of biscuits she had prepared.

"She's quite right actually, so what are you trying to draw me into," Jack remarked, attending to his sweet tooth also.

"Nothing really... my main objective was to seek your advice."

"Why would you need my advice?"

"Well... as you are probably aware, I run several courses and I'm fortunate enough to know several professionals capable of overseeing them, but unfortunately, as you might expect, my own group suffers badly from the lack of professional assistance."

"And which of these extracurricular activities do you wish my advice on?" Jack asked, still unconvinced, as he poked amongst the biscuits.

"Why... my pet subject of course; criminology." The Vicar said.

"That's a very big subject Vicar. Do you have any particular speciality?"

"Why is it Superintendent that I get the feeling you find this amusing?"

"I apologise if I give that impression, but you have to understand, I don't take lightly to armatures in my profession, even if I am now retired. It's far too serious, and certainly no comparison to a detective novel."

"I know that, Superintendent. I have been a regular prison clergy for five years now, the last two in the prison for the criminally insane at Hatchwood. So I am quite aware of the serious nature of my hobby."

"I stand corrected. Hatchwood is not a place I would wish my worst enemy... how come you're there?"

"You mean they have little hope of redemption?"

"Exactly."

The Vicar thought more carefully this time before answering.

"There are a lot of old inmates who funnily enough need

some form of solace in their final years. They are no longer a threat to society, especially the terminally ill who are too old to seek parole and have nothing left to face but more years or confinement. Besides, who would have them?"

"And you're their next best thing."

"Yes... I like to think I manage to give them some hope in the after-life, even if most are sure they'll end up in the eternal flames."

Jack looked at him suspiciously as he sipped his tea.

"So this experience got you interested in criminology?"

"Not quite... I've always been an avid reader of detective novels, and yes, I wanted to find out how like real life they were. This actual contact and listening to the inmates' tragic stories, only reinforced that."

Jack unintentionally found himself drawn to the chocolate biscuits and rummaged as discreetly as he could through what was left on the plate.

"I can understand the outpourings of those desperate men; I've never known one yet who couldn't resist telling everyone all the gruesome details after he was convicted. But I have to say, they could also tell some whoppers."

"Quite so, Superintendent... my last terminal patient may well fall into that category; a story I might interest you in later."

"That's all very interesting, Reverend, but you still haven't told me how I fit into all this," Jack continued, now more suspicious than ever.

"It's quite simple really, I have this small group who are also interested in criminology, and we meet once a week to discuss anything from recent news of criminal activities, to books, and of course my own experiences with my inmates. And I just thought I might persuade you to join us one evening and enthral us with a short introduction into the intricacies of homicide investigations and... if possible, an insight into what it's like to be a real detective."

"You may find a lot of my work very mundane, Reverend, it's not quite like you read in your novels you know."

"I know that, Superintendent. So do I take that as an affirmative reply?"

"I don't see why not, as long as you don't expect me to give a lecture."

The Vicar's eyes lit up with excitement.

"That's grand, Superintendent, I'll let you know when."

He quickly finished his drink, stood up and attended to the duffle-coat he opened, then throwing the scarf around his neck with a flourish; he made his way towards the stile in the fence. "You don't mind me taking a short cut over the paddock do you?" he asked, climbing into the field.

"That's all right by me, it's not my land but Marjory will be disappointed. I'm sure she wanted to say goodbye."

"Give her my apologies, I'll see her later," he shouted back, already half way across the paddock towards the small pine plantation.

"Did I hear the Vicar shouting, Jack?" Marjory said, coming down the path to where they were seated.

"He had to go dear... he said he was sorry and would talk to you later."

"At the hall?" she questioned.

He was becoming aware of the new busy village life she was getting involved in, "I'm not sure dear, he didn't say. Going out again, are you?"

"Yes... didn't I tell you? I joined the theatrics class, it's on this afternoon."

"Good... I'm glad one of us is fitting in," he commented.

"Don't be like that, Jack, just give it time, you'll see," she hesitated before continuing. Jack could be so difficult at times, especially if he sensed he was being manipulated. "Are you going to join the Vicar's criminology group?"

"So you did discuss it with him?" he said, letting her know he was wise to her manoeuvres. He looked at her suspiciously as he put the cup to his mouth and took a sip, then screwed his face up. "Ooh... it's getting cold."

"He just asked me if I thought you would be interested in his little group. I told him I couldn't say; he would have to ask you." Knowing Jack, she was very defensive. She picked up the tray and turned back to him. "I'll make you a fresh pot."

He stood up, stretched his arms and took hold of the tray while he kissed her on the cheek, "Don't bother dear, he sighed. I've decided to come in now... I've had enough fresh air for one day.

CHAPTER 2

It was late morning, almost lunch time when Marjory rushed in expecting Jack to be waiting wondering when she was going to start his lunch. She had been to her flower arrangement class and her gossiping had driven the time right out of her mind.

With no response from Jack she went upstairs half expecting to find him lying on the bed; a practice that he was falling into more often these days, and it was beginning to worry her. She hoped the Reverend's criminology group he was to attend this afternoon would stop that before it got worse.

Not finding him in the bedroom either, Marjory went over to the wardrobe thinking he might have put his anorak on for a walk. She glanced out of the window and there he was in his recently adopted place at the bottom of the garden.

"Is this what your retirement is going to amount to, Jack?" she asked on approaching him. "Sleeping in, eating, sitting here for hours and watching TV?"

Without looking at her he answered in a manner she had not heard before.

"Marjory... I don't question how you waste your time with all those village meetings, so please refrain from criticising mine."

It hurt to see what was happening to him since he left the force; he had always been such an active man, almost hyperactive. Now he was the direct opposite.

She sat down closely beside him on the bench, placed her arm across his shoulder, realising this present frame of mind was not that of a lazy, mawkish person, it was more like someone with a deep yearning for that which he had lost.

"Jack I'm not criticising you, it's just that you have to motivate yourself again. You can't continue like this, you'll just sink further into depression. Come and have some lunch, and then you can take a leisurely walk over the park to the church hall.

"Why would I want to do that?"

"Have you forgotten?" she turned him to face her. "Oh, Jack, you have."

He looked questionably into her eyes, "Forgotten what woman?"

"You were going to attend the Reverend's criminology meeting this afternoon."

"Oh that's great, I did forget," he admitted. "I'll make it next week."

"No you won't," she told him angrily. "You'll get your lunch, tidy yourself up, and get over there." She dragged him up from the bench. "Besides, you know what will happen if you don't."

"Yes I know... no need to remind me. He'll be round here like a shot wanting to know what happened to me, giving me a sermon as usual."

"He will."

As Marjory said, there was still plenty of time, so they had a casual lunch. Afterwards he did as she suggested and took a long stroll over the paddock, through the copse into the back of the church cemetery.

Still being early, he decided to take a wander through the old stones, something he had not done since his father died, and was buried near his grandparents eighteen years ago. On that occasion he remembers having difficulty finding them; the stones were so black with London's pollution, that was when the city was constantly bathed in smog, before the days of smokeless zones.

Now he found himself surrounded by white marble, older grey granite, the occasional black slab that looked out of place, and at his feet, weathered stones that went back centuries.

It was interesting, tracing the villager's history, and reading what they said about each other back in those days; nothing had changed; things were said in death that were probably unsaid in life. As he slowly sauntered on, head down like a beachcomber; he heard the melodic voice of the Vicar up ahead: he was checking the stones and talking to a few parishioners.

"That's what I like to see, Superintendent... enthusiasm," he shouted out, finishing what he was doing and walking towards him.

"And that's very encouraging also, Reverend," Jack commented, continuing to read the stones, trying to look interested.

The Vicar arrived alongside him, and glanced at the stone Jack was reading.

"In what way, Superintendent?"

"Well I gather you're watching over your silent parishioners also."

"Oh yes... very good," he laughed. "No, unfortunately I have to start thinking about moving some of the older sites to make way for the new inhabitants; we're getting a bit full." He looked down at Jack's feet. "And as you can see, this isn't the first time." He started laughing again.

"So I see... it's fascinating reading some of these older ones," Jack remarked, placing his hand on a lichen encrusted stone nearby, with a tale of lost love and expectations of togetherness in the afterlife. "Life never really changes, does it?"

"That, Superintendent, I try so hard to get into my sermons each Sunday. Since the Old Testament we've been making the same mistakes, mankind will never learn."

Jack stood up and looked the Vicar squarely in the face.

"One thing Vicar I would like to correct straight away. I'm not a Superintendent anymore; I'm just plain old Jack Hammond. So I'd appreciate it if you'd call me Jack from now on. And while I'm on the subject, do I have to call you Reverend?"

"I know exactly how you feel Jack, I sometimes wonder if I have a Christian name myself. Do you know shortly after we married, my wife started calling me Reverend? It took me ages to remind her of my first name."

For that moment Jack could visualise the awkwardness of the moment.

"I can imagine how embarrassing that must have been," Jack commiserated, holding a clenched fist over his mouth to cough, smothering a laugh.

"It was, Jack," then turning his head. "Oh, here are the others," he said, looking up towards the hall where they were gathering, waving to him. "By-the-way, I'll introduce you once as Superintendent, then refer to you as Jack from then on, and if it makes you feel more comfortable, you can call me Peter."

"I will, Peter, unless it's in front of my wife," they both laughed.

The Vicar's criminology meetings were only an hour long, officially that was, as Jack soon found out after the majority had left. It appeared they were double sided, although he had difficulty finding out whether this was intentional or simply something that had developed as the group's interests expanded.

The main hour this week was taken up with the Vicar's introduction of Jack as 'Superintendent Jack Hammond,' cleverly announced to add significance to the surprise and subsequent admiration of the group. Following the flattering exaggerations of his importance in the CID, Jack was coerced into spending the whole period giving a brief discourse on what it was like being a Superintendent in the world's most famous police force, coupled with examples of his recent cases.

It was not until the end of his lecture, when he stood with the

Vicar at the entrance shaking everyone's hand as they left, that he noticed three of the group had stayed behind and were slowly folding the chairs and stacking them into a small storeroom. Their manner was unlike that of church helpers; he sensed they were killing time until the last of the class had left.

While in the cottage, or on his frequent walks, his mind slowed down and he found it extremely difficult to remember his recent past. But in the company of new acquaintances, or unfamiliar places, his mind came alive again, and he began picking up on every nuance like he used to when he was deeply involved with a complex case.

Jack's suspicious mind filled with silly images of secret handshakes, burning candles and covert incantations. As it turned out, most of the members in the first hour were simply interested in the general picture of criminology, while the remaining group, including the Vicar, wanted more.

They all aspired to the thrill of amateur detection, despite the limits of their individual professions, and studied the subject of criminology seriously. They examined every case they came across in the media and researched microfilm of old cases in the local library archives to wet their appetite.

When the Vicar introduced each of the three in more detail than he had at the original session, Jack once again became occupied with the suspicion of being drawn into some covert activity. There was a noticeable return to the use of Superintendent, as if he was being reinstated, and the members of this elite group thought of themselves as his special CID team.

The one female member of the group was called Janet Donald: the principle of the local school. In the Vicar's introduction it was emphasised that she specialised in maths and languages, and Jack immediately found her a trifle too tweedy, but not to the same extent as the farmers wives.

Jack guessed she was about his age, greying hair, with virtually no makeup that he was aware of, and as best as he could make out, under her thick jacket and skirt, she had quite a good figure. Something else Jack found he had become obsessed with since his move to the country.

As she gathered the chairs he thought she looked athletic, a guess on his part until he found out she organised the local squash team. She overshadowed the men, with her speed and agility; an exhibition Jack felt was not unlike the signs he had noticed in the new breed of young women entering the force.

Then he noticed her deep blue eyes; they were like windows, inviting him to see how intelligent she was; piercing, almost calculating but devoid of any sexuality.

Of the two men, Arthur Sandhurst made the first impression. Maybe it was his loud tie, but Jack opted for his personality. Before he was introduced, while Jack was analysing the participants, he guessed like he always did, that this was a commercial man; a salesman or executive.

So it was no surprise when Jack found out he was in Real Estate, and that his company had been the only estate agent in this area for over one hundred years. He was a fifty-year-old clean shaven man with well groomed hair and stylish clothes befitting the social class he mixed with, but somehow he looked out of place in the nave of a country church.

As for fitting into social profiles, Dick Meadows was his own walking advertisement, and there were no prizes for guessing he had to be a shopkeeper. He was the exact opposite of Arthur; a prosaic man, totally without style. He wore baggy grey trousers with a heavy knit jumper, around sixty, but difficult to judge, as he had gone to seed. He was jovial, and with his white hair, bushy eyebrows and a ruddy complexion he would make a good Santa Claus.

Jack later found out that Arthur's special contribution to the group was his skill at searching records, a valuable asset in the Real Estate industry. Dick was a natural medium; something Jack thought would not have mixed too well with the Vicar's religious opinions.

"So there you are Jack," the Vicar exclaimed. "What do you think?"

"Ah… well, I'm very pleased to meet everyone," he replied politely, a little lost for the right words, if in fact he had no idea what was expected of him.

"No Jack, I mean what do you think of our 'Profiles'? is that what you say?"

"We do use the word profiles, but not in that context," Jack answered abruptly.

"That's why it's so important for you to join us Jack," Arthur said, we need that professional input. At the moment all we seem to be doing is copying what we read in the papers or hear on the television. I'm not surprised you look suspicious."

"Yes… exactly," the Vicar agreed, with the others nodding their heads.

"Look, what is it you really want, you haven't actually told me what this little elite group of yours does, other than your introduction."

"I thought you picked up on that Jack," the Vicar said. "The main class is simply a matter of interest, this one's more serious."

"I'd put it a bit stronger than that, Peter," Janet grunted. "We can't expect to be taken seriously if we're just playing at it… can we, Jack?"

Jack leant forward on the table spreading his hand out in front of them, patting the surface to emphasise his intent. "There… that's the part I can't come to terms with, what does being serious mean?"

They all looked at each other in surprise. The thought that they were doing anything unusual had not occurred to them.

"I thought we had made our activities quite plain," Janet said. Dick and Arthur preferred to stay silent.

"Have you a problem with that, Jack?" the Vicar asked.

"If you're only playing at detectives in this room to amuse yourselves, then that's fine, I have no problem with that. But if you intend any serious research into areas outside, such as people's lives and police cases that have already been before the judiciary, then you had better be aware that you are possibly breaking the law."

There was silence at the table; they had not expected Jack to take as official a line as he did. They had obviously thought, in his retired state, he could advise them on their course of action, without any consideration of the legal issues involved.

"Truly, Jack, we had no idea we were breaking the law in our activities," the Vicar explained. "We obviously need your professional advice."

"Very well... as I see it we're talking about old cases here," he questioned.

"Most definitely," Janet said, glancing at the others who nodded in agreement.

"Good, then your researching can come under the same category as any author, newspaper, filmmaker or historian but venture into the area of questioning people involved in the case or living relatives, then beware. They could sue you or worse still, inform the police, who take a dim view of meddlers resurrecting old cases. That's why private detectives have to be licensed."

"Private detectives?" Arthur questioned. "Is that really necessary if all we're doing is reviewing the evidence?"

"It is, if you intend doing anything about it."

"Most of what we've done so far, Jack has been at least a hundred years old," Janet remarked. "Certainly no modern cases."

"That's good if you stay in that time period, but you'll be

amazed what problems you can get into, even turning over hundred year old stones. As a matter of fact there's no better example than the case of the 'Yorkshire Ripper'. The press soon made the similarity with 'Jack the Ripper'... no comparisons please," they all laughed.

Jack was not amused by the interruption and continued, "... simply to drum up more sales for their newspapers. Anyway, without getting too involved, once the media got their teeth into the people involved, they dug up all sorts of nasty innuendoes, even involving Royalty."

"Yes I remember seeing a documentary on that," Dick said.

"So what do you suggest, Jack?" the Vicar questioned, not wanting his pet idea to be squashed by such a trifling problem before it really got started.

"Well I'm prepared to oversee anything you want to do, and advise you accordingly. But I certainly suggest you get yourself some credentials, such as in writing or history, better still something involved in criminology perhaps. Janet, your experience in education should help there."

"Yes... I'll look into it straight away, that's a good idea. It's quite easy to become a society these days I hear, as long as you have enough members."

"Oh dear me," the Vicar suddenly exclaimed looking across to the large clock on the far wall. "Look at the time, it's six o'clock already."

They all had other engagements and or wives to go home to like Jack, so they started to collect their books and things hurriedly, and followed the Vicar through the large doors out into the chilly night. Jack smiled to himself, thinking that was the difference between amateurs and professionals. The amateurs get to go home.

"By... you certainly know autumn's arrived," Arthur commented, pulling his collar up around his neck, "Would you like a lift Jack?... I pass your place."

"You know where I live then?" Jack replied. Everyone roared with laughter. "Of course, how silly of me, you probably handled my mother-in-law's affairs."

"Sure did... come on then," he called, stepping smartly towards the Lichgate.

The others quickly set off in the direction of the town, except the Vicar, all he had to do was cross over the small green in front of the church to the stone cottage by the main gate and he was home.

"I'll call and see you tomorrow, Jack, see what you think. My regards to Marjory," he shouted, as he disappeared inside.

Arthur already had the car warming up when Jack climbed in, another icon to establish his position in the community.

"My first drive in a Rolls Royce, it's very nice," Jack commented.

"Only very nice, Jack?" Arthur unashamedly answered back as he sped away up the hill, "It's bloody fantastic."

After walking from the cottage to the church Jack had forgotten how close it really was, as the Rolls slowed down and turned into his drive.

"Well that was very nice. How about saying hello to Marjory and a drink?"

"I'd love to, Jack, but I really do have a pressing engagement, and to be honest, she's much prettier than you but I'll definitely call in for a chat soon."

"That's fine, Arthur, I'll see you then."

As Jack was getting out of the car he saw the curtains move and thought Marjory would be bursting with questions when he got in. It was one thing to have to face the barrage of questions about his meeting, entirely another to explain coming home in a Rolls Royce belonging to Arthur.

"Isn't Arthur coming in?" she asked, leaning out of the door.

"No, he had to get off to a more pressing engagement," he shouted back from the lounge, where he was pouring himself a stiff drink.

"You weren't persuasive enough, more like it," she shouted back.

"Believe me dear, the pressing engagement sounded very important."

"Oh there you are... hitting the bottle early aren't we?"

"I need this after that bunch of amateurs."

"Oh, Jack, they're a nice group of people," she said, putting the stopper back on the decanter, and then sitting down opposite him.

"Their bloody dangerous," he went on.

"That's not very nice after they invited you to join them. I suppose as usual, you upset everyone and they won't have anything to do with you"

"Well you're wrong there. Looks like I shall have to join them, if only to keep them out of trouble. Anyway, how did you know the Rolls was Arthur's?"

Marjory suddenly blushed with embarrassment, although she had no need to, it was just Jack's way of inferring something into nothing. "Everyone in the village knows Arthur's brown Rolls Royce," she explained.

"Very well, I'll let you off this time," he jested.

As Jack finished his drink, he let out a long sorrowful sigh, got up and made his way back towards the trolley as if he were about to pour himself another. Marjory doubled back around the couch and stepped in front of him.

"You're too suspicious, Jack," she said. "That's what comes from being a policeman, you have to question everything," she continued, taking the glass out of his hand. "And that's your lot till later. Get ready for dinner."

"I suppose your right, dear," he said starting for the door. "I even suspected Arthur had some young female on the side... his pressing engagement."

"Why, what did he say to make you suspicious?

"Oh something about her being prettier than me... certainly not his wife."

"Why not... she was his young bit on the side."

CHAPTER 3

The autumn sun had arrived, and the first leaves were falling amongst the stones as an urgent voice rang out across the cemetery, "Peter."

The Vicar looked up from his continually disrupted attempt at cataloguing the older tombstones, thinking another widow was trying to catch his attention.

"Peter," the voice called out again, closer this time. He stood up from his hiding place to see Janet strutting in his direction, as she did.

"Ah, Janet, I thought you were a dear departed loved one, how are you?"

"Fine. I thought you'd like to know I sorted out our problem."

"What problem? I didn't know we had one."

"You know... the thing with the Superintendent."

"Oh... you mean our credentials?" he remembered.

"Yes," she blustered, a little disgruntled after all her effort. Then, after brushing away the imaginary dust with the end of her long scarf, she sat down on the stone next to him brandishing a manila folder, from which she extracted a magnificent heraldic looking document. "There you are, I told you it would be easy. You are now a member of The Historical Criminology Society, and you owe me one pound."

The Vicar scrutinised the paper looking impressed.

"Good heavens, is it that easy?" he uttered. "No wonder there's so many of them about. Didn't you have any problems at all?"

"No... I just had to wait while the woman checked the ledgers and paid the fee. Then she just said, 'Go around the shops for an hour and it'll be ready', and here you are. Something you can get framed in your woodwork class."

"No thank you," The Vicar cried. It's bad enough me condoning the interest."

"I was only joking," Janet scoffed. I'll frame it myself and bring it along each time we have our meetings."

"I suppose you have to."

"Oh yes, it's part of our charter now, it has to be openly displayed at every meeting. That's what it says here."

While the Vicar was trying to get rid of Janet so that he could get back to his onerous task he spotted the postman arriving with a parcel.

"Excuse me, Janet," he said jumping up from the stone. "I must catch old Fred. I think you've done a marvellous job, simply marvellous... see you later."

Fred was gasping for breath as he entered the church, after pushing his bike up the hill, when the Vicar caught up to him. "Ah, Fred, just in time," the Vicar exclaimed.

"How's that, Reverend?" Fred answered back sitting down on the nearest pew. He dropped his canvas bag down by his feet and searched for his hanky to wipe his brow, despite the noticeable chill in the autumn air.

The Vicar was also trying to catch his breath as he sat down opposite.

"Just trying to escape from, Janet," he said.

"Ah... I understand," he replied, with a big grin on his face.

"When are they going to get you a motorbike, Fred? You can't keep dragging yourself and that old bike up the hill every day."

"It does get harder each time, Reverend, but I think it'll be like waiting for the cows to come home if you ask me. Still I can always rely on a rest at the church."

"Can I get you a drink, Fred?"

"That would be nice, Reverend,"

"Is that parcel for me?" the Vicar said before leaving.

"Good heavens, Reverend, I'd forgotten all about it, as big as it is. All the way from..." he glanced at the label, "Hatchwood Prison an' all."

The Vicar took hold of the parcel stamped with the unmistakable black crown and portcullis over H.M. Prison, and went into the vestry for Fred's drink. Before returning he glanced once again at the twelve by eight by four-inch brown paper package, and wondered if he had left something behind on his last visit.

"Here we are, Fred, this should cool you down, he said on returning."

"Thanks, Reverend... oh by the way, I forgot to get you to sign for the parcel, it was recorded delivery. Who do you know in prison?"

"A lot of people, Fred, I visit there every week."

"Oh I see," he replied, easily satisfied. "Well I can't sit here all day gossiping," he continued as if nothing was unusual to him. He gulped down the last of the orange, and handed the empty glass back to the Vicar. "Thanks for the drink, Reverend."

"Bye, Fred, the Vicar shouted," watching the postman push his bike up the hill.

He had a quiet chuckle for the old man's dilemma before suddenly remembering the parcel. He made an excited turn, his cassock flaring as it did, and headed back inside to see what his package had in store for him.

In the security of the vestry, he carefully examined the parcel as if it was a mysterious gift, trying to imagine what could possibly be inside and hoping it was not, as he first thought, something he absentmindedly forgot.

The common brown paper was tightly folded over the sides and held in place with old-fashioned manila sticky tape. He reached into his desk drawer for the Stanley knife and carefully slit along the edge of the wrapping until the two sides suddenly sprang apart, revealing an unexpected flash of bright orange.

On closer inspection it turned out to be a battered shoebox with an official looking envelope attached. As he started to open the envelope his eyes were constantly drawn back to the shoebox, which looked familiar to him. It was on the tip of his tongue; something to do with the colour.

The letter was from the Warden of Hatchwood Prison and read:

"Reverend Jay,

I don't know whether or not you are aware, but on the form the inmates have to fill in for medical treatment, Samuel named you as his next of kin.

Following his death, his cell was cleared out and his belongings were brought to me for disposal. I didn't think you would want any of his clothes so I had them destroyed, and a few small items made in the prison workshop, I distributed amongst his fellow cell mates. The only items I felt he would want you to have were those he kept in this shoebox on the shelf above his bed.

He was always protective of this, carrying it everywhere with him, so its contents must have meant a lot to him.

I would like to take this opportunity in thanking you for your weekly effort with the inmates, and look forward to your future visits.

Warden Richard Brewer. H.M. Prison Service.

The Vicar immediately remembered the brightly coloured box on the shelf above Samuel's bunk, but had never seen what personal treasures lay inside, so it came as a surprise when he lifted the lid; his anticipation was quite excruciating.

On the top was Samuel's cherished bible, the edges of its leaves burred with constant use, which he reverently lifted out and placed to one side on his desk. Next was an abridged volume of the Collins English Dictionary, which, unlike the bible, was surprisingly still in good condition.

Underneath the dictionary the Vicar came across a bundle of folded blue-lined papers that were yellow with age, looking as if they had been torn from a school exercise book.

The intriguing bundle of sheets momentarily distracted the Vicar's attention from the remaining contents of the box. Carefully he lifted the bundle out discovering the yellowness was confined to the open surface only, and curiously raising the bundle to his nose, he realised it was in fact years of nicotine.

He unfolded the sheets, two in all, and spread them out across his blotter, noticing each one was covered with densely scribbled numbers, line after line, in various pens and pencils, as if written over a long period.

Interested to find out what was left in the box the Vicar put the sheets to one side for future consideration and pulling the box closer he began to examine the collection of bizarre objects that remained.

A brass cartridge caught his attention first, probably for a rifle bullet, it was too big for a pistol; A receipt, funnily enough for a dictionary, dated last year and issued at the prison shop; A leather purse, the type you fold the front over the back to close, with three stamps, six pound in notes and forty pence in change inside; An assortment of pens and pencils neatly bound together with an elastic band and finally, the most mysterious item of all:

a strangely shaped key.

The Vicar held it up to the light in front of the small stained glass window. It was about three inches long, too big for a normal lock, with multiple notches down the whole length of one side and only three notches at the top of the other. Along the lower smooth side was an engraved number: 04-173-8030013 / S. He studied the key for a moment alongside the other items and was intrigued.

Once the last item was removed, there was nothing left but the scruffy interior, caused by years of taking things out and putting them back again. The one thing that did terrifyingly strike home, as he gazed into the emptiness, was the fact that the emptiness reminded him of Samuel.

There was nothing to say this was his, no papers certifying this man lived, no documents, nothing but these few belongings and even those were only identified as his, because they were found in his cell: number 45997.

He returned the items back to the shoebox in exactly the same order they had been removed and stared at the orange and black object with tears welling up in his eyes for someone he hardly knew. Why, he had no idea. Probably the pathetic nature of the man, finally at peace, pleading his innocence for as long as he had known him, yet suddenly confessing to many killings and his promise to this man; how was he to keep that promise?

The Vicar thought only of Jack Hammond as his salvation.

Above the sound of the traffic Arthur Sandhurst called out from the front gate.

"Good morning, Marjory."

Marjory looked up from her gardening, surprised to hear his voice.

"Oh, Arthur... you did startle me, I didn't hear the Rolls drive up."

He opened the gate and walked casually down the path admiring the roses. "And here's me thinking it was my personality that startled you."

"You better not let Jack hear you talk like that, he hasn't any sense of humour."

"Does he know I've known you longer than he has?" he continued, giving her a peck on the cheek on reaching her.

"Ooh... careful of my gloves," she said, trying to take them off without getting mud all over his new suit. "We are looking smart today."

"Thank you. I'm going up to the Squires place later; he wants to sell off some more land. Poor soul, he's feeling the pinch."

"I wish I could feel as pinched," she said, taking his arm and leading him towards the front door. "It's difficult trying to reorganise yourself into a retired lifestyle."

"I'm sure it is. But surely Jack would have come out of the force with a good pension? He was a Superintendent."

She left the gardening things by the front step, slipped her feet out of her Wellingtons, and led him inside.

"Oh look it's not so much the money; we manage fine. It's having to think about it all the time," she continued as they moved into the lounge. Arthur chose the comfortable chair and Marjory went over to the drinks trolley. "How about a drink?"

"Who's having a drink at this time of the day?" Jack's voice echoed from the kitchen, as he was removing his boots.

"It's all right dear, it's only Arthur," Marjory shouted back.

Jack walked into the lounge, Marjory was standing by the trolley, "Hello, Arthur, how's things?" he said. "Have I interrupted something?"

"Don't be silly, dear, Arthur and I go back a long way."

"How come Arthur gets a drink this early, and I don't?" Jack questioned.

"Because he's a guest."

"Look you two, I'd much rather have a cup of strong coffee," Arthur said.

"And tea for you, dear?" she asked on her way out.

"Er... yes please."

"So, Jack, doing some gardening I see."

"It's not really gardening, more a cleaning up exercise," Jack said, as he looked him up and down. "Why are you looking as if you're going somewhere?"

"I am... to the Estate."

"The Estate?"

"Yes, the Squire's Estate."

"Who is this Squire actually," Jack enquired, as Marjory returned with the drinks, placing them on a coffee table and then sitting down opposite the men.

"Brigadier Mathew Chomley-Pitt," Marjory answered for him. "I thought you'd like some wholemeal biscuits, plain or with chocolate on one side."

"He's not a Lord then," Jack commented, stirring his tea. He circled his fingers above the plate and went for the chocolate variety. Marjory glared at him.

Arthur took a biscuit then answered, "Afraid not, second son and all that. All he got was this small estate; his brother, Lord Chomley, got the rest."

"So when you talk of the Squire's Estate, you're not talking about some great edifice of a Stately Home surrounded with acres of manicured lawns and flower beds."

Arthur laughed, and then realised Jack had no idea of country life.

"No, Jack... just a mere mansion standing in a few hundred acres of pure bred stud country... oh and some farm buildings, cottages here and there, half of the village and not forgetting the park he donated at the bottom of your garden."

"Sounds like being a second son isn't that bad after all," Marjory said.

Arthur took another drink to clear the biscuit between his teeth.

"Are you aware that this cottage belonged to the estate at one time, it was the gamekeeper's home, when he had one."

"I had my suspicions," Marjory said.

Jack looked blank. They were talking about a time that had nothing to do with him, and it irked him. He didn't like the idea that someone knew her before him.

"Yes... the Squire put this little triangle of land up for sale when he turned the bottom paddock into a park. I grabbed it for your mother; she was living in the village then and always loved this cottage. She was a good friend of the gamekeeper's wife before she died. Poor fellow... he never got over it."

"Yes I remember that time, just after the war," Marjory said. "You remember Jack, we had just met while you were on leave."

"The war?" Arthur questioned.

"Yes... sorry, the Korean War," Marjory corrected herself.

"So you're off to this mansion now, are you?" Jack asked.

"Yes," he glanced at his watch. "I saw Marjory in the front garden and thought I'd pop in on my up to the estate and here I am having tea and biscuits when I should be on my way." He emptied his cup and made for the front door.

It was plain to see Marjory would have preferred it if he stayed all afternoon instead of visiting the Squire. Jack was still thinking about their past when they saw Arthur out to his Rolls. It was a quick goodbye and he whooshed off up the hill and out of sight. Marjory was still standing there uninterested in lunch.

The Vicar was breathing a little heavier than usual, as he trudged out of the copse across the paddock towards the Hammond's.

Most probably because of the excited state he was in, brought on by the thought of the shoebox he had stuffed under his arm, and the anticipation of what Jack might make of its contents.

Half way across the field he suddenly became uneasy. Jack was not sitting on his bench as he had done regularly since arriving. At first he thought they might be out, then inside having a late lunch; but he carried on since he was almost there.

As the Vicar neared the fence, Jack suddenly popped up from nowhere; his back towards the Vicar, yanking at something out of sight. There was a loud whoosh, and Jack swung round with a dead shrub in both hands.

"Good grief... sorry, Peter, I didn't see you there," Jack shouted.

"You gave me a shock too, Jack. When I didn't see you on your bench, I thought you might be out," he said, climbing the stile and dumping his backside and the shoebox down on the bench.

Jack dumped the dead shrub, "No time to sit down today, Peter," he said.

"Has Marjory actually got you gardening again?"

Jack brushed the earth off his gloves and started removing them.

"Clearing the rubbish more like it... what brings you this way? and what's that?" he pointed to the brightly coloured box on his lap.

The Vicar placed the shoebox on the bench. "This Jack, I suspect, is our next mission; a real mystery adventure."

Jack looked at him and then the box suspiciously. "Oh yes..." then decided to sit down on the other side, with the mysterious box between them.

As the Vicar removed the lid and started to take out the contents, he suddenly realised there was a slight breeze cutting across the paddock, immediately catching the bible and fanning its wafer thin pages across to the other side. Jack court the golden edged leaves with the side of his hand, and gently closed the lid.

"I think we'd better go inside, Peter, before you lose this lot."

44

"I think you could be right."

As it turned out the unexpected breeze was the forerunner to an autumn downpour. It was such a surprise, they turned and stood for a moment watching the savage rain pound the garden with merciless disregard, tearing at the soft leaves of the geraniums and quickly flooding the patio where they stood.

"Quick, Peter, before you get your feet wet," Jack shouted.

Passing through the open French windows Jack called out for Marjory. "We've got a visitor, dear... it's, Peter," forgetting her preference for Reverend, "I mean the Reverend." There was no answer. "Make yourself comfortable, Peter; I'll see what she's doing."

He soon found her in the bedroom, with clothes strewn everywhere.

"The Reverend's here," he said.

She gasped, grabbing at the clothes on the floor. "Where?" she shrieked.

"Steady on, he's down stairs," Jack reassured. "What on earth are you doing?"

"I decided to get rid of some of our old clothes."

Jack checked the pile, "I hope some of my things aren't amongst that lot."

"I haven't got to your stuff yet."

"Anyway, are you coming down to see the Reverend or not?"

"Has he come to see me?"

"No, I don't think so."

"Then why ask?" she answered, returning to the wardrobe.

"Last time you told me off when he left without seeing you," Jack said.

Downstairs Peter looked embarrassed. "Have I come at an awkward moment?"

"Pardon?" Jack replied, distracted.

He eased himself into a chair on the other side of the table.

"You're not having a domestic are you? I couldn't help hearing the ruckus, my visits sometimes affect people that way."

"Oh no, it's nothing like that," Jack said, sitting down at the table opposite him. "Marjory has decided to give away some old clothes."

"Sorry, Jack, I think that's my fault," Peter said.

"It's not important, Peter," Jack assured him.

Jack suddenly realised they had drifted somewhat from the main point of the Vicar's visit. He was now sitting at the table with the open shoebox to one side, and its contents already neatly arranged in front of him, with an expectant look on his face.

"I thought I would save some time," he said.

"Just get me back on track, Peter, what is all this stuff and why did you come over? Not that we're not happy to see you of course."

The Vicar handed him the warden's letter, then relaxed with his hands together on the table in front of him, fingers entwined as if he was in prayer.

"Just read this, Jack, it explains everything."

Jack frowned and looked at the Vicar suspiciously. Then unfolded the single sheet and read the Warden's short note. "That's it... a dozen or so lines?"

"Yes, although I don't think he could have said more."

Jack looked across the top of the letter to the scattering of belongings that the Vicar had carefully arranged in his own order of importance, a subconscious action but one he hoped would not go unnoticed.

"So this is all this man's got to show for his life... not much is it?" Jack said.

"No... that's exactly what I thought but on closer inspection I think you'll find there's a lot here we can't see."

"And what does that mean?"

"Why don't I go through these things and you'll see," the Vicar said.

This was going to be interesting. Jack relaxed back in his seat and crossed his arms loosely over his chest. To him the small group of objects meant no more than just that, except maybe the unusual key, that intrigued him.

From his experience, keys left behind under these circumstances invariably opened up a whole new dimension to the previous owner: derelicts turning out to be multi-millionaires, safety deposit boxes with hidden stolen property and on one occasion that crossed his mind: a front door key to a different identity.

"Right... the first item I took out of the box was this bible. Now I'm familiar with this, because he always had it close by on my visits, he cherished it. You can see by the burred edges it was well used."

"What did you mean when you emphasised you were familiar with it?" Jack asked, interrupting him; becoming a policeman again.

"Because it was all I saw him with. I remember seeing the orange box on the shelf above his bunk, but he never showed me what was inside."

"That's not unexpected," Jack remarked.

"Why do you say that?"

"Well long term prisoners usually end up with a box which they never let out of their sight. That proves what we have here was valuable to him."

"Next was this dictionary, which I found very unusual."

"Why would you say that?"

"He didn't strike me as an educated man."

Jack noted how pristine it was, "It looks new, it's hardly touched."

"Exactly... and here's the receipt, it was only purchased last year."

Jack studied the computerised till printout, "Yes... which means he must have bought it specifically to find something out... I wonder what that was?"

The Vicar pushed the dictionary to one side and picked up the folded yellowing exercise sheets covered with the jumbled numbers. Unfolding them, he flattened each sheet out with the palm of his hand in front of Jack, "What do you make of these?"

At first Jack simply cast his eyes across the rows of unintelligible numbers, without touching the sheets, and then he allowed his fingers to gently kiss the surface of the handwritten scrawl.

The Vicar was fascinated, and sat watching him, waiting for his opinion.

"Interesting," Jack said. "I notice he's written this code with several different coloured pens and pencils."

"Code?... what makes you think it's a code?"

For the first time Jack took hold of one of the sheets. His pupils flashed back and forth as he perused the first few lines before he looked up at the Vicar. "I admit, Peter, at a glance this scrawl looks no more than a bunch of nonsense but if you examine the different coloured segments carefully," he prompted him to do so. "You will see it contains a kind of formality."

"I wondered why he needed so many pens and pencils," he said, pushing forward the tight bundle held in place with an elastic band.

"Maybe..." Jack guessed. "Each different writing tool possibly indicates an individual section of code. I doubt if he just ran out and started another. In that case the different writing would end and restart again anywhere, not like this at the beginning of each line."

"I didn't think of that, Jack... marvellous!"

"That's why he still has all these pens and pencils."

Jack was thinking again, the grey cells were beginning to firm up, no longer jelly like. He could feel the creative matter coming alive and filling his thoughts with a myriad of possibilities. He was beginning to feel like a detective again.

"So you think its code, Jack, not just the gibberish of a demented mind?"

"Oh, Peter, you could well be right, all this could in fact just be the meanderings of a lunatic, playing out some fictional game with himself; I did this often at school."

"You did codes at school?"

"Didn't you? I thought all boys played the game of secret agent."

"I'm afraid my childhood was less imaginative, Jack."

"Still... if that were the case, why bother at all. No, the function of a good detective is to assume these things have a meaning, just as one assumes innocence before guilt. With that in mind we can eliminate the impossible until we are left with only the truth." Jack raised his hands into the air, opening both palms questionably, "Only then can we say these cherished possessions really meant something, and this scribbling no more than the ramblings of a lunatic."

They both roared with laughter, Jack because he felt he was over his depression and the Vicar because he was so happy at the prospect of him joining them. Little did they know they were each laughing at something totally different.

"What do you make of these numbers Jack?"

"Could be anything, numbers were never my forte."

The Vicar pointed at the first sheet. "Have you noticed how they all seem to start with three digits?" then glanced at the others.

"That's what I meant by formality."

"I thought at a glance they were from the bible, the three digits followed by a colon, then one or two others," he tapped the bible.

"So?" Jack questioned.

"It doesn't make sense. It's not referring to the bible."

"Don't concern yourself, Peter; I'm sure Janet can solve it."

"Janet?" the connection was not apparent.

"Well she is supposed to be good at numbers, isn't she?"

"Yes of course," that was something he could do later this afternoon.

The purse was of no interest to Jack, but the key was. He had seen something like it before. He picked it up. "I've seen a key like this before... or something like it, but when?" he commented, flipping it over and over between his forefinger and thumb.

It was too long for a house key, and the unusual teeth had him puzzled. They were angular and intermittent, not like the typical saw tooth pattern of a normal key and the fact that they were on both sides baffled him.

"It's most unusual, isn't it?" the Vicar commented as he drew Jack's attention to the engraved numbers. "What about these?"

Jack turned the key sideways, "04-173-8030013/S... that's it... I remember. It's the 'S' on the end I remember, it stands for storage. It's a private storage key."

"Not a safety deposit?"

"No... they only last a short time without re-renting. Whereas a storage warehouse deposit is usually rented for longer periods, say three to twelve months," he placed it back on the table. "All we have to do is find out the what and where; then we might find out if these were all his possessions."

"Can we ring around the warehouses and ask them to check the number?"

"Peter... there's hundreds in London alone, and what about the other cities?"

"It isn't as easy as I thought," the Vicar said, disheartened.

"As I told you yesterday, it's a professional's job."

"I know. I suppose I got a bit carried away but I'm back to earth now."

Jack reached across and placed his hand on the Vicar's shoulder. He said nothing, his look of understanding was enough, and the Vicar drew satisfaction from that. It was enough to know Jack was finally interested.

Jack's attention was now drawn to the cartridge. It would have been his first interest if not for the fact that it had rolled behind the dictionary when the Vicar moved the bible. It looked familiar to him. It brought back memories. "Well, well," he exclaimed knowingly. A 303 cartridge, I haven't seen one of those in years."

"You know what it is then, Jack?"

"Yes... it belongs to an old rifle bullet; there's still some of them in use today."

"Would a sniper use one?"

"Oh yes, most certainly. Why?"

The Vicar had left the story Samuel told him about being a sniper till last, until he was sure Jack was interested. He was still not fully convinced it was true. Bearing in mind Samuel's chequered past, he had no intention of being laughed at until he knew Jack's suspicions about the contents of the box had begun to fester in his mind. He felt the coded sheets and the unusual key had done that.

Telling Jack how Samuel was used during the war for purposes other than just fighting was something he had to play by ear, and the consequences of his recruitment into something he did not explain when he re-entered civilian life; not to mention the two hidden corpses.

As far as Jack was concerned, regardless of whether or not he believed Samuel's tale, he told the Vicar that this information placed a different light on the subject, along with the importance of decoding the two sheets. If there were any credence to his story, the implications would be paramount.

Although Jack neglected to mention this would mean the police would have to be informed if Samuel's story was confirmed, the first thing they had to do, above anything else, was to find one acceptable fact, either through the coded material or what they might find in the warehouse.

"Before we do anything else, Peter, we have to call a meeting with the others to discuss the ramifications of this, and what we do next if anything; and not in the church hall, it's got to be separated from your class. I don't mind the first one being here; we can make it more permanent later."

"That sounds a good solution, Jack," the Vicar agreed. "I'll go and see Janet now; she'll be still at the school. I'll see if she can throw some light on these figures before our meeting. I'll also contact the others and ring you regarding a good time."

"I'll leave you to it then," Jack said.

The Vicar gathered Samuel's possessions, placed them back in the shoebox and left the way he came through the French windows. He seemed too preoccupied for small-talk and Jack understood that he had a lot to come to terms with. Not to mention the possibility that Samuel was telling the truth.

CHAPTER 4

School had finished, although there were still a few children playing in the yard, which meant the teachers hadn't left yet, when the Vicar pushed his way through the swing doors. They opened onto a corridor of administration offices and the main notice board on the wall.

A few mothers were standing by the board as he passed and he had a few words with them before continuing on to the principal's office. He noticed Janet was talking to one of the teachers and hovered impatiently.

"I want you to arrange for a coach to take the team over to Guilford at the weekend, Pamela. I've got a couple of meetings and I just can't attend to everything," Janet was saying to her physical education teacher as they walked back from the main hall along the corridor where the Vicar was waiting. "Oh, Reverend, I hope you haven't been waiting long," she said, on catching sight of him.

"I'll attend to that, Miss Donald," Pamela said, nodding to the Vicar and continuing on down the corridor.

She said nothing as she passed him; she felt he was too familiar for a man of the cloth. She had seen him several times with the principal and knew they had a relationship that wasn't entirely to do with the school's activities.

"Well, to what do I owe this pleasure," Janet said, now that they were alone.

"I know you must have had a hard day, Janet, but I was wondering if you could spare me a few moments of your valuable time."

Janet was curious, seeing him standing there clutching an old shoebox.

"Of course, Reverend, anytime... you know that," she blustered, making him regret his decision already. "Let's go into my office, we won't be disturbed there."

The Vicar had to admit Janet was a remarkable woman but she had the awful habit of treating everyone as if they were still at school and that sometimes meant she was a little overwhelming.

She sat him down, switched on the percolator, brought two cups and some biscuits from her cupboard and stood looking at him while she waited for it to bubble, "Are you going to sit clutching that box all day or are you going to tell me what it is? Presuming that's what you've come here for."

"Sorry, Janet," he said, placing it on her desk.

She poured out the coffee, brought it over to the desk and sat down looking at the orange box in front of her, "So, Reverend, you said a few moments."

"Yes" he said, not knowing where to start. He had it all worked out on his way over but as usual as soon as he saw her it completely left his mind.

"Is there a problem," she urged again.

"Sorry, Janet," there he goes apologising again. "I mean it's difficult to know where to start, it's so complex."

"Usually the beginning is a good place," she said, trying her coffee.

"I know, but if I started there I'd be here all night. I've just come from Jack's and that was a two hour session."

"Well, Reverend it's up to you, I'm happy to wait."

"No... that's alright. I'll make it brief."

"Very well, Reverend, I'm enthralled."

"I would wait until you hear what I have to say first."

He calmed himself, took a drink of his coffee, which seemed to help, then started. "Okay, you know that I regularly visit the Hatchwood Prison and in particular, how I've often mentioned Samuel and his problem with thinking he was innocent."

"That's right, sorry," she interrupted.

"Well he died of cancer last week and the Warden sent me his bequest, this box." He paused as he placed his hand on the lid.

"That parcel you rushed off to get from Fred this morning?"

"Yes," he opened the box and placed the contents across her blotter. She didn't look too happy at first, as if they may be contaminated or something.

"Jack and I discussed each item at length, prompting the decision to call a meeting at his place to go into them in more detail but before that time, we felt you should look at these sheets with numbers on. We already discarded the idea that they may refer to the bible," he unfolded the pages and passed them over to her.

She noticed the yellow stain and poked at the top sheet, "Mmm... very interesting. I can see the reason why you first thought they might have had something to do with the bible; they look like chapter and verse numbers up on your board by the pulpit."

"Exactly but I can't make any sense of them, I've tried."

"Well I'll have a look at them tonight if you like but I wouldn't hold my breath if I were you, without a key, and I don't mean that peculiar looking thing either, I mean a pattern or keyword to start us off. She picked up the security key and twirled it in her fingers.

"Another mystery?"

"Yes... Jack says he thinks it belongs to a warehouse storage deposit."

As with Jack, the Vicar had omitted to disclose his prime objective: to find out the identity of the two victims and where their bodies were hidden.

"To what end?" Janet interrupted his thoughts.

"I beg your pardon?"

"What is the purpose of finding out what all this means? ...if it means anything."

"Of course, I didn't finish my story. Samuel was still emphatic about his innocence on his death bed but surprised me by confessing to other murders; two that were hidden which he wanted me to find and say the words over."

"Say the words over?... you mean the Last Rites?"

"Yes, he didn't know what they were."

"If you say he was criminally insane, how can you believe him?"

"I can't... that's why it's so important we find out what all this means."

Janet picked up the cartridge, "A 303," she said, causing him to open his mouth in surprise. Everyone except himself appeared to know what a 303 was.

"That's what Jack said. You know about these things?"

"I should do, my father was a member of the local gun club when I was a bit of a girl. We used to spend hours there and I always had to collect all the spent cartridges like this one before we left. In those days country folk filled their own shells."

"Is that so... how interesting."

"Yes... and he used to keep me occupied loading his clips and belt."

"Clips?" he questioned in his ignorance.

"Yes clips, the metal thing that holds the bullets."

She put the cartridge to her nose, sniffing the old cordite. "What's this?" she said, looking inside, picking up her paper knife and poking it into the cartridge.

"What have you got there?" the Vicar asked, as a thin white tube began to appear.

"I don't know, weren't you aware of it?" she said, letting it fall onto the blotter.

"No... I wasn't... what is it?"

Janet picked it up and begun unrolling the tight coil that turned out to be a slip of paper about six inches by two. On the internal side was written the words, 'Collins English Concise Dictionary' in blue ink and underneath, two sets of similar number groups as on the sheets but this time in red.

"Things get stranger," the Vicar commented, looking quite perplexed.

Janet on the other hand, took on an air of confidence as her manner changed on seeing the numbers. "Well as far as I'm concerned, Reverend, this is our key. This paper tells us the Collins Dictionary here is our source, and you did say you were looking for two victims?"

"That's right."

"Then I wouldn't mind betting these two sets of numbers refer to them."

"That's fantastic Janet! I told Jack you would be the one to help us," he said, diverting his eyes slightly and forgiving himself under his breath for that very small white lie, knowing it was for the greater good.

"Good... you leave this lot with me, Reverend and I'll make a start tonight," she said condescendingly. "What about this meeting? Tomorrow afternoon's fine with me," she continued, helping him pack the items back into the box.

"I'll have to contact the others. I'll get back to you."

"Be forceful, Reverend. Next week I've got the education authorities here doing an audit, so my time will be pretty well occupied," she blustered.

The Vicar nervously looked at his watch, it was getting late and his wife would be wondering where he'd been all afternoon. He finished off with Janet, leaving Samuel's shoebox with her, and made his way back to the church.

Jack had made two mugs of tea and was just about to check on how Marjory was doing with the evening meal when the phone rang.

"Hello," he said.

"Jack... it's Peter, sorry to call you now but I'm trying to pin everyone down to a time for this meeting at your place. How about tomorrow afternoon?"

"Tomorrow?... yes, that'll be alright,"

"Good, say about two. Thanks a lot... oh Jack, are you still there?"

"Yes, Peter, I'm still here."

"I nearly forgot, I went straight round to Janet's as you suggested and guess what, she found a piece of rolled up paper inside that 303 cartridge with wording and numbers on indicating that the dictionary was the source."

"Well there you are, Peter, I told you she would help. Now can I please have my meal, I'll see you all tomorrow."

"Oh sorry, Jack, see you then."

As he returned the phone Marjory was already placing the plates on the table, "What's this about tomorrow?" she said.

It's a long story, dear, let's have our meal and I'll tell you all about it later."

The following day Marjory was more interested in shopping than the meeting of the criminology group regardless of him trying to persuade her to be there in the capacity of a scribe. He said if she wanted him involved, it was going to be done properly.

Despite Jack's pleas Marjory had better things to do than getting involved with a bunch of amateur detectives. She planned to be out shopping when they arrived and if he wanted to get himself strung out over it, that was his business.

The first to arrive was Arthur; majestically gliding up to the front of the cottage and parking the Rolls in the open area to one side of the garage. Jack was there to greet him after closing the wooden garage doors for Marjory, who had just left.

"Arthur... nice to see you," Jack called out.

Arthur shook Jack's hand, "Did I pass Marjory back there?" he said.

"You did... she's getting out of making notes."

Arthur laughed, "I can see her point."

They were distracted by shouts from the back garden; the others had arrived. They had decided, as it had turned out to be a fine autumn afternoon, that they would walk across the now favourite route from the church, leaving their cars behind.

"Do you think you're beginning to create a public right of way, from the church to my place?" Jack commented, cutting round to the back through the side gate.

They all laughed, shaking each other's hands and generally going through the usual ritual they did each time they met; except now Jack was involved, as if he had been unceremoniously enrolled as a new member.

"Very good of you to let us have this meeting at your place, Jack," Dick said. The others let out a loud, "here, here."

They went into Jack's study; a small back room Marjory converted into a den. The walls were covered with pictures of ceremonial police gatherings, his academy photographs with his parents, his old colleagues in Uxbridge, a few in the local next to Scotland Yard with the CID mob and some images of Korea.

They were all instinctively drawn to Jack's past.

Up until their move to Lower Cheedam the photographs had hardly seen the light of day until now; tucked away in an old album Jack had started but lost interest in when he moved to Scotland Yard. During Marjory's redecoration, while Jack was still struggling with his desk job, she dug them out, had them mounted and framed in the village and on the wall before she invited him into his new den.

Everyone was quite impressed, especially with his framed commendation, awarded at Buckingham Palace for bravery in disarming a gunman in a public place, alongside his war ribbons and campaign medals; neither of which he could be drawn on, preferring to pass on to other things.

They soon settled down expectantly around his small desk, bringing chairs from the dining room to compensate for his singular furnishings. Janet helped Jack move the tortoiseshell desk set Marjory bought him for his last birthday, a small table lamp, the telephone and a pile of old files he brought back from the office as mementoes to while away his boring afternoons.

"Well... here we are then," the Vicar began, not sure how to start, this being a special meeting, and the first one Jack was involved with. "As you are all aware from my telephone call yesterday, Jack has asked for a special meeting to discuss my bequest from Samuel in the prison... so over to you, Jack."

Jack looked speechless. He didn't know why he expected to maintain a low profile, as Marjory suggested, during a meeting he instigated. He hesitated.

It was as if his chair had been kicked from under him. Yesterday it was all so clear, why they needed to talk and what they had to decide before these incorruptible eccentrics went too far.

"Well, Peter... I don't know so much about me calling this special meeting, I know it was of consensus during your visit yesterday that everyone should be aware of what happened, so I think you should get the ball rolling and explain what this bequest is all about; assuming I'm the only one you confided in."

"Oh for heaven's sake, sorry, Reverend, let's stop all this waffling," Janet jumped in, obviously anxious to get to her part in all this, by the mass of papers she had.

No one seemed surprised at her outburst except Jack; he was used to women being less assertive around him and it came as quite a jolt to his senses. The Vicar sheepishly tilted his head in agreement and opened the shoebox Janet had placed in the centre of the desk. He pulled the box closer to him, removed the lid, and spread the contents in a row across the desk in front of them.

Mainly for the benefit of Arthur and Dick, but not wasting time saying so, he explained how he came by the box, the discovery he made about Samuel's past, and Jack's reference to the significance of the coded papers and unusual key.

Not surprisingly, Arthur picked it up immediately; it appeared to have that affect on people, whilst the Vicar continued with Janet's recent discovery but didn't elaborate on that, instead concluded with Jack's reason for this impromptu meeting.

"Now, Jack, I think you can continue," he said with relief.

"Before I start, I think you should be reminded that I made two provisos when Peter asked me to conduct this investigation as professionally as I would have done with the police... if these deaths are to be taken seriously..."

"Deaths!" Dick interrupted."

"Don't alarm yourself, Dick," the Vicar said with his usual calming voice. "All will become clear as we progress."

Jack sat patiently until silence fell across the group again. "Firstly, and most importantly, we must not do anything that in any way would conflict with police business or give cause for any interested party to take legal action against us. As I explained, amateur detection is frowned upon and requires at least a licence to do so; or some form of historical research or media publication..."

"Sorry, Jack," the Vicar interrupted. "I forgot to tell you, Janet managed to make us a society," she passed the certificate across to him, he handed it to Jack.

Jack almost burst out laughing but halted himself, other than his expression, which he had no control over. "Well... I suppose this could loosely fit into the category of historical research, I only hope we don't have to use it."

"I take it you think it's bogus?" Janet commented.

"Don't misunderstand me, Janet; I think it's great that you were able to at least give us something to work under. But don't take my advice lightly in this, as a retired policeman I can assure you, the police don't like amateur detectives meddling in their business. So let's get that quite clear.

"But what if, as Samuel said, the bodies were hidden? The reason for him wanting me to find them, surely the police wouldn't know about them?"

"Hidden or not, Peter. People disappear, and if someone has reported them missing, the police have to investigate and that constitutes a case file."

The others had been silent until Dick half-heartedly raised his hand, as if he needed permission to interrupt. "Surely there are instances when these missing people aren't missed, if you understand my meaning?"

"Then that poses somewhat of a problem, because we shall be investigating a new case, which I shall be duty bound to report to the police if it proves to have any validity. However, I suggest we worry about that issue if we come to it."

"But you'll keep us right on this, surely, Jack?" the Vicar questioned.

"Of course I will, Peter, but everyone needs to be aware of our situation. Anyway, enough of that, the second point is that if we are to do this properly, it must be conducted professionally. If everyone agrees, I will take over the strategy of this investigation and co-ordinate each phase, just as if it were a police case."

"That was going to be my point, Jack," Arthur said.

"Oh... what was that?"

"At what point would you think of contacting the police?"

"As I see it, that probability is some way off yet. We have to establish that we're dealing with a real issue here. I'm still not convinced all this isn't the fanciful meanderings of a demented mind."

The excited look drained from the Vicar's face, "Oh, Jack, I thought you were actually convinced yesterday?"

"I told you then, Peter, I'm not convinced easily. What I said was, I find sufficient evidence to warrant an inquiry; not an investigation."

"Oh dear."

"Should this inquiry establish a basis for me to suspect there might be some truth in these deaths..." he looked at Arthur, "then I shall have to give consideration to an investigation on our part or informing the police."

"I told you Reverend, it wouldn't be that easy," Janet remarked.

The Vicar was not going to be deterred by Jack's threats of police involvement or a long drawn out procedure before they got started, as long as they did start. He put on a new front, "That sounds excellent, Jack."

Everyone gestured with a nod of agreement.

If Jack had been honest with them he would have admitted he had no confidence in this becoming any more than a good exercise in investigative procedure. He was positive the clues they were about to discuss were no more than what he had already intimated: a group of highly imaginative 'Red Herrings'.

CHAPTER 5

Suddenly Jack didn't see a bunch of county bumpkins anymore; they were his investigative team, much as he had at the Yard, only this group needed coaxing. They had no idea of procedure, of weeding out clues or how to approach a crime scene; it was like being back at the Academy again.

"Now to start our first official briefing I shall nominate major roles to everyone, although we'll all chip into the general program so to speak. Then I'll go over these items one by one, and we can all input any ideas we have. By the way, should any of you object to their speciality speak up, I don't want any problems later. Right... Janet," she looked at him apprehensively. "You can look after the code breaking aspect of this investigation; I understand from Peter, you've already made a breakthrough?"

"Yes... I found a piece of paper rolled up in that 303 cartridge, which I'm sure is the key to the code; I've already made a rough start."

"Hold it there, Janet, sorry to butt in, I need to keep this in order so I'll get back to that later... okay?" he had to control this women.

"Yes fine," she said, a little uncomfortably. She was used to dictating the pace. Someone else telling her what to do was a new experience for her; she wasn't sure whether she liked it or not. Jack opened his note-pad and started making notes; cursing Marjory.

"Okay, Arthur, I think your role should be as our researcher," everyone verbally agreed with his choice, "You can liaise with Janet as she gradually unfolds the code, with regards names and places." He turned to Dick who appeared happy just to sit and listen, "Dick... I can't see a great use of your augury talents generally but certainly I shall consult you when it's appropriate with some profile work. In the meantime I'd like you and Peter to join me in some good old legwork."

There was very little reaction to the suggestion, which interested Jack.

"Time isn't a problem, now my son's taken over but what do you mean by legwork?" Dick questioned. "And what's a profiler?"

Jack indulged him, "Okay... by legwork I mean running down leads, checking if the address Arthur gave us is correct and so on."

"That sounds easy enough."

"Believe me it can get extremely boring. As for profiling, it's guessing what the suspect's character is like from available evidence. Usually the job of a psychologist, who can define the suspect's temperament, hang-ups; that sort of thing, you know?"

"Not really," Dick said unenthusiastically.

"Well I don't know how you became known as a medium then, I'm only going on Peter's introduction of you but I presume you get impressions of people and things you come in contact with."

"I don't really know what I do; I'm semi-unconscious most of the time."

"Well don't you read anything into people when you meet them?"

"I suppose I do, I just thought it was something most people did."

"Well I'm sticking my neck out here but do you get anything strong from me?"

Dick closed his eyes and paused for a moment.

Everyone looked embarrassed at the possibility Dick might say the wrong thing. "It's difficult to say, but there is a very strong image which I had the first time I met you, and it's there again now. It looks like a curved sword and yes, a wooden 'T'" he looked at Jack, who had turned quite ashen.

"Enough to convince me you can perform a profiling job under guidance."

"Is that it?" Peter exclaimed. "Are we not going to know what these things mean? Jack don't keep us in suspense. I thought our involvement with you as a member of our group was going to be a learning experience."

Jack thought about whether he should tell them, he had been desperately trying to drive the image from his mind since it happened. It was as if Dick had plucked it from his subconscious: an unhappy experience with no real closure for anyone.

"It was my last case, a particularly nasty one, and before you start, there's no way I'm going to tell you about it and resurrect that memory I've been trying to erase since I retired. What I will say is the curved sword was a Japanese Samurai, and the 'T' was in fact a crucifix."

"Crucifix," the Vicar cried out, his curiosity bristling. "Sorry, Jack, I respect you not wanting to go any further, but how do you relate a 'T' to a crucifix?"

"The old style crucifix. The one with a bar across the top of a stake. It was a reference to the way the victim's in my last case died."

"Yes of course I remember now," the Vicar agreed.

"Thank you. Now does that answer your question?"

"Yes, Jack."

"Right, back to the agenda, how's the time. Three thirty... everyone okay?" they all nodded to continue. "Now let's look at this lot." He continued as he passed his hand across the contents of the shoebox.

Jack rearranging them to suit the way he wanted to introduce them. It was an exercise he always found himself doing back at the station, when evidence was brought into the squad room.

"A bible which, on the face of it, looks like having no bearing on our case. I gather you went through it Peter?"

"Yes, it obviously wasn't the source as you say and didn't look as if it had any other significance than to give Samuel comfort," he replied.

"Okay... remove it, we don't want anything that won't help us". He placed the bible back in the box.

"Next we have the dictionary that Janet has already stated looks like being the source for these sheets of code, according to this piece of paper she found in the 303 cartridge," he slid it and the two sheets over towards Janet.

"We'll return to that later. Now what's next? The receipt can go with the dictionary. That leaves the purse. You did say it only contained money?" Jack asked the Vicar.

"Yes, his only monitory possession, no ID or anything else," he confirmed.

"Okay that only leaves the 303 cartridge and this unusual key."

"Don't forget the pens and pencils," Janet pointed out.

"Again, they serve no purpose, but I would like you to check if in fact they actually made the notations, whilst you're deciphering the code, Janet."

"Do you doubt Samuel did this?" Arthur questioned. He had little to contribute to the proceedings so far, but was curious to establish who created the code.

"To be frank with you, Arthur, yes I do."

"I thought so... I know I would."

Jack continued, "The first impression I got from Peter's description of this man, was that he was inarticulate, not the sort of personality that would be capable of such an obviously complex creation. Would you agree, Janet, from your first encounter?"

"I have to agree, unless he did this in better times, I doubt he was capable. I also think it's a good idea to check the handwriting."

"Do we have any other examples, Peter?" Jack asked.

"I'm afraid not."

"Back to these other two items then. Wherever he got this cartridge from, it's certainly a 303 shell, which ties in with Peter's story about him being a sniper. Other than that, there's not much we can get out of it; too many people have handled it,"

Jack rubbed the back of his neck.

"Although the hairs on the back of my neck tell me to hold on to it," he placed it in front of Dick.

"What do you think, Dick?"

Dick looked apprehensively at the cartridge standing upright on the green leather inset in the top of the desk, reflecting the light off its shiny brass surface and gingerly placing his forefinger and thumb around the crimped end, he closed his eyes. After a few seconds, he suddenly opened them again with a shocked look of awareness and released his hold, knocking the cartridge over as he did so.

"Good grief," he exclaimed. "I never experienced that before."

"What happened?" Arthur asked him.

"I actually had a thought that wasn't mine when I touched the cartridge," he continued, still shaken; looking quite ashen.

"What did you see?" Jack asked.

"It was a fleeting image of a man sitting on a bed."

"Can you elaborate?" Jack asked.

"He was sitting on one of those blue grey woollen blankets. He picked this cartridge up from the bed where there were many others, or at least one like it."

"No, that'll be the one. Did you see the man's face?"

"Not really, it all happened too quickly, but I remember his hand. It had a bad scar above the knuckle of the forefinger."

"Did you actually see this," the Vicar questioned.

"Not really," Dick replied, screwing up his face, feeling unsure. "It's not unlike when I contact a channel that takes control of my thoughts. Except that way I relax and wait for him to speak, instead of touching something," he paused, thinking. "When you come to think of it, I must have had these thoughts all the time without knowing, whenever I touched anyone or anything... it's eerie, now I'm going to be conscious of that all the time, I don't know that I like that at all."

Jack cut off his rambling, "There you are, Dick, you're earning your keep already but you're not doing anything different to any of us if you think about it. As I said myself a moment ago; when the hairs stood up on the back of my neck. I had a premonition. You're just more sensitive than most."

The others were getting excited. "Now we just need to channel this more professionally," Arthur said.

"I never knew I could do this," Dick continued. "I normally just sit still, close my eyes and wait for someone to contact me. I've never associated what's in my mind with the object I'm touching before."

"I read once that this type of cognition could be triggered by a violent act," the Vicar pointed out. "Maybe you didn't come across any violent vibes before."

"That's quite true," said Jack. "The profilers I've worked with say it takes a tremendous energy to stimulate a past act from an object, extreme hate or violence."

"But we all think things all the time," Dick pointed out. "How can we be sure it has anything to do with an object?"

"We can't, we can only go on the assumption that your thoughts are more significant than ours, and see if they pan out," Jack assured him. "We'll soon know."

"But how does this help us?" Arthur questioned.

"By getting Dick to fine tune his gift."

By now they were all staring at the last two remaining objects on the desk; in Jack's mind probably the two most important ones. Nothing was said as he instinctively slipped a pencil into the cartridge, as if not wanting to contaminate it any further, and let it slip into the shoebox beside Peter.

Jack now returned to the key, holding it upright in his hand for everyone to see, "As I pointed out to Peter when we first saw this, I was sure it was a storage depository key. It was the letter 'S' at the end that I recognised. However, it'll be a mammoth task to find out what it fits, even if it's still there."

"Would you like me to research the depositories?" Arthur asked.

"That would be a good start but I don't think you appreciate how many there are in England. My suggestion is that we hold off on that until we get some more information from what we have. It's surprising how often one thing leads to another." Jack saw the disappointment on Arthur's face. "Of course, I suppose it wouldn't harm you trying London first. It would give you some good practise."

"Right, I'll do that," he said more optimistic, and picked up the key. "What if I'm lucky first time and find something?"

"Don't pursue the matter, just take down the details."

From the corner of his eye Jack could see the anticipation on Janet's face. She had been so patient while he passed her over for something else on the desk and was bursting to tell everyone what she had discovered.

"Okay, Janet, it's over to you. Tell us what you've made out of those codes."

They all watched impatiently as Janet withdrew the rolled up piece of graph paper she was working on and placed it in front of her along with the dictionary. She then arranged the two original sheets to her right.

She sat looking at the array to make sure she had everything she wanted, then snapped her fingers and pulled out the piece of paper she found in the cartridge. "When I found this piece of paper," she passed it round for them to read, "I was pretty sure it pointed to the dictionary as being our master source. As you can see it's written there at the top alongside the two codes."

When the paper was passed back to her she continued.

"Assuming this piece of paper was in fact the key to the code, or at least its subject matter, I decided that the numbers underneath represented the index of the two sheets: Two sets of numbers... two sheets."

"How clever, Janet," the Vicar interrupted. She scowled at him. "Sorry."

"Armed with this assumption I set about breaking the code. As Jack speculated earlier, I made the mistake of thinking this was a complex one, when in fact it turned out to be quite simple; one might say quite school-boyish."

"Comparable with Samuel's intelligence?" the Vicar interrupted again.

"Yes, Reverend. I was forced to change my opinion that he was incapable," she checked the dictionary. "I worked out the first code as follows: (1174:4 / 405:5) represents Watt-ford, although I think he's trying to say 'Watford', and (317:4 / 124:14) stands for East-bourn... or 'Eastbourne'. Working on the assumption that these two names had to correspond in some way with something on these two sheets and since Samuel told the Reverend about his two victims, I think it is reasonable to assume each one of these sheets represents a victim."

"I could have done with you at the Yard, Janet."

Smiling at him she cleared her throat and continued. "I scanned the two sheets into my computer and converted the images of the numbers to text, once I had done that it was comparatively easy to scan for a corresponding number representing the word 'Watford'. Once I established that, I checked the other sheet and found it also corresponded with 'Eastbourne', and titled each sheet accordingly with its prefix. Satisfied that I had interpreted the code correctly, I began translating the first sheet. I still have some way to go yet."

"Well done, Janet," the Vicar complimented, everyone all acknowledging how well she had done. "Of course you do realise, that breaking this code could be all we need, the dictionary equivalent to all these numbers should spell it out for us."

"It's not quite as easy as that," Janet said. "Whoever did this picked only key words, which means the blank spaces are going to leave a lot to our imaginations and I found out another thing; the code is synonymous with this dictionary only. By chance I tried to match it with another version and it didn't work."

"Nevertheless," Jack started again. "What you've come up with so far gives us a pretty good lead. At the Yard we frequently had far less to go on."

"What do you make of it, Jack?" Arthur asked.

"It's early days, Arthur. We all need to think about it."

"Maybe we'll have a better idea by our next meeting" the Vicar said.

"Janet you continue with your decoding. I want one full victim's profile, if what you said is true, before we go any further. Arthur, you look into London's storage depositories until we have more information, and Dick, I want you to take charge of this shoebox and its contents."

"And what do I do with it?"

"I want you to check it out and write down anything you imagine, no matter how ridiculous or bizarre you think it might be. That's everything, even the box."

"What about me Jack," the Vicar said quietly, feeling left out of his own show.

"I'm leaving you to come out on our first field trip, Peter but first I need to be sure where we're going. We need a few more facts behind us."

The Vicar's expression confirmed he was satisfied with Jack's evaluation of the situation. He would be the first to acknowledge the worst thing would be to go into their investigation unprepared.

When Marjory finally arrived home she called out for Jack, anxious to show him all she had in her boutique bags. There was no reply, and the house at the front was in darkness, which worried her. At the back, opposite the kitchen, she was relieved to see a thin line of light under his study door, but could hear no voices.

"Jack... are you there?" she called as she pushed the door open with her elbow.

There was no answer and her first thoughts were that the room was empty until she saw Jack's reflection in the window, crouched down in his easy chair with his arms crossed tightly over his chest. His eyes were closed; deep in thought.

"Jack, why don't you answer me?" she called again, now becoming anxious.

He opened his tired eyes, lolled his head to one side so he could see her, his expression didn't change, "So you're back then."

"Yes, are you all right? They've all gone I see."

He still didn't reply, just continued staring out into the darkness of the uncurtained windows. There was nothing he could see; nothing she was aware of.

Marjory placed the bags on the floor and walked around the chair so that she could kneel down in front of him, rested her hands on his crossed arms, and looked up into his face. His eyes said nothing; they were still occupied with his thoughts.

"What am I doing, Marjory, for a while back there this afternoon I felt alive again, as if I was back at the Yard. Then when they left, taking their enthusiasm with them, I suddenly went flat and panic took over."

"What do you mean, dear?"

"I thought, 'What on earth am I doing playing detective with this bunch of amateurs?' They're not satisfied with just toying around with old crimes; they have to get involved with something real... untouched."

He shook his head back and forth, in bewilderment.

"Maybe a visit to the Yard to see what they think would help?"

"How would that help? They'd probably laugh me out of the place."

"What have you arranged with the group?"

"I've just gone and given them all tasks to do, that's all. I've got a bunch of novices running around getting into heaven knows what."

"Then just leave it like that for the moment, Jack, they can't really get into any trouble. Then after the weekend, if you still don't feel good about it, drop it; or as I suggest, go and have a drink with your old Sergeant."

"He's an Inspector now."

"Better still. His suggestions will carry some weight."

Jack looked at his long suffering wife and wondered why she put up with him, then down to her bags lying across the floor.

"Oh sorry, dear, you wanted to show me what you'd bought, and as usual I spoilt everything. Show me now."

"Do you really want to see, Jack?"

He bent down and kissed her forehead, and then she turned her face upwards and kissed him passionately on the mouth.

"You bet," he said firmly, getting up and grabbing the handles in one hand, and her in the other. "Come on let's go upstairs and you can show me all these new clothes you've bought."

CHAPTER 6

The weekend turned out to be a restful stroll through the Squire's acres. Jack persuaded Marjory to venture over the stile she simply peered over occasionally; despite the Vicar's constant short cuts lately.

Then to their surprise, as Jack and Marjory casually sauntered back to their cottage after evensong in the church, Arthur slowly drew alongside them and tooted his horn. Marjory melted on seeing the Rolls.

"If you haven't got anything better to do," Arthur called out. "How about drinks at my place?" Arthur was keen to have a word with Jack.

His casual weekend had been occupied on the computer looking up all the storehouses in London and the suburbs. As Jack warned him, it was a daunting list but checking the number on the key, he had narrowed the search down to a mere twenty-two sites.

Jack glanced at Marjory; she looked as if she needed no persuading, "Sounds good to me, Arthur," he said, and they climbed in.

His mansion was an exciting finale to the weekend; at least to Marjory it was. Two drinks turned into a meal and more drinks until Arthur was too drunk to drive and Jack too conscientious to drive under the influence; they ended up walking home.

Jack suffered for it the next morning when Marjory pulled the curtains back, letting in a light brighter than he had ever seen before, blinding even with his eyelids closed, he turned away from the window and pretended he couldn't hear.

"Come on, Jack, I told you not to have too many whiskeys last night, even if Arthur was driving," she called out, as he slipped further under the covers. "You said you were going to call Sergeant Binstead first thing."

"Oh hell, I did, didn't I," he baulked, throwing back the sheets. "I'll make my call first; he might have a busy day ahead of him."

As Marjory tidied the bed before starting breakfast, Jack called his old Sergeant. He was naturally apprehensive about ringing him after all this time to ask a favour, not just to see how he was and began to feel guilty. As it turned out he was pleased to hear from Jack, more concerned in how he had settled into retirement than his own worries; which Jack was unaware of.

They agreed to meet at lunchtime in their old favourite pub around the corner at the usual time. Apparently things weren't that busy at the moment, he pointed out. It was good that Jack rang now. Jack thought his last statement unusual; it was never quiet at the Yard, even at the best of times. They were usually so far behind with their inquiries, if not the paperwork, he guessed Brian had other things on his mind.

"All settled, dear?" Marjory commented cheerfully, taking his bacon and eggs out of the oven just ready for him as he sat down.

"It's not the weekend, dear," Jack pointed out, taking up his knife and fork.

"I know... this is my little thank you for my new clothes," she answered.

"Well I hate to burst your bubble, Marjory, despite your

apparent rejuvenation from the experience, but we can't use the card for the rest of the month; if you know what I mean," he sheepishly continued with his breakfast.

"I guessed as much when I saw the look on your face when you saw the bill. Never mind we'll manage, we always do," she said.

"It's not as if you do this sort of thing every day," Jack commented.

"I should hope not," she joked, sipping the coffee she poured herself. "So... what did you manage to arrange with the Sergeant?"

"I'm meeting him for lunch at the pub," she threw a sharp glance at him. "It's all right; he can't drink on duty so it'll be orange juice... I promise."

After breakfast Jack got ready and drove down to the station at the other end of the village, and parked the car. As he turned, he saw the train was already standing at the platform and leapt up the wooden steps, with just enough time to get a paper before the guard enthusiastically blew his whistle for it to leave.

On the half hour journey to the city Jack intended to read the paper and catch up on any lurid crimes the Sergeant might be involved in. Then he realised he wasn't a Sergeant anymore; he was an Inspector now.

No longer could he shout Sergeant do this and Sergeant do that, he had to face this man who had put up with him for so many years, on equal terms.

Jack was also uncertain about the; 'What's it like being retired,' syndrome. He could hardly tell him he was now big in this or that, just as he couldn't bring himself to admitting the trips to the shops with Marjory and the gardening. However, he did have to tell his friend about the criminology group and their current investigation.

Jack sat in his usual place in the pub and casually looked around at the new crowd. He couldn't recognise anyone, although he knew the CID were about by the occasional word 'Guv' that kept catching his ears.

"Superintendent, how are you?" a familiar voice came from behind.

As Jack turned around, he saw his loyal assistant had not changed, his fears of jokes and laughter about his retirement all disappeared. It was just as if it was a normal day, and the last eighteen months had never happened.

"Sergeant... sorry I mean, Inspector." Jack replied, his eyes getting moist. "I've missed you... by God I've missed you. What have you been doing with yourself?"

The Inspector sat down opposite him, "Not much, Guv', things are about the same. Mind you, the squad's changed now you're not about."

"Thanks for that, you don't know how much you miss things until they're gone and you're an Inspector now... how about that?"

"Yes. It's a bit difficult to get used to. I keep expecting to hear you shouting Sergeant from the office. Then I realise I'm sitting in your seat now and I'm the one who's shouting Sergeant."

"I hope he's as good as you were for me."

"He's a she and she's got every qualification under the sun."

"Oh dear... that doesn't sound good." he said with a grin.

Jack moved round the booth and let his old friend sit down beside him. It was beginning to feel like old times again, and he soaked in the atmosphere.

"Oh it's not bad really. She doesn't have to look things up like I did. It's all changed now, Guv'. The place is full of smart boys... and girls. The Academy is training little wiz-kids now. I find it hard just keeping up with them."

"I don't care what you say; good police-work will win-out every time."

"True... they do seem to flounder a bit if there's no forensics." He looked Jack in the eye. "I won't ask you how it is, you must

80

be sick to death of hearing it. So... why the call? You could have knocked me over with a feather when I heard your voice."

"Marjory twisted my arm."

Jack got the Inspector a pint of his favourite and an orange for himself; at the same time he tried quickly to decide how he would broach the subject in question.

"Before we say another word, let's drop all this Guv' and Inspector stuff; it's Brian and Jack now that I'm out of the force... okay?"

"Fine with me, Jack, but old habits die hard."

"Well I don't know... you didn't have to get used to Superintendent for long."

"No... and we all felt terrible about that, you taking the can an' all".

Jack sipped his orange juice.

"Oh I don't know... I deserved it. It was bound to happen sooner or later. So learn a lesson from me... and Stone. He got his as well. Do you hear much about him now? Is he still wheeling and dealing?"

"No, Jack, not since that last case you were on. I saw him at the Christmas party and I must admit he had the decency to come over and say hello."

"Well that's something. I never heard from him again."

They nattered for a while, Brian didn't seem to be looking at his watch, which Jack was grateful for but he had to bite the bullet sooner or later, if he was going to get him on his side; he needed some professional support.

"Brian as you can imagine I've got myself drawn into all sorts of things in the country life of our village now that I'm retired. There, I've actually said that nasty word" they both laughed. "But one thing in particular worries me and I thought I just had to pass it over someone in CID, and I immediately thought of you."

Brian took a drink, looking extremely puzzled, thinking, 'What on earth could he get up to in a sleepy village?' "Sounds very mysterious, Jack, you haven't run across a couple of old lady poisoners have you?"

"At the moment it isn't quite like that, it's more of a legal issue," Jack stated.

"I was only joking, Jack, you haven't really got a case?"

"Look just bare with me; I don't know what I've got yet. Is your time all right?"

"Fine... I'm out doing some research, which no one really thinks much of anyway, so you just take your time... I'm glad of the change."

Jack didn't want to ponder too much on Samuel's past, he preferred to concentrate on the area they would be involved in, so he briefly outlined the circumstances leading up to the Vicar's group taking on the task of finding the two alleged victims.

He told him of all the evidence they had, and the clues Samuel had left that would presumably lead them to the gravesites, and how the other members of the group were determined to track them down. Finally Jack pointed out his own loose connection with these people, and the subsequent advice he had given them regarding the possibility of stepping on the toes of the police.

Brian looked genuinely interested as he sipped his drink, which heartened Jack, and he allowed him to finish before he decided to speak.

"Well, Jack, as far as I'm concerned, although it defies me to think why you should ask my advice when you must surely know the answer yourself, your problem is more one of controlling these enthusiasts, than breaking the law.

"As I see it, no crime has been committed yet, because we have no bodies, no unsolved report of criminal violence and no official complaint of anyone being missing, at least not published generally.

"Also, these alleged murders appear to be in the past," he took another sip of his beer, "In fact, I lay you odds that if you came back with me now and told the Super what you've told me he'd die laughing. It's taking us all our time to clear up the current stuff. Let sleeping dogs lie, Jack... I say."

"Okay, I thought that might be your reaction, but as a retired person now, I had to put it right, I needed you to confirm that," Jack emphasised.

"Oh look, Jack, don't let me steer you wrong, if it's security you want you have to do it official, and put up with the stick, we're just a couple of old colleagues having a drink and talking about old times now" he openly confessed.

"I know that, and it's not really what I want, I just needed you to know where I'm coming from," Jack stated; now the real talk begins.

"I thought there was more to this visit than old times, you don't change do you."

"I suppose not, deep down."

"Well what do you really want," Brian asked, back on familiar ground.

"What I always want from you, Brian... a little support."

"Now, Jack if it's what I think it is; it's not on. We're watched like hawks now."

"Come on, Brian, all I'm asking is the use of your general network now and then; I already decided not to ask for any forensics or pathology."

"You can't pull that one on me any more, Jack, I learnt all about that trick a long time ago; you tell me about something much worse to get me to do the lesser thing; which turns out to be the worst thing all the time."

"Sorry, Brian but I had to get things done in those days, with my limited resources, it meant bending the rules slightly, but it worked, didn't it? You want to try it sometime," Jack laughed to try and soften the instant.

"Oh I do, I wasn't going to be the only one used in the CID."

"Look, Brian, all I want is you to run a name or two or three through your files now and then, no more... how difficult can that be?"

Brian finished his pint and pushed the empty glass across to Jack.

"Get me another and I'll think about it. Oh... make it a bitter this time."

"Well... have you made up your mind?" Jack said when he returned.

Brian laughed, "What's with the orange juice?"

"It's all right; I haven't given up drink yet."

"Marjory's done that for you."

"Half right. I had a big night last night: a few too many whiskeys."

"Say no more," Brian commented after his first gulp of his bitter. "Well as far as helping you is concerned, I can only say it will have to be on a 'one by one' basis. There's bound to be times when it's just not safe, if you know what I mean."

"Look, Brian, this is always going to be an anytime situation, I'm in your hands."

"Another thing, Jack, you're going to reach a point in time when this gets awfully close to being a police matter, so I stress that you keep me informed of your progress, unless you want to deal with the locals."

"Good heavens no, I'd rather keep this low profile as long as possible. I'm not looking forward to the time when I have to contact two different CID's."

"Two?"

"Yes two. Oh sorry, in my summary I omitted to tell you the bodies are alleged to be in Watford and Eastbourne."

"Now I understand your reluctance to advise the locals."

Brian's so called casual research outing came to an abrupt

halt with his bleeper sounding off, drawing attention from the occupants of the bar.

As far as Jack was concerned the timing couldn't have been better, he had got what he wanted and was finding it difficult to continue their conversation, and as far as what was troubling Brian, he was not forthcoming. Jack did persevere but not wholeheartedly. He had the feeling that although Brian wanted his opinion on something, for some reason the time was not right.

Back in Cheedam, Jack found Marjory unusually quiet. It didn't concern him too much as he got ready to attack the garden again. She was fussing and when she fussed Jack knew something had upset her but for the life of him he could not think of anything he might have said or done recently.

Jack tried to tell her about his meeting with Brian and how he would have to lay the law down with the group but it seemed to be going over her head.

"You don't mind if they come over here after the normal group meeting dear," Jack continued after a somewhat lengthy discussion about his involvement.

"Jack, you do whatever you want, you always do, as long as you don't expect me to get involved. No taking notes or running around making drinks, in fact I shall organise to be out when they come like I was last week."

"Well that's put me in my place, I'll just tell them to take a running jump," he snapped, storming out of the room to put on his Wellingtons.

"Jack... don't you walk off like that just because I don't suit your plans."

"Well I don't understand what your problem is," he barked, nearly falling over with one foot stuck in the top of the boot.

Marjory followed him into the kitchen.

"This was supposed to be a way of you getting out of the house and meeting a group of people from the village but what do I find? you're only meeting a select group and worst still arranging for them to meet here."

"So you expect me to sit with a group of people I have nothing in common with, who aren't really interested in criminology in the first place, just so I can get out of the house? I can do that with long walks." Jack stopped putting his Wellingtons on. "In fact I might decide to go on a long holiday somewhere... broaden my mind... get away from everyone telling me how to run my life."

"You're missing the whole point, Jack. This wasn't meant to be an extension of your working life, it was to develop new horizons," Marjory stated.

He finally stamped his foot down the damn Wellington.

"I've only known one thing for over thirty years Marjory," he called back at her.

She leant back into the kitchen, "Does that mean you have to try and manufacture something to continue until you die. Retirement is supposed to be your rest period after all that hard work."

Jack turned and faced her in the doorway, "Okay... what's all this about. You've been full of hell ever since you got back from that dramatics class."

"I was talking to Arthur's wife if you must know."

"So."

"I embarrassed myself by asking her how she liked Amsterdam."

"You didn't," Jack exclaimed, sitting down in a chair, "I told you he had a fancy woman on the side. Why couldn't you leave well alone?"

"I thought you were joking."

Jack went silent for a second.

"Well... I know now why you don't want to be here when they come round."

"Oh it's not that, Jack."

"What does that mean?"

"Apparently she knows all about his philandering, they have an agreement."

Jack burst out laughing, then stopped abruptly when he saw her face.

"I was embarrassed because she didn't think there was anything wrong."

He paused and thought for a moment about what she had said. He still thought the whole idea was funny and bent down to find his other Wellington but as he was about to utter his reply, he heard the front door slam.

"Well Jack Hammond, that's put you in your place," he said out loud, as if he was still talking to her, "In the doghouse," he shouted again, now trying to put the other Wellington on. He lost his temper and threw it out of the open door into the garden, where it landed with a thump in amongst the azaleas.

Looking through the front window, hoping Marjory might have had second thoughts and he would see her little Morris Minor return into the drive, he saw the brown Rolls draw up instead.

As the merry band of sleuths made their way down the path to the front door, he could see what she meant. He had nothing in common with any of them. They were in their own little world and were about to drag him along with them.

THE WATFORD VICTIM

CHAPTER 7

Jack opened the door and they all filed in as if they were attending church.

"Good afternoon, Jack," the Vicar greeted him first, the others followed behind in single file down to his study. "In here all right?"

Jack nodded as he began to close the door. "Yes that's fine."

As they removed their coats and dropped them onto the spare chair Jack had hoped Marjory would use, they turned and stared at his feet. He looked down and realised he was standing with a Wellington on one foot and a thick sock on the other.

"Is this some form of new initiation, Jack?," Arthur said as seriously as his face would allow, then burst out laughing, he caused the others to follow suit.

"Oh very funny, I'm sure," Jack replied. "I was just about to do some gardening."

"Does that mean you had forgotten our meeting, Jack?" the Vicar asked.

"Of course it doesn't... I mean... oh it doesn't matter."

Jack stormed from the room back into the kitchen looking for his slippers. He took a little time trying to regain his composure and returned as if nothing had happened. He had no intentions of being drawn on the subject.

"What happened to you earlier?" the Vicar continued, taking

the same place he had the previous week.

Jack was horrified, suddenly realising a routine was developing already.

"Quite frankly, Peter, if we're going to have this meeting afterwards each time, I see little point in me being at the criminology meeting in the first place. I see this as a temporary meeting dealing with a different issue altogether."

"Oh very well, as you please but we are continuing with our meetings in the church aren't we?" the Vicar questioned.

"Of course; but I foresee, as we get more involved and our investigations become more of a day-to-day routine, there'll be fewer reasons for regular meetings like this... except in the case of emergencies."

"Do you see many emergencies, Jack?" Dick interrupted.

Jack scowled. This was going to be a fine afternoon.

"How do you see it working then, Jack?" Arthur questioned. He had to know, he didn't want this to interfere with his business and he didn't quite expect it to become a day-to-day affair as Jack suggested.

"Look..." Jack started, "there's a difference between an investigation and an arranged meeting to discuss criminology in general: one we communicate one-on-one wherever we are, or on the phone as may happen, the other is just a regular meeting."

They all nodded their heads, obviously satisfied with that initial scenario.

"Before we start," Jack continued apprehensively. "I have to tell you the overall concept of what we're doing didn't settle well with me, I think I made that clear last time, before Peter told me about our society status."

"Yes, Jack... and we understood and agreed with your fears," he replied.

"I know... but I just had to go and have a discreet word with one of my colleagues at the Yard." No one said anything but they looked concerned. "He agreed, so long as this remained research, our activities would not concern the police."

"That's a relief," Arthur interrupted.

"However," Jack continued, "as soon as our suspicions were confirmed, we would have to notify the authorities."

"What should we do then?" Janet asked.

"Yes, Jack," Arthur jumped in, "I can't get involved in any lengthy inquiries."

"It would take its normal course as a CID investigation."

The Vicar could not hold his tongue any longer. "After all our hard work?"

"I'm afraid so, Peter," Jack said. "However, let's not get ahead of ourselves."

Jack glanced around the table for any further outburst.

"Fine... then let's proceed," he said, opening a new manila folder he had prepared, revealing a pristine note pad inside. Everyone braced themselves seriously, it had started. "Since the whole investigation is to be generated from what Janet interprets from the coded sheets, I think we should hear what she has to say regarding the first sheet we named 'Watford', analyse her interpretation and plan what investigation and research is necessary to develop this information into a directive towards finding our victim. Or at least verifying there is one."

Janet hesitated a moment and looked at Jack, "Oh sorry, you mean now?"

"Yes please, Janet, if that's all right."

"Certainly," she said, fumbling with her notes. "As I said last time, the author of this code has deliberately left out essential information, creating a disconnected array of singular words which don't make much sense. However, if we look between the lines and use our imagination it is possible to build a picture;

whether it's the right one or not is anyone's guess."

"Why did you say deliberate, Janet?" Jack asked. "Why couldn't it simply be a case of expediency?"

"Because it would have been so easy, using this basic code to spell out the whole story. He obviously didn't want anyone to know directly."

"I felt you were looking for a word to describe these notes," Jack continued.

"I was... you're right."

"Would that word be 'shorthand'?" Jack said.

"Yes... exactly, this is in shorthand, basic key-words to document an event," she said, with a satisfied look on her face."

"Why should you choose that word Jack?" the Vicar asked.

"It was the first word that came into my mind when Janet read out her original translation. This man, for some reason, had the compulsion to jot down the details of his kill. Maybe it was because, according to Peter, they were his only hidden kills and he needed to record their resting place quickly."

The Vicar gestured with his hand while still obviously thinking, "Er... Samuel seemed very agitated towards the end, not at all concerned in the many others he admitted to killing, only the two that he had hidden."

"Which only reinforces the premise that Janet has indicated, so we'll stay with that until we know otherwise," Jack made notes on his new pad. "Right, Janet... sorry for the digression; I told you this would happen; see what you can do with it."

She nodded placing a copy of her notes in front of each person so they could all digest its composition and hopefully add to the process.

"Now, Dick," Jack continued. "What have you got for us?"

Dick jumped. He had become noticeably complacent, "Me?"

"Yes, Dick, you were going to check the items in the shoebox,"

Jack reminded.

"Ah... yes, well I didn't get much really, well I don't think I did."

"Whatever you have, Dick," Jack said patiently.

He wasn't as organised as the others, who all came prepared with clipboards and manila folders and rummaged for something in his pockets, before bringing out a crumpled looking piece of folded paper.

Unfolding it, he mumbled under his breath, "Let's see now."

At least he remembered to bring the box back and began rummaging through its contents after he had removed the lid and discarded it on the floor beside him. The Vicar was sitting next to him and checked his action with some concern, as if the box meant as much to him as it had to Samuel. Dick brought out the 303 cartridge and stared at it.

"The cartridge... I can't say much more about it. It still gives me an idea of a man on a blue blanket loading his rifle, except I did think of a dark blue cricket bag." Jack was frantically writing all this down, wishing he had learnt shorthand. "The purse which I know you said wasn't of much importance, did surprise me though."

"How so?" the Vicar questioned, before Jack got the chance.

"Well it wasn't his?"

"What do you mean?" Jack asked this time.

"The 303 cartridge and the purse didn't belong to the same man... the same for the papers, the key and the others."

"Place the items in two groups, unless more people are involved," Jack said.

Dick took the items from the box and assembled three groups; the cartridge, papers and key in one pile; the bible, purse and bundle of pens and pencils in another; and the third, which surprised Jack, he placed the dictionary and its receipt.

"Why the third?" he asked.

"These two items have no aura at all but if pushed I'd put them in the pile with the purse." On second thoughts he moved them over.

"What difference is there, Dick?" Janet asked him, touching both piles.

"This one," he pointed to the one with the bible, "has no violence attached to its aura; in fact all I can feel is a pathetic insignificance. Whereas this pile," pointing to the one with the cartridge, "Is devil-incarnate itself. I feel terrified of whoever possessed these items... his life was full of violence."

"Reverend," Janet interrupted. "Is it possible for the same person to possess both these characteristics? To be violent one moment, meek the next?"

"I suppose schizophrenia could be a possibility," the Vicar replied, only guessing. "What do you thing, Dick, have you ever come across these feelings before."

"I did get confused on one session, although the different auras were not as defined as this. It turned out some months later when this person had to be taken into hospital; she did suffer from schizophrenia."

Jack began writing again, "Let's just say for the moment, until we have any more evidence, that Samuel had a split personality. At the same time though, I want you all to keep an open mind to the possibility that more than one person may be involved here. There's always the man Samuel killed?"

"He said he was innocent of that murder, Jack," the Vicar reminded.

"We have only his word for that," he turned back to Dick. "Anything else, Dick?"

"Yes actually, I suppose I should have pointed this out at the beginning," he reached into the box. "Do you realise this has a false bottom?"

The shock on everyone's face was unmistakable. Their jaws fell open and stayed that way until he pulled the box into the middle of the desk. It looked like a common or garden thin cardboard box as they all leaned forward to watch Dick lift up one corner with his forefinger, then peel the inner layer backwards to reveal a neatly folded piece of paper, the exact size of the base. He lifted it out and unfolded it. It was a photocopied map of London.

"Good heavens," Janet exclaimed, expressing everyone's feeling.

Jack quickly examined it. It was a map of metropolitan London with the familiar image of the river Thames running across the sheet horizontally. "I know this area; it's the patch between Westminster and the Tower of London."

"Oh yes, there it is," the Vicar said. "I never knew it was opposite Bermondsey."

"And if you look closely, there's a square with an arrow pointing to it under the overpass to London Street Station. Oh my God... what a coincidence," Jack uttered, open mouthed, with his face quite drained of colour.

"What's wrong, Jack," the Vicar asked.

"The square is opposite a small street called Crucifix Lane."

"That is strange, Jack, is the square in that street?" the Vicar asked again remembering the effect Dick's earlier comment had on him.

"No, I know this area very well; there are quite a number of lines running over the roads at this point leading directly into London Bridge Station. There's a small underpass between this Crucifix Lane and Tooley Street opposite the river. The last time I was in the underpass I noticed a lot of large lock-ups either side of the road. This could be where our man used to hang out... it's worth looking into. Maybe you could check the real estate Arthur and see if anything turns up?"

"Great, I'll do that, it won't take long."

"And if Dick's finished, we can have your input now Arthur. By the way, Dick that was very enlightening, you see how these things contribute to the whole."

"Oh... I'm glad I could help," he said.

Arthur opened the manila folder in front of him and took out a bunch of typed lists, impressing everyone. "You were right, Jack; this lot is only the City of London. So I got in touch with the Federation of Warehouses with this number and their reply was," he looked for the piece of paper he scribbled it down on, "are yes... they had to have the actual storage facility as the key numbers kept changing."

"Yes... I expected as much, Arthur," Jack sympathised. "You can check the map Dick found... you never know we might get lucky."

"I thought you said we can't rely on luck, Jack," Janet reminded him.

"That's quite right and I stand by that. What I was referring to was the luck we generate ourselves in good investigative work and a keen eye for possible connections, no matter how diverse."

"What an excellent analogy," Janet said, "I shall have to remember that the next time I'm lecturing my history class about research... quite excellent."

Jack smiled as he glanced back and forth over his notes, "I certainly miss my whiteboard in the incident room," he said. "You could see everything that was happening at a glance, no flicking through notepads and bits of paper. You mark my words; by the time we're finished we'll be knee deep in scraps of paper."

"I've got one if you want," Dick offered.

"Have you really... how come?" Jack said, expectantly.

"I bought it, with all the fancy pens and things a few months ago, to stand at the back of the shop with specials noted on each day but my son thought it was a waste of time. He said by the time people saw it they could be on their way out."

He said everything in those few words without knowing it. His son was taking over the business he spent half his life building up to what it was today, giving him a secure life, the best schooling and it all stood for nothing.

Jack saw all this, he felt Dick was losing interest; he had to do something before he stopped coming altogether. "That's great, Dick, sounds just the thing," he said.

"Good... I'll drop it by later this evening."

"That'll be fine, I'll start straight away getting these facts on display," Jack said. He expected someone to say something but they didn't, and he immediately turned his attention back to the manila folder and the notes he had been making.

"Right... new duties," he said, changing the subject before he got too maudlin. "Arthur can you get me that detail on the warehouses in that underpass?... I'd like to go over there in the morning."

"Sure thing, as soon as I get back to the office."

"Can I come with you, Jack?" the Vicar asked eagerly. "I'm free tomorrow."

"I don't see why not," Jack said, glancing back at his notes.

As Jack was saying goodbye to his guests at the front door Marjory's car pulled into the drive and not wanting the embarrassment of her coolness to show, he left them to meet her outside on their own while he returned to his office.

"Were they all happy with their meeting then Jack?" she said walking in.

"Aren't they always dear."

"It took long enough," she said, walking through to the kitchen.

"If you bothered to attend one of these meetings, you would know, most of the time is spent with them asking silly questions."

"You should come to mine sometime Jack," Marjory called out from the kitchen. "They seem to like everything in detail in the country."

No sooner had Marjory started to prepare the evening meal when the phone rang; and just as Jack answered it, there was a loud knock on the front door.

"Get that will you, Marjory... it'll be Dick."

Marjory opened the door to find Dick struggling with a large white board.

"Hello, Dick... what's all this?" she said.

"No time to stop Marjory," he blurted out, "Jack knows all about it."

As Jack finished his call and walked out into the hall he saw Marjory wrestling with the board, looking puzzled. "I'll take that, dear."

"Who was that on the phone?"

"It was Arthur; he was looking into something for me."

"By your expression it looks like he had good news."

"Yes... he did. I'll be going up to London in the morning."

CHAPTER 8

Jack drove slowly through the damp underpass, checking out the address Arthur gave him. He glanced across to his left while the Vicar keenly leant out of the window searching on his side for the storage warehouse.

"Look up ahead, Jack," the Vicar said.

A traffic warden appeared from nowhere and was aggressively marching towards them. Jack switched on the engine and pulled away before she arrived and was forced to turn right into the one-way system of Tooley Street.

The last time he was in the city with a car, life was so easy, he simply showed the traffic warden his warrant card and everything was all right. Not having police immunity was going to make things that much more difficult.

As Jack turned towards the blue 'P' above the street sign, he suddenly stopped. "Are omens accepted in your faith, Peter?" he asked, smiling.

The Vicar looked puzzled, "Hardly, Jack; we're guided by divine providence."

"Then look up at the street sign." It read 'Potters Field'. "Now is that eerie."

"I fail to see your point, Jack."

"Potters Field, Peter. It's the name for a place where they bury unknown or derelict people. I would imagine without the words as you say.

"Oh dear... I see what you mean; like Crucifix Lane over there."

"We should have had Dick with us. I'm sure he could have made something of all this," Jack mentioned as he parked the car.

Walking through the underpass Jack sensed the Vicar wanted to say something, he was very quiet, hanging back just behind his elbow and Jack's old instinct could feel the Vicar's tension in the back of his neck.

"Is there something troubling you, Peter?"

"Yes, Jack... it was your last comment about Dick."

"Did I say something out of turn?"

"Oh no certainly not," he assured.

"Then what's the problem?" Jack said, stopping.

"Dick spoke to me after we left your house yesterday. He's not at all comfortable with this case... it's effecting him badly."

"I don't see the problem, Peter; he's not bound to doing anything he doesn't like. He can do something else, chasing information down for instance."

"I don't think it matters what he does Jack, he's getting a lot of bad vibes."

"Fine, tell him to visit the general group only, if he's still interested."

"You're not upset?" the Vicar asked, as they started walking again.

They finally reached the entrance to the underground labyrinth of the storage warehouse and the female traffic warden still standing where they left her. As they passed the curved archway supporting the bridge they came upon a vast open space, broken only by the occasional concrete pillar and row upon row of lock-up containers as far as they could see.

Jack looked up at the name on the sign above the arch, 'Mason & Stephenson, Long or Short Term Storage'. "Well this looks like the place."

To the left of them was a 'Portacabin', which doubled as a checkpoint and an office by the looks of it. Inside was an arrogant young girl, chewing what appeared to be the biggest mouthful of gum they had ever seen. Her mouth was so full she could hardly open it when she asked what they wanted; or to be more accurate, the only word they clearly understood was 'Yeah'. Jack still carried his old warrant card in his wallet, he knew he shouldn't use it but couldn't resist with this insolent girl. She needed teaching a lesson. He flipped the old warrant card open so she could clearly read his name.

"Police?" she mumbled, "What can I do for you?"

"I'd like to see whoever's in charge."

"That'll be Tommo... I mean Mr Colliver," she replied, getting up from her little desk and going over to the door between the drawn blinds behind her. There was a gruff reply and she entered, returning seconds later. "You can go in."

"Superintendent Hammond?" the dull looking man called out from behind his desk when they walked in; his east-end accent almost as out-of-date as his bizarre appearance.

Colliver reminded Jack of a man who kept pigeons near where he lived as a boy: a crumpled dirty look, 1940's cardigan, blue striped shirt with white collar and cuffs that were now a grimy grey and an equally crumpled grey suit. He was clean-shaven, but for some reason wore his sideburns down to the line of his jaw.

"Now Superintendent, how can I help. I run a clean ship here," he added.

Jack smiled to the Vicar; he had heard that one too many times before.

"It's all right, Mr Colliver, I haven't come to check into your warehouse, it's your help I want for Reverend Jay here," Jack fabricated.

He went on to tell him a story about a parishioner who had

died leaving a key which they thought might be a storage key, with no next of kin to pass it on to."

Jack took the key out of his pocket and slid it across his desk.

"Let's have a look at this key then," he replied, picking it up.

"Mmm," he uttered, then reached down for a binder in his bottom draw. "It's one of ours all right, it's a five year lease key," he said, flicking through the pages. He ran his finger down the list to a corresponding number, "Yes, it's got another six months to go." He looked up at them from under his hat. "What name did you say it was?"

"Er..." the Vicar glanced at Jack, who nodded. "Alluche," he said.

"That's him... Bay 36, aisle 3," he answered, handing back the key.

"Is there an address with that?" Jack questioned, making notes.

"No, we don't keep addresses here, too much paperwork. Our customers pay cash up front for as long as they like. Then after thirty days, if they haven't renewed, we open up and dispose of the contents. It's all in the conditions."

"What happens now?" Jack asked.

He walked them to the door leading out into the warehouse, gestured with an outward pointing arm saying, "be my guest... it's Bay 36, aisle 3. You'll find that four aisles down and to your left." He then disappeared back into the Portacabin, leaving them to find the bin for themselves as a train rumbled passed above their heads.

After some fifteen minutes of going back and forth from one aisle to another, the Vicar finally shouted, "I've got it, aisle 3."

They eventually found Bay 36 at the far end of the large containers, which took some time re-checking the numbers. It was amongst a group of small lockers tucked up against one of the pillars. There, almost in the middle was Bin 04-173-8030013/S. They looked at each other; this was the first piece of evidence they had been able to unravel.

"Well, Peter, since the key really belongs to you now, I think you should have the privilege of opening the locker," Jack said, handing it to him.

The Vicar hesitated, not sure that he wanted to enter Samuel's private world, then thrust the key deep into the lock and turned. The lock must have been spring loaded, as the eighteen by twelve inch door immediately sprang open, causing him to jump backwards with shock. They peered inside; it was quite cavernous, maybe four or five feet deep, revealing something that surprised them.

Not having much time for clairvoyants or mediums Jack took Dick's interpretation of Samuel's belongings with a pinch of salt; but Crucifix Lane, Potter's Field and the contents of the locker gave him reason to think again.

Jammed into the narrow space was the triangular end of a dark blue sports bag, similar to the one Dick had described earlier. How long it was could not be seen; Jack betting on the length of a cricket bat, if he were to believe the rest of Dick's prediction.

In his excitement, the Vicar couldn't wait to grab a loose flap on the end and tugged at the bag with all his might but it was no good, it was too heavy for one person at this height.

Jack leant a hand and together they gradually eased the bag out of the narrow opening with a zig-zag motion until it suddenly broke free, slipping off the edge and plunged towards the floor.

In that instant, Jack snatched at the handle, taking its full weight as it dropped back-end downwards, and arrested its fall just as it reached the concrete. The Vicar didn't have the sense to let go, and was almost trapped as it swung across his body, narrowly missing his leg and landing between them.

"Good heavens," the Vicar cried... shocked at its weight.

He had forgotten Jack for the moment.

Taking the full impact left Jack with one knee on the floor

out of breath, "You can say that again, it's certainly not full of cricket gear."

"What could it be?"

"We'll soon find out," Jack replied, sliding the bag around at right angles. He pressed the catch on the brass lock with no effect, "Locked," he stated, not surprised.

"The locker key was the only one in the box," the Vicar stated before Jack asked.

"Never mind," Jack said, fumbling in his pocket. "We'll soon see to that, I've been getting into these things since third grade."

"We can't do that, Jack... it's breaking and entering."

"That's when you break into a house," he said sharply, bringing out his multi-purpose pocketknife. "This is only petty theft," then he stopped and looked at him. "What are you talking about? The bag belongs to you anyway."

"Oh... sorry, I keep forgetting."

Jack let out a sigh of impatience as he sorted through the mass of miniature implements fanning out from both ends of his knife and looked up at him. "Look, Peter, you opened this bin with your own key, so it stands to reason anything inside is yours, even if we can't open it... okay?"

A timid, less assuming Vicar nodded silently and had to agree.

"Ah... here we are, just the thing, I knew it was here somewhere," Jack muttered to himself as he poked the desired instrument into the lock.

To the Vicar's surprise the brass clasp flew open with a resounding clonk.

"What's wrong?" Jack questioned, undoing the leather straps at each end.

"I feel as though we're opening Pandora's Box."

"I hope not," Jack said, and then laughed as he prised open the long bag.

The sight that greeted them might as well have been the contents of Pandora's Box; as neither was prepared for the shock of what lay inside the cricket bag. Although Jack knew he should have guessed from Dick's description.

Jack reached inside and began naming each item as he laid it out on the floor between them, not so much for his own sake; he was more than familiar with them, but to head off a barrage of questions he was sure would be forthcoming.

"One 5.5mm AR-18 Armalite rifle with scope; One AK-47, 7.2mm rifle with night sight; One 9mm Browning automatic; One Walther 9mm P38 automatic; one 7.6mm Mauser automatic, an Enfield 303, assortment of silencers and two, four, six, eight... twelve boxes of shells; presumably for these weapons," he struggled a moment with two black rods, while the Vicar appeared to have difficulty in coming to terms with their find, then gawking, open mouthed at the tripod Jack was bringing out of the evidently bottomless pit. "Not the snakes you expected, but just as deadly."

"Is that all, Jack?" the Vicar asked sarcastically. "There aren't any grenades hiding away in there, are there?"

Jack light-heartedly looked back inside, and laughed.

"No, that's it, Peter, just your average assassins kit," Jack said, rummaging about at the bottom of the bag. Then he turned back to the locker. "There's lots of packets of nails and screws and of course a hammer and screwdriver," he demonstrated. "A ball of string, tape measure, and..." he paused a moment.

"What now, Jack?"

"Oh it's just a plastic box of fishing gear: weights, floats, hooks and a real of line, he was certainly well prepared. There's also a medical kit and a bunch of maps."

"What of? They might be important."

"Yes you're right, Peter, I didn't think. We'll keep these."

"What do you mean... keep them?"

"Well we have to inform the police about the weapons."

"I suppose we do. We've hardly started and we're bringing them in already."

"We have to, Peter," Jack said, looking over the guns again,

"How come you were so informed about what type of weapon they were?"

"Well I was in the Military Police," Jack reminded. "We had to know all this lot and more off by heart; there was plenty of contraband going about in those days."

"I suppose we couldn't just leave them here?"

"It will only be a formality; they still don't really want to get involved."

"What's all this at the bottom of the bag?" he pointed out, still suspicious.

Jack at first had taken all the paper in the bottom of the bag to be protective waste to combat dampness. Drawn to a closer inspection, he found it to be an assortment of invoices, receipts, business letters and hand written notes; probably the remains of discarded transactions, tossed there after each mission.

"These look important, Jack," the Vicar commented, picking them up and placing them on one side with the maps.

"Yes maybe, but we can't take them; they belong with the guns."

"But they might give us a lead, Jack."

"I know that, just let me think will you."

"There was a copying machine in the office," the Vicar interrupted.

"Good... you take this lot and fit as many as you can onto their largest sheet, otherwise we'll be here all day... and don't forget, both sides."

"What are you going to do?" he asked, gathering up all the pieces of paper."

"I'll put this lot back and make it look as if it hasn't been disturbed. Then I'll see if I can get hold of my friend at the Met. There was a public phone by the door, I don't want the others getting wind of this lot."

It must have been one of the shortest calls he ever made. Just the mention of guns and Inspector Binstead was jotting down the address and he was on his way.

"What's the matter now?" Jack asked, seeing the look on the Vicar's face."

"Do you know they had the audacity to charge me five pounds for these copies?"

"Did you question that?" Jack asked.

"Yes I did... he said it was a case of supply and demand."

Jack was just about to recompense the Vicar, but thought better of it.

"What he meant, Peter," Jack said, placing his arm around his shoulder, as he relieved him of the older papers found in the bag. "He had the copier and you wanted copies. Unless you were prepared to shop around, he was your only choice."

"I see... I suppose one should expect this sort of thing with these people."

"Hang on, Peter, if you expect us to carry on with this investigation, you'll have to learn the way of life, and that doesn't usually apply to certain types. Just think about that when you pass the plate around your congregation this Sunday."

"That's a different situation altogether, Jack; it's for God's work."

"I'm afraid it's not. You're doing exactly the same thing; gathering your flock in for faith and scriptures and then once you have a captive audience, they are expected to put something on the plate if they want salvation."

"That's something we'll have to discuss later, Jack."

"Good," Jack said with a sigh. "Now while I return these papers to the bag, you put the copies in my boot, and don't forget the maps."

"Why can't I wait for you?"

"Do you want to bump into the police with that lot?" Jack pointed out.

He didn't answer; instead he rushed off out of the warehouse, looking both ways as he left, while Jack walked over to where the young man was still reading his magazine to wait for the police.

The spotty-faced youth looked up lethargically, "Yeah," he said.

Jack smiled back at him, "Just wanted to make sure you were still alive."

"What does that mean?"

"Well I don't want the police thinking they have a dead body to investigate as well. Things might get complicated."

The young man thought a moment, then suddenly jumped up, dropped his magazine and dived into the Portacabin.

Jack was enjoying the state the sharp warehouse man was in when a car pulled into the entrance. "Jack," Inspector Binstead called out as he rolled down the window.

"Brian... thanks for coming. I hope this isn't going to be a wild goose chase," he answered, walking just a little beyond the car to see if the Vicar had left.

"I hope so too," the Inspector replied.

"I didn't expect you to be quite as efficient as this."

As they walked towards the Portacabin Jack could see all three outside.

"Neither did I until I realised my Guv' was eavesdropping. As soon as he heard guns he went berserk, I thought he was going to call out the SAS; he got so excited."

"How come only you then?" Jack asked, furtively looking about for Brian's female Sergeant; he was dying to see this intelligent woman he spoke of.

110

"I just mentioned your name and he tossed the worksheet back on my desk."

"We don't even know each other," Jack remarked.

Brian looked embarrassed and stopped for a moment as if he didn't want the suspicious looking group outside the Portacabin to hear.

"Well I think it was partly my fault. As I told you, Jack, I had to give him some background on what you were doing, and in the process of trying to lessen its importance, I intimated you were humouring a bunch of amateurs."

"Oh thanks a lot, my credibility just went to zero."

"I'm sorry Jack but if I told him what you were really up to, he would have dropped on you like a ton of bricks. As it is your activities are blackballed."

"So I'm down to using local sources am I?" Jack remarked, impatiently.

"Well how was I to know you found a stash of arms straight away?"

"Yes all right, it gave me a surprise too. I mean how many times did we come up with results as fast as this?"

"Never, Jack... then again we never got it handed to us on a platter either."

"What does that mean?"

"Well this Samuel fella did lay it out for you."

"Hold on, we only got coded messages, they have to be broken down."

"I still say you had it easy," Brian laughed, looking over to the nervous trio."

"That's the proprietor and his staff," Jack said.

They ignored the blustering con-man for the moment and Jack took Brian back into the labyrinth of storage containers, to the group of small bins where the guns were found. The first thing Brian did was to smell the barrels, something Jack completely forgot about, which only went to show how quickly he had lost his touch.

"Nothing here, Jack, these haven't been fired in years."

"Don't forget, if he was a professional hit man, they would have been cleaned."

Brian passed his friend the Armalite, not only didn't it smell of being fired recently, there were no signs of it being oiled either. Its action was extremely sluggish, and to his embarrassment there was a small white cottony ball of spider's eggs in the breech; not to mention the firing-pin was missing.

"Okay, it's obvious these weapons haven't been used for five years," Jack had to admit. "But it's proof that an assassin did exist."

"Why so certain of the time?"

Jack swung the door over and checked the card in the holder and pointed.

"Because this bin was only taken out for five years, and it's almost due for renewal, assuming he rented it at the time of the killings."

"Well I can't help you here. All I can do is take this lot to the pound, out of harm's way. They're all illegal anyway."

"Are you not even going to check them out?" Jack asked.

"I told you, Jack, we haven't got the resources."

"Okay, but don't blame me if we turn something up that might embarrass you."

"Damn you, Jack. You always manage to find a way to get what you want. I'll look into the papers... satisfied?"

"That's all I ask Brian, thanks."

On Jack's return to the parking area, he was surprised to find the car empty, until he heard his name being called from a distance. Turning in the direction of the voice, he saw the Vicar standing by the water's edge leaning on the railing separating the end of

Potters Field from the river.

"Breathtaking isn't it, Jack," he remarked, looking over the barges marooned on the mud flats, back-dropped by the magnificent structure of the Tower of London across the river. "You saw your friend in the police then?"

"Yes, for all the good it did, he wasn't interested one jot."

"Does that mean we've reached one of those brick walls?"

Jack laughed at the Vicar's innocence, "No, Peter it doesn't. It just means we're on our own again... and we start looking for the next clue."

CHAPTER 9

As Janet explained to everyone, her time would be restricted this week with visitors from the School Board going about their yearly audit. She was finding it difficult to concentrate; splitting her attention between agitated teachers and her efforts to solve the mystery code of the Watford Victim.

Then the phone rang, it was the Vicar on his way back to Lower Cheedam. He was so excited about his trip to London that it was difficult for Janet to understand what he was trying to say.

"Calm down, Reverend, I can hardly make out what you're saying," she said.

He told her they found the warehouse and its uncanny similarity to Dick's vision; along with their surprising find in the bin. He was babbling a bit, as usual, and she found it difficult to understand the point of the call.

"I still can't understand your reason for ringing me, Reverend," she said.

"Jack's filling the car with petrol, and he asked me to ring you and see if you can arrange a meeting in the church hall this afternoon. Can you ring the others?"

"Oh very well... I hope it's important."

"It is, Janet. We opened Samuel's storage box and you wouldn't believe what we found inside. It was the last thing in the world that I expected."

"Well... what was it?" she asked.

"Must go, Janet... Jack's in a hurry to get back."

On his return Jack stopped off at the cottage to let Marjory know what had happened. He was about to tell her he had arranged a meeting at the church when she interrupted; telling him Janet could not get away until four.

They had an hour to fill, so Marjory invited the Vicar in for an early tea. He was grateful, telling them his wife would be away most of the day. In the meantime Jack persuaded him to sort through the papers they had brought back from London.

It was an unusually fine afternoon and they decided to walk over to the church where they saw the others looking at the stones as they made their way through the cemetery. As everyone was getting reacquainted on their passage down the nave into the vestry, no one realised Dick was not with them.

"Has anyone seen Dick?" Jack asked.

Janet looked up. "I rang him as the Reverend asked."

"Did you tell him about the meeting?" the Vicar questioned.

"I did, Reverend, and I didn't think anymore of it."

"I don't think we'll see much of him in the future," the Vicar remarked.

"Pity, I had some further plans for his talent," Jack continued. Then as if it were all in the past, he quickly turned to the point at hand." Okay everyone, shall we get down to business. If Dick has decided to call it a day, we're going to be one short, an important one I might add," they all agreed. "However, Marjory has agreed to sit in on our meeting today and who knows, we might be able to persuade her to join us."

Marjory glanced at Jack as she politely smiled at the group.

Jack pulled out the notes he had roughly prepared.

"Firstly I must say how surprised I am in how quickly this case has progressed; we still have some clues to run down but so far, things are working out. Our trip into London was bizarre to say the least. We found the locker Samuel rented and discovered a cache of weapons inside; mostly sniper arms... which proves that part of Samuel's story was true.

"Weapons?" Arthur interrupted. So we are on the right track.

Jack jumped in, "Inspector Binstead, my friend in the CID, pointed out that they hadn't been used for ages. Of course this in itself means nothing."

"So the police are involved now?" Janet asked.

"We had no option, Janet. Firearms have to be reported to the police. However, my old colleague still hasn't any interest in the case, so for the time being we're still in charge." Jack poured himself a drink, "Anyway, to the most interesting part of the morning. We found a lot of paperwork, something we can go into later... Janet?"

"Oh yes... well... my first task if you remember was to clarify whether or not we were dealing with more than one person. I went to see a friend of mine in the local museum who specialises in old manuscripts, with samples for him to check."

"Was he able to help?" Jack asked.

"Yes... he was sure they were written by two different hands."

"What was his actual comment?"

"His comment was that the note for the Reverend and the notations in his bible, did not match the coded pages. He went on to say the level of skill in the writing differed remarkably."

"You said Samuel didn't appear intelligent enough to be a sniper, Jack," the Vicar pointed out. "So we are looking for another killer."

"So it seems," Jack said, pondering on the possibility. "Samuel may well have admired this man's life-style and took on his responsibility."

"I knew Samuel wasn't a killer," the Vicar cried out excitedly.

"It could also be blackmail copies of the man who employed him, knowing he was dying and seeing no further use for them," Arthur spoke out.

"It could be all of those things," Jack said, "It could also bog us down in weeks of useless investigation. No, we need to concentrate on the task at hand and continue looking for the site. That means we need some more input from you, Janet...I know you are busy with these people, but we can't move forward without you."

"I appreciate that... they'll be gone tomorrow."

Jack looked down at his notes, then over towards Arthur sitting next to Marjory, who seemed eager to get started. He had glanced at her on occasions and was pleased to see she appeared more interested.

"Good... as soon as we have that I'd like you Arthur to look into this Scratchwood Service place... see what you can find out."

"Why don't I do that tomorrow ?... I have some spare time."

"No... let's see what Janet comes up with first. Now the paperwork."

"Why don't I have a go," Marjory said.

"Yes, I think that's a good idea," he answered.

They looked at each other and smiled.

"Now... the last thing before we close," Jack said with some reticence. "I have got to go up to London tomorrow to make a statement about the guns Peter and I found. I don't think it will amount to much, but you never know; they might want to take over. I'll keep you updated on that."

"Does that include me, Jack?" the Vicar questioned.

"No, Peter. I made the disclosure so I am responsible."

The following day Jack was only allowed to make another trip to London if he agreed to take Marjory with him; not to visit the CID as it turned out but to spend some time with her good friend Rhonda. She was waiting for them at the station when they arrived and with her usual breezy temperament, she talked their heads off all the way to Scotland Yard where she dropped Jack off before they went on to their shopping.

Jack stood in the car park watching Rhonda's old Morris Minor break out into London's busy morning traffic, winced at the sound of horns but really more occupied with that feeling of apprehension that was taking hold of him once again.

Jack did not have to wait long for Brian to pick him up in the lobby. "You were quite right as usual," Brian remarked casually, as they stood in the familiar lift on its way up to the CID squad room.

"I'm glad you think so, after your scepticism last time we met.

Brian laughed, "We were able to trace some of those weapons. He'd been a busy little beaver in the cold war days."

"Counts for nothing, now he's dead," Jack replied, a little nervous. He didn't really want to run into anyone from the old CID. "Where are we going?"

"My Guv' wants to be in on this meeting and he wants it to be kept away from the usual routine," Brian answered, looking a little embarrassed.

The lift stopped, and the doors opened to an attractive civilian female. "I think he wants to go a bit deeper than a statement, Jack," Brian continued as they stepped out of the lift, brushing past her and catching the thick scent that pervaded her space.

"Am I getting older or are they hiring younger policewomen these days?" Jack commented, glancing back before the doors swished shut.

"It's this new private enterprise thing; the place is filling with non-police personnel, and they don't quite follow our old dress code."

"You can say that again."

On the occasions Jack visited Scotland Yard he had never been on this floor before and was curious. They turned right into a long carpeted corridor where Brian stopped by a panelled door titled Detective Chief Inspector R.V. Grant and knocked.

"I'd love to know what the 'V' stands for," Jack whispered as a voice from inside shouted enter. He could almost imagine the man behind the door.

"Whatever you do don't ask... it's a sore point," Brian said, leading Jack into what looked very much like an incident room; only stripped of its paraphernalia.

"This is Jack Hammond Guv," Brian said, introducing him.

The stylish man in his early thirties looked awfully like Stone's assistant Mark. He dramatically tossed his sharp yellow pencil onto the pristine blotter in front of him, making little impression on Jack as he stood up and moved around his desk to greet him, same hand outstretched. "Jack... I've heard so much about you. You don't mind me calling you Jack do you?"

"No of course not D.C.I." he replied, not knowing what to call him.

"Just call me Reg," he said grabbing his hand in a vice-like grip.

There was a moment of rugby contact while they both measured their man, then the Chief Inspector let go and they all moved over to a table in the centre of the room, choosing their seats for the interview; Brian and Reg on one side, Jack on the other.

"It appears your little group opened a real can of worms," he started, glancing at the notepad Brian pushed in front of him.

"An alleged one I might add, Reg." Jack said.

"Yes of course, we can't chase a case we don't know exists, can we," he referred to the file Brian dutifully placed in front of him alongside the pad.

The procedure going on in front of him had not slipped Jack's notice; it was quite obvious Reg had Brian well trained. Unless it was a lesson he should take note of.

"What actually do you want to question me about, other than my statement?" Jack said up front, removing the document from his briefcase and sliding it towards him, making sure it nicely lined up with the pad and the unopened manila file.

After completing his customary power play, the Chief Inspector carefully read through Jack's statement, occasionally glancing in his direction in a non-committal manner. "I can see your little group have been very busy, Jack... most commendable, and very quickly achieved. I wish we could turn things around so well, sometimes," he remarked unnecessarily, glancing in Brian's direction.

"As I tried to make the point in my statement, Reg, all the facts were in our hands, all we had to do was unravel them."

"Yes... and I understand you have two victims to find?"

"We do... unless you'd like to take over yourself."

"Oh no," he exclaimed most emphatically. "As you said, they don't constitute a case as far as we're concerned; there are no consequences to these old murders, just the fact of finding them and giving them a decent burial."

"What about accomplices?" Jack interrupted.

"Accomplices?"

"Yes... our paperwork tells us there is more than one involved."

Chief Inspector Grant looked towards Brian for support.

"I wasn't aware of anyone else."

"I gave you all the original paperwork."

"Quite... well we're still digesting that," the Chief Inspector acknowledged.

The remaining part of their discussion centred on the two

victims, and it was Grant's furtiveness that made Jack suspicious of the fact that there was a hidden agenda here. He immediately suggested that he handed over all the material and they continued with the cases themselves.

Grant's transparent cleverness turned to an almost cloying smugness, gratuitously pointing out that Jack's initial success gave him an advantage on any newcomers. Brian was unable to hide his obvious contempt for his superior's attempt to hoodwink such an experienced detective.

Jack wasn't about to play his game. "Alright Reg... tell me what really concerns you about these two victims, and why you don't want to get involved? Otherwise I walk out of here and leave this lot with you."

Reg knew Jack was in earnest, and he didn't have a leg to stand on. He in fact was the one who had been handed the sticky pole and had no one to pass it to. "Okay, you win. But what I'm about to tell you must go no further than these walls."

"Very well, but if I don't like it, I'm out of here."

At great pains Chief Inspector Grant told Jack of the can of worms he had opened by finding the weapons secreted by Samuel. His words immediately reminded him of the Vicar's statement regarding the opening of Pandora's Box.

As soon as the serial numbers and corresponding rounds of ammunition for ballistic testing were sent to Interpol, all hell let loose. Not only the British MI5, but most of Europe's security agencies were interested in how these weapons had fallen into Scotland Yard's hands. Apparently they had been looking for the owner of the weapons for several years.

It appeared each weapon had in fact been used in the assassination of an important figure, the detail of which was ominous by its absence, and they were more concerned in the background to the ballistic information getting out.

The items in question immediately disappeared along with all relevant files, pictures and test results. Grant's superiors were satisfied that this was now secure until they learnt of the Vicar's two victims.

"Surely, that in itself constitutes a closed-shop investigation, instead of a bunch of local amateurs blundering about," Jack stated, after hearing his story.

Brian just stared across at Jack's persistence, but remained silent.

"That's just it, Jack, we cannot be seen to be associated with...," he glanced back at his notes, "Samuel Alluche's past deeds."

"Oh but a retired Superintendent and a bunch of crime-buffs can, I suppose?"

"You know the establishment, Jack."

"Yes I do, too well." He couldn't forget the rough deal he and Stone were doled out by the same people. He also knew you couldn't fight them. "But why don't we simply drop the search for the bodies, destroy all the evidence and get on with our lives as if this had never happened?"

Chief Inspector Grant glanced over at Brian, who had been avoiding the issue ever since they entered the room. "What about your little band of amateurs, and their wives, and their friends, or anyone else they happened to tell?"

Jack had forgotten about them. He suddenly realised they were in grave danger; Marjory was in grave danger. If Samuel's International victims were that important, the authorities would stop at nothing to cover this up. Jack had to find the easiest way out of this dilemma, or at least suggest the quickest way of muddying the waters.

"Okay, Reg... but as I said; one hint of trouble and I'm out."

The Chief Inspector weighed Jack up suspiciously. He knew nothing of him personally, only what was in the records and Brian's annoying reference to the way Jack always handled things.

Smugly relying on the very establishment to protect him, he agreed. "Oh... by the way," he said. "No more official statements. From now on, everything is verbal only, that goes for any dealings you have with these locals also."

"Don't worry; I know how important secrecy is just as much as you. I shall destroy everything as soon as we have finished with it."

"Excellent, Jack... we understand each other."

Jack had to have one last word. "As a matter of interest, why do you really want us to continue? If the guardians of our security were simply worried about an old retired policeman and a bunch of eccentrics, they would soon find a more convenient way of covering this up... another Samuel perhaps."

"Jack... I can see your reputation was no idle myth. You really are an inquisitive bastard aren't you?" Jack smiled back. "If you must know, that scenario was considered, but only briefly. The powers to be finally decided it would serve them far better if your little band of detectives continued with their amateur pastime, under your guidance of course. After all, they have no connection to the victims, and as I understand from your report, once this Vicar has given them their Last Rites, the matter is closed. However, the people Samuel came in contact with in the course of his... occupation, shall we say, they're a different story. We shall be very interested in them, and expect you to keep us informed as you find them."

"Have I your word that after the Vicar's Last Rites, that will be the end of it?"

"It isn't up to me, Jack, as I'm sure you well know. However, if it is of any consolation to you, my superiors gave me that assurance."

"Then we have nothing more to say, Chief Inspector."

"No, Jack, this will be our last meeting. In future you will deal directly with Inspector Binstead, he has my full authority."

Brian had kept out of the discussion as much as possible, only offering support or information when obviously requested. He only returned to his old self after leaving the incident room to escort Jack back off the premises.

"So what do you think of the little shit?" he asked, on their way down in the lift, "Do you trust him? Because I don't... not for one minute."

"That's a bit harsh, Brian," Jack said, surprised.

"He'll drop you in it if it means saving his own skin."

"I'm ahead of you, Brian," Jack said, reaching into his pocket.

He brought out a small recorder. Reversed the tape a short distance and played it back. It was the section where he implicated his superiors.

"You crafty old bugger, did you get everything?"

"I hope so," Jack answered.

"Back in the lobby away from prying ears, Brian pulled Jack to one side, obviously wanting to tell him something he was unable to in front of his superior.

"You know what they want don't you?"

"They want a scapegoat if anything goes wrong," Jack answered.

"That's part of it, but they're also hoping you'll dig up something better to tie this man in with the sensitive killings the DCI mentioned. They want to extricate themselves from the continuing international investigations."

"How's an English assassin going to do that?"

"With a name like Samuel Alluche, what do you think?"

Brian had ventured to alert Jack in a way he hadn't expected, suddenly filling him again with a new anger against the establishment. Was he never to rid himself of these people? Now he needed to beat them at their own game.

"Will you do me a favour, Brian?" he asked.

"If I can," Brian answered more affably.

"I want to beat these people, or at least leave enough egg on their face that it will take the rest of their lives to wash it off."

"I'm all for that, Jack, what can I do?"

"Dig up as much as you can on Samuel Alluche, not just his record, but everything, his family, education, military service... anything and as quickly as you can. Who knows, we might come across some skeletons."

"Okay I'll do what I can. I'd like to stick something on this character."

"Don't let him get you down; you just concentrate on keeping your nose clean. Scotland Yard's not the only midden... you were happy enough in Uxbridge."

"Yes but I won't get many opportunities there."

"Opportunities are for the making, Brian," he grabbed his arm before he left. "I mean it. When this is over I want you to come out and see me, I'll help you."

"I know you're right, Jack, and I thank you for that, but I better get back before grumble-guts misses me. I'll get back to you on Samuel."

"Do that, I think we've got something going for us there."

Jack glanced at his watch as Brian headed back to his office. It was almost lunchtime and he promised he would meet Marjory and her friend in the cafeteria of Marks & Spencer if he finished early enough.

As it happened the girls had just arrived themselves. They had found a secluded table in the corner of the room with plenty of space for all the bags they had. Marjory was the first to spot Jack looking around the room and waved, as he headed in their direction, managing to disguise his feelings with a broad smile.

It was going to be difficult hiding his fear from her. Somehow he had to keep Marjory and his group of investigators safe. He had to steer them through the unravelling of these two victims as quickly and calmly as possible and despite the Chief Inspector's warning; he had to keep every scrap of evidence.

CHAPTER 10

The Vicar, Janet and Arthur were sitting gazing into the lofted beams above and most dramatically of all, there was absolute silence. It was apparent that they had been discussing the possible outcome of Jack's visit to Scotland Yard. He had no idea what conclusion they had arrived at, but he was certain of one thing; they deserved the truth.

"What happened in London, Jack?" the Vicar said first.

On seeing Jack's expression it was evident that he was about to tell them something they were not prepared for. Jack had not prepared for this and hesitated, replaying the whole fiasco, snatching at relevant parts that might explain his dilemma.

He stared at the three individuals in front and then started. "I hadn't intended telling you of the outcome at Scotland Yard, but when I saw your faces, I remembered one thing we agreed on at the beginning; and that was honesty above all."

Jack waited for the usual interruption... they remained silent.

"I was lead to believe they were not interested in our investigation, so long as we notified them of any victims we found. However, the Chief Inspector admitted they had set up their own full scale investigation into Samuel Alluche and his guns. Apparently that set off alarm bells with M15 and Interpol. I was told the weapons were used in several high ranking assassinations."

Jack took a moment to collects his thoughts. "When I suggested we hand over all we had on the two victims so that they could continue, I was told that was not an option. The people in high places said we had to take this case to its conclusion. I was also told... no threatened, that should any of this get out into the public domain, everyone involved would be held responsible."

Janet could no longer hold her tongue. "What does that mean, Jack?"

"It means, Janet... we have run up against the establishment. So many top persons have been killed that they are extremely embarrassed. Not only have they got to be sure the assassin is dead, they have to be sure he never existed. As far as we are concerned... we could end up as the scapegoats"

"They couldn't do that," Arthur said.

"Believe me, Arthur... they could."

"Oh I'm so sorry I got everyone into this," the Vicar cried.

"You weren't to know, Peter," Jack said.

"So what do we do now?" The Vicar continued.

"Well we have no option but to continue," Jack replied. "However, I'm sure you'll appreciate we'll have to be very clever. We have to be extra careful who we contact and what we tell them."

"Are we still calling the first one 'The Watford Victim'?" Janet asked.

"Why not... it doesn't implicate anyone," Jack said.

Jack returned home exhausted. He had just sorted out one problem and now he had to face another. Things had turned out pretty much as he expected, although he had the feeling there was still work to be done with Peter's conscience. Marjory, on the other hand, was another kettle of fish. She could go either way.

"Is that you, Jack?" Marjory called out from the kitchen.

"No it's your secret fancy-man."

She dashed out into the hall drying her hands, "Oh lucky men... you silly man," she said.

"Well who did you think it was?" he replied, hanging up his coat.

"I expected you across the paddock. Why have you come in the front way?"

"Arthur offered me a lift in his Rolls."

"Oh getting used to stylish living are we?" she joked. "Where is he?"

"He couldn't stop, 'Pressing things', he said. If you know what I mean?"

"Is he still messing on with that woman?"

"I wouldn't know dear and I don't care," he replied as he went into the lounge for a drink. "You'll see him soon anyway," he called out.

"How's that?"

"When Janet's got the Watford profile done I invited them over to discuss it, and I might add, see where your findings fit in."

"Is that one of your clever tricks to get me involved in what you're doing?" Marjory said, following him into the lounge.

"No it isn't. As far as I'm concerned this can be your one and only contribution, if that's what you want," Jack replied, putting the stopper back on the whisky decanter.

"Why are you drinking so early, Jack? You don't normally touch the stuff until the sun goes down."

"Well it's almost down, look how the nights are cutting in now."

"Yes... I suppose you're right, we'll have hardly any daylight at all soon."

"Besides," Jack continued, "that was all tied up with not drinking on duty; I need a drink after that lot. They're driving me crazy."

"I thought you got them organised?"

"This time was different. I had to brief them on my reception in London. It didn't turn out quite as I expected."

Marjory suddenly realised she forgot to ask Jack what happened.

"Oh, Jack I'm so sorry. I was so wrapped up in my shopping spree; it went right out of my head. How did you get on?"

"How long before dinner?" Jack said.

Marjory glanced at the clock, "I thought you'd like a Sheppard's pie tonight. It's in the oven now... about half an hour yet... why?"

Jack poured Marjory a port and handed it to her. "Take this and sit down on the couch with me," he said.

"Why? I don't have a port till later."

"Take it and be quiet until I've finished."

It took Jack almost the half hour when the Sheppard's pie was cooked before he finished telling her what happened in Scotland Yard. She said nothing, but her expression changed several times from surprise to sheer terror. By the time he reached the part about keeping quiet, she had relaxed.

"Oh, Jack I had a bad feeling about this when you first told me. Is there no way you can get out of it? Tell them you couldn't find them."

"I'm afraid not dear. That's not an option."

The Sheppard's pie was not the special treat Marjory had hoped, despite Jack's performance during the meal. The rest of the evening went by much the same way. Sitting in front of the open fire, the first of the year, making uninteresting conversation until it was time for bed. Jack fortified himself with another good shot of whisky.

The following day Jack woke early to the smell of bacon and eggs. He roused himself, put on his dressing gown and checked the weather. Winter was almost upon them. The sky was dark and his breath was fogging the window.

"Are you up, Jack?" Marjory called from downstairs.

He walked out onto the landing, "Yes I'm up... why the hurry?"

"I'm going to the Women's Institute this morning and I don't want to be late."

Jack decided to go down to breakfast before he showered, "I won't expect you at the meeting then," Jack said walking into the kitchen.

"Like last time it has to be four Jack. Janet rang earlier to say that's the earliest."

"Right then," Jack said, scratching his head and sitting down.

Jack felt like a frump seeing how smart Marjory looked all ready for her meeting with the women of Lower Cheedam. She looked in a good humour also and he decided to forget about yesterday, and hope she had.

Jack decided to spend the time before lunch preparing the white board for the Watford victim, and after lunch he persuaded Marjory to bring him up to date on what she had deduced from Samuel's papers in the cricket bag.

At four o'clock everyone arrived from across the paddock and Jack was particularly interested in their expressions. It seemed, like Marjory, they were back to normal and settled into their usual places in his study ready to start; like a group of regular card players.

He attributed this calm atmosphere to Marjory's grasp of the situation; taking control, arranging drinks, putting everyone at ease with idle chatter about her morning with the Women's Institute and drawing the Vicar into the conversation with his part in the proceedings. Jack was thankful for her presence.

When everyone had settled, and Marjory's banter had petered out, eyes began to converge on Jack, as if asking; 'Well are we going to start?'

He faltered slightly and then started, drawing strength from Marjory's smile.

"Well it appears everyone is ready to start our investigation."

"I'll say," the Vicar answered, chuckling as he did; the others nodding.

"Okay," Jack continued, opening his prepared note pad to the new section titled the 'Watford victim.'"

Janet noticed the title on the white board, "Are you sure we should call the investigation the Watford victim?"

"I thought that was everyone's choice. If you remember, Janet, it was you who revealed the two victims locations... Watford and Eastbourne."

"So I did, you're right. Our first body then will be found in Watford."

"One moment, Janet," he said, turning to Marjory who was sitting silently in the background by the window. "What do you want to do dear?... stay with the meeting and introduce your input as required, or give it to us now, so that you can get about whatever you had planned."

"Oh... I'd much prefer to hear what you're up to, at least for this meeting, if that's all right with everyone," she replied.

Everyone showed their eagerness for her to stay, to the point that Jack had to call the chatter to order, gesturing to Janet to continue.

Janet fidgeted with her notes and her usual confidence had left her. "This clue sheet was much more difficult than I expected."

"When we saw it the first time it seemed simple enough," Arthur interrupted.

"Well I might have been a little eager," she explained. "The difficulty I referred to was not in the deciphering of the numbers, but in their meaning."

"I was able to locate and understand all the words, even those that could easily have been surnames, but then it got difficult.

It could be an unfortunate combination of double words... I don't know."

"I hope this isn't going to cause a problem?" the Vicar said.

"It won't... I assure you," Janet snapped back.

"What do you mean by double words?" Marjory asked.

"When two dictionary words are used to convey one," Janet answered impatiently, then noticing the blank look on Marjory's face, she explained, "The dictionary has been used as the code source."

"Don't worry, Janet," Jack said. "Read it out and see what happens."

"Very well," she said. (1174:4 / 405:5) - WATT FORD, (152:13 / 349:29) - CAMEL ERIS, (375:12 /137:13) - FAST BUCK, 1125: 50 - UNDERGROUND, (565:31 / 15:9) - KYRI ADZE, 424:6.1 - GAMBLING, 178:19 - CHIPS, 116:31 - BODY and finally 1024:3 - SUBSTITUTE. What do you think?"

As Janet feared the group simply looked dazed. She had no idea what they expected and tried her best to point out the simple divisions in the code.

Jack spoke first. "My first impression, funnily enough, is drawn to the notion of a casino. We have Fast Buck, Gambling and Chips."

"Underground could be a reference to the Tube," the Vicar commented.

"Yes... it could be that the body is close to an underground station," Jack agreed. "So let's put underground and body together." He turned to the board.

"Here... let me do that Jack," Marjory volunteered, picking up the black marker and quickly jotting down the casino link and followed with the other two.

Jack glanced at the board and nodded his satisfaction.

"What about Camel-Eris and Kyri-Adze," Arthur noted, still studying his sheet of paper, "They don't seem to fit any pattern."

"In that case, as Janet suggested, we assume they're surnames. Cameleris and Kyriadze," Jack said.

"That sounds better," Marjory interrupted, "Almost Greek.

"Maybe you're right, Marjory," Janet agreed. "Greek surnames."

Down they went on the board in their own group.

"Okay what does that leave us with," Jack checked his copy; "Substitute. It could be a link-word; linking the casino with the names."

"How do you mean, Jack?" the Vicar questioned.

"Well haven't you realised, it's the only word relating to an action. So whatever happened was related to something or someone being substituted."

"I would bet it's a something" Arthur commented.

"I'm inclined to agree with you," Janet said, nodding to Marjory.

"Is there a problem, Jack?" Janet asked.

"You know... I've got that feeling again, that this is far beyond Samuel's ability. If you look at this closely you can see a pattern forming: The place, the participants, the scenario, where and why," he looked for support but only saw blank faces.

"That's all," Janet said. "It's not much but it's all I could get out of this one."

"I think you've done well with what Samuel's given us. I feel he must have had difficulty with this himself. Anyway, what have we got?" Jack questioned.

Marjory had done a neat job; better than he imagined. She had picked up on his grouping, itemised each section and left plenty of room for notes.

That looks excellent, Marjory. See how simpler it is now."

"I'm sorry Jack, I can't see it," the Vicar commented.

"Okay" Jack started. First group Marjory has headed as Casino:

Gambling, Fast buck and Chips. Next, Victim: Underground and Body and finally, Greek names: Cameleris and Kyriadze."

"Seeing it like that, it makes better sense." Janet agreed.

"I must say I can see a pattern now," Arthur said.

Jack glanced over in the Vicar's direction. "Well?"

"What can I say, Jack. The white board puts a whole new light on it."

Jack studied the board for a moment, "We've forgotten something."

"What's that dear," Marjory said, following his eye.

"In my opinion the most important word: Substitute. I think this word is a key-word, which would explain the apparent lack of association."

"Yes I see it now," Janet interrupted. "I was looking for a more direct link."

"That may have been your problem," Jack commented.

"I could kick myself, it's so obvious now, Jack. We have two key-words. Gambling, which could signify we're looking for a gambling house called the Fast Buck and the chips may play an important role in this victim's death. Then the substitute must be the reason for his death, maybe he was a spy or something, planted in this club."

"Don't stop, Janet," Jack prompted. "You're on a roll... I think you're right."

"Well I was just going to say the two surnames must be the leading characters in this scenario and then there's just the word underground, which I feel is the site. Of course it could just be what it is, you know, underground; buried, but I feel the Reverend's right, it has to do with a tube station."

Jack could feel the atmosphere stirring; everyone was beginning to get excited. What was once a jumble of words was now making sense, all they needed was to get them in the right order. He glanced back at Marjory.

"I think this is the best time to bring you in dear," he said. "Marjory spent some time breaking all the papers from Samuel's cricket bag into two groups associated with the two locations.

"Read out what you have on Watford, dear."

Marjory checked the two bundles held together with paperclips and slipped the clip off the one marked Watford. She suddenly began to see what it was that intrigued Jack; what kept him vital all these years.

"It appears the papers generally fall into three categories: meals, travel and accommodation. I don't know whether or not he had his own car but he never bought any petrol," she paused a moment, staring at her notes. "He travelled quite a lot on the underground. Oh... there's that word."

Jack jumped up and turned towards the white board, scribbling in the area left for notes; that Samuel used the underground a lot.

Marjory continued looking much more confident. "He spent a number of nights at the Scratchwood Motel..."

"Excuse me, Marjory," Arthur interrupted. "That's at the large complex on the M1 above the Watford bypass. Maybe he used that as his base."

"Very possible," Jack said, noting it down on the board.

Marjory continued, after glancing at everyone for any further remarks. "The meals were fairly scattered, a number at the Scratchwood, some in London, and unusually one invoice for sandwiches from a bar on the other side of Deacon's Hill."

"Why should that be unusual?" Jack asked.

"Well by the looks of these other invoices he enjoyed a good appetite but on this one occasion, by the size of the order, he appeared to be stocking up for a picnic."

"Very interesting," Jack commented.

"Maybe he expected to be away in the country for the day," the Vicar said.

"Or maybe he was going somewhere without ready access to eating-places for a number of hours. Say underground," Janet chipped in, with a grin on her face.

"I've already mentioned the accommodation at Scratchwood," Marjory continued. "The only other place he stayed was in London for a few days and as far as travelling was concerned, that was mainly on the underground between London and Watford, with the occasional bus journey... oh... I almost forgot, he hired a taxi."

"There's your picnic," Janet prompted.

Jack raised his eyebrows and twisted round in his chair to jot down the word taxi under sandwiches at Deacon's Hill. He paused; looking at the group, then bracketed the words and drew an arrow towards picnic.

"That's looking better," he said, and turned back.

"And that's about it," Marjory said, "except for these marks on the map. They appear to be concentrated around each of the two locations." Jack glanced in her direction with a proud expression on his face, and she looked pleased.

"Well... it didn't start so good but it's finished better than I expected. We have identified three main areas of concern, with two key words. Now our first priority is to investigate each area and see if there is any link; nothing too aggressive mind, just a casual nose around to try and put some flesh on these bones."

Jack glanced at each one in turn expecting someone to say something. They didn't, they seemed to be waiting for him to start issuing his instructions.

"Okay... Arthur I want you to have a nose about at Scratchwood, Marjory has the receipts, see if anyone remembers Samuel and more important, see if you can find any reason why he should pick that spot for a base. And checkout the nearest underground at the same time."

Arthur quickly jotted down a few notes on his pad and then looked up with a puzzled look on his face, "What's my cover?"

"Cover?" Jack replied, caught off guard by the remark.

"Yes... you said no aggression yet you want me to ask a lot of questions around Scratchwood. What reason do I give?"

"I see what you mean," Jack said, then thought for a moment.

"Arthur's an Estate Agent, Possibly he could be looking for someone who's been left some property in a will," Janet suggested.

"Good idea," Jack said, relieved." What do you think, Arthur?"

"It might work... yes, I think it would."

Jack then turned his attention to Janet and the Vicar. "You two can check out some of these other places he visited. Try and build up a picture by following the pattern from the earliest of these invoices," Jack tapped Marjory's pile with his finger, then pushing it between them to make their notes, he thought out loud; "Why would he want to keep all these? That's what I want to know."

"Maybe that's something we'll stumble across," Marjory said.

"Maybe you're right," Jack agreed. "Anyway... I think we're done for now."

"I'll put the kettle on," Marjory said.

As they left for the kitchen Marjory held Jack back.

"What would you like me to do, Jack?" she said.

"I didn't think you were interested in the legwork dear."

"It sounds more interesting than I expected."

"Well I've left the gambling side for myself, I should be able to get the information I need from Brian, but it would help if you could run down those Greek names for me, I know it's a bit laborious, but it's important information we need."

"That's fine, Jack, I don't mind checking out those names for you, how much detail do you want," she asked, confidently.

Jack was surprised. He only expected her to glance at a

telephone directory. He knew Brian would probably have the names anyway, "Er, as much as you can."

"You forget, dear, I worked for the Civil Service: in statistics. I know where to look; you'll be surprised how much the government knows about you."

Jack had forgotten, "Great, dear," he exclaimed. Then suddenly realised her sources would provide a lot more information than just people's ID's. "What sort of information are we talking about?"

"Everything... I think."

"Then that would include contracts, wills, land titles... you name it."

"Oh yes, Jack... anything that needs an official stamp would have to go through my department. You have no idea the information they store."

The expression on Jack's face said it all. "And you can get at this information?"

"They asked me to pop in anytime after I retired, I just wasn't interested. I'll give my friend a ring; see if she can arrange something."

"You know what I'm looking for?"

"I have a pretty good idea, Jack."

"Great... just remember what I said about keeping a low profile. No paperwork, no signing anything and above all no one is to know why you're curious. I mean it, Marjory. If you get the slightest attention, drop it. It's not that important."

"I know, Jack... don't worry."

"But I do worry, Marjory. After my stern briefing when I got back from London I expected everyone to be on tenterhooks, and what do I find... you all going about your business as if nothing happened. It's quite bizarre."

Marjory took hold of Jack's arm with her usual consoling look, "Jack... can't you see. They're all putting on a brave front. They know what the consequences will be if they don't tidy this mess up quickly."

"Does that include you, Marjory?"

"Maybe not as personally... but I do understand."

Jack kissed her on the cheek, "What would I do without you?"

"You wouldn't last long without feeding the troops."

They needn't have worried. Janet had the kettle going as the rest made themselves comfortable around the kitchen table.

"Just one thing, Jack," the Vicar said when Jack arrived.

"And what's that, Peter?"

"I'm a little confused. You keep saying Samuel did this and Samuel did that. Then in the next breath, you say you don't think he was capable of this."

"I don't. I have this feeling Samuel is sitting up in heaven laughing at us but instead of saying the perpetrator all the time, until I know otherwise, Samuel will have to do. After all, Peter, he did tell you this story on his death-bed."

CHAPTER 11

Jack was beginning to think he should change his meeting place with Brian in the old local around the corner to the Yard: too many of Stone's old colleagues were recognising him and asking awkward questions.

"We'll have to stop meeting like this, Jack," a familiar voice came from behind.

Jack swung about in surprise, he knew it was Brian but didn't expect him to come from that side. "I was watching the door, what are you doing over there?"

"Sorry, my need for a leak was greater than my need to see you. In fact we have to talk about that, find a new meeting place," he explained, walking around the booth Jack was sitting in.

"Yes, I was thinking as much myself. Too many people are recognising me," he gestured to the other glass. "I got you a drink in, it might be a bit flat though, you're half an hour late."

"Sorry again, I was waylaid by you know who, he wanted to know why I wanted this information. I'd swear he's got eyes everywhere, he doesn't miss a thing."

"I told you, Brian," Jack commented, sipping his lager.

"I'll have to be careful in future."

"I thought we settled all that at our last meeting."

Brian tried his beer, "We did, Jack. It's just that he doesn't want us to get too involved. You know he wants to keep a low profile."

"Well if he wants this thing tied up quickly I need this information."

Brian took a long swig from his pint and then opened his manila folder. "You understand I can't let you have this, but you can take notes."

"Yes okay, what have you got?"

"Not much... these boys play it very cool. Everything all above board as far as the Gaming Authority are concerned, except one thing that was very unusual."

"What was that?"

"Well it appears a couple of years ago the owner, Arthur Kyriadze, called in the authority to check his chips... some irregularity." Jack's attention sharpened, it was one of the names on his list.

"Is that it, no detail?"

"Well this is only a summary. The contact name at the authority is James Fisher; he should be able to fill you in. The club, one of several across London owned by Kyriadze, is in St. Albans Road near Watford Junction station. Here are the details if you're interested," Brian said turning the folder around for Jack to copy.

There didn't appear to be a lot of pages and looked as if it had been specially prepared for Jack's benefit. Reading the meagre few lines of information Jack noticed Kyriadze had a record and pointed it out.

"It's an old one from his early days. He did five years in Dartmoor for GBH, got such a shock inside he's been clean ever since. We suspect he gets others to do all his dirty work now. Maybe that's where your Samuel fits in. If you can tie Kyriadze in with what Samuel did, we might have enough to put him away for good."

"Has he got connections?" Jack asked casually.

"Let's put it this way, if he's not actually in bed with them, he's very cosy."

"So we've got to do what you haven't been able to."

"Are you finished with my folder now?" Brian asked, finishing his pint.

"Yes of course," Jack replied pushing it back. "So, Brian, where are we going to meet in future? Somewhere less conspicuous I hope."

He thought for a moment until he was disturbed by his bleeper going off. "Sorry about that," he said looking at it. "It's him; he wants to know where I am."

"So where do we meet?" Jack said impatiently.

"How about the pub by the Tower Marina complex?"

"Sounds fine to me," Jack said, he could see he was becoming anxious. "Go on, don't get yourself in trouble over me and thanks for the info."

"That's okay, although it wasn't much, wish I could have done better."

He stood up and glanced round to see if any of the others were still around.

"This is plenty to go on, you know me. I can always make something out of nothing. Now be off, before that thing goes off again."

"Okay, good luck... see you soon." Before Jack had turned back to his drink Brian had returned. "Oh sorry, Jack, I almost forgot," he said, diving into his inside pocket for some folded papers. "This is the stuff on Samuel, as much as it is but it makes interesting reading." He dropped it in front of Jack and left.

Jack hadn't finished his drink yet, so with the help of a telephone directory borrowed from a kiosk behind the booths, he set about finding the number of this Gaming Authority and James Fisher.

Janet and the Vicar had independently decided to turn their simple task into a major exercise. Janet had called early at the church, knowing Peter would be there preparing for the evening service. She found no difficulty in persuading him that they should prepare their map, as suggested by Jack, and establish a route of inquiry.

Some time later they both sat and stared at the pattern of Samuel's stay in the area, during which time he did what he did. For some reason Samuel had used public transport most of the time, with only a few invoices covering taxi journeys.

This turned out to their advantage. The bus tickets were punched with the start and finish of each journey and the start of each underground journey was indicated by the printed name of the station of purchase. As for the taxi receipts; all they had to go on was the mileage and the cost of the fare.

They dramatically highlighted the underground route in red and the bus in green, there was no indication as to what he did at these junctures but with some careful analysis they were able to associate other invoices and notes to specific points.

It appeared that he started from Kings Cross Station in London where he had a receipt for a counter lunch and a luggage storage bin ticket on the same day. He then travelled on the underground to Kensington South station where stay at a local hotel in Thurloe Place for two days. The number of entrance tickets to the Natural History Museum and similar venues confirmed that.

By this they deduced he was filling in time till his journey on the underground to Watford Junction. There was no indication where he went in Watford but they were certain from a second ticket that he returned to Kensington that afternoon. He then disappeared for four days until he took a bus from Victoria Station to the Scratchwood Service Area on the M1 near Watford.

Over the next ten days he made several journeys from the service area by bus to Watford, with several taxi receipts mixed into his itinerary. Janet suggested to the Vicar that he was possibly using the taxi to scope out the area.

The most unusual thing to evolve from this exercise was the fact that he simply disappeared while still at the Scratchwood Service Area–with no further information on him travelling away from the area or back to London.

It was now lunch time as Janet began folding up the map. "Well, Reverend, shall we grab some lunch before we set off on our journey."

"Journey?"

"Yes... to verify his route and try and gather some information."

"Yes, but I thought we had pretty well covered that on the map."

"Well if you don't want to come that's fine with me. I'll do it myself," she replied.

"Oh very well, but I must be back before my service."

"You didn't think I meant go round the whole route this afternoon did you?" she said, looking at his expression. "You did, didn't you?" she said rolling her eyes.

"I don't know what I thought, what exactly did you have in mind?" he said.

"Well there's no need to follow the whole route, we just need to concentrate on destinations. I think we should go to this hotel in Thurloe Place; they may remember him, or at least have his home address details. We then need to spend some time at Watford, who knows what a stroll around the town will reveal."

"What have you got planned for this afternoon?" he said.

"How about a train ride to London, then tomorrow we can go by car to Watford, that'll be our biggest challenge, where we need to keep our eyes open."

For his part, Arthur was settling down to 'Roast of the Day' and a nice light Riesling to wash it down at the Scratchwood Service Area restaurant. As he pointed out to Jack, he was familiar with the place; but omitted to tell him it was where he took his latest lady-friend on his way up north.

He had managed to get a seat beside the window overlooking his parked Rolls, which was attracting the usual number of admirers, when the cork to his Riesling squeaked its way out of the bottle, and a smartly dressed man poured him a taster.

"Yours, Sir?" he said, admiring the Rolls from the window.

"Yes," Arthur replied, taking a sip.

"We should get more cars like that out front, it's good for business," the man in black said, topping up his glass after Arthur nodded his approval.

Arthur turned to examine the man with more than the usual good day conversation; he wasn't surprised to see by the plastic lapel-badge that he was the manager. This was one of the perks of owning a Rolls Royce.

"It's funny you should say that. My local fish and chip shop says the same."

The manager looked somewhat bemused, but hesitated to continue the conversation. "Will there be anything else, Sir?"

"Yes actually, I'm interested in some real estate around here, and wondered if you could fill me in with some history? That's if you've been here that long?"

"I've been here since the place opened, Sir, was there anything in particular you had in mind?" he said, sitting down opposite. "You don't mind?"

"No... be my guest."

"You continue eating, Sir... I don't think I can help you much."

"I was really interested in any future developments, something that I should know about if I were to invest in the area, if you know what I mean?"

The manager gave him that knowing look.

"I would be happy to pay for your advice," Arthur prompted.

"I know what you mean, Sir, but I don't think I can help you."

"Arthur had misjudged this man and tried a new tack."

"I was thinking of getting involved in something that might take advantage of the motorway. Surely an important junction like this would have future plans."

"There's nothing that I know of planned for the future, Sir... this is it now. After the fiasco a couple of years ago I don't think the developers dare try anything else."

"Oh, that sounds interesting, what was that?"

"I think you need to talk to the management office, they would know better than I. All I can say is the developers wanted to bring the underground up to here, but the authorities said no; the service area was only for the traffic coming off the M1."

Remembering the small plot of land that brought about a similar catastrophe, Arthur felt he had struck gold, and had to find out more.

"The management office you say?"

"Yes, Sir, they should be able to give you better information than I can."

"Thank you, you've been a great help. By the way the roast is delicious."

"I'm glad you like it, Sir, do enjoy your meal," he replied, and then left promptly.

The management offices were only two doors down as it turned out and Arthur made his presence known by thumping the brass bell on the counter. A very attractive girl, albeit a little young for him, entered the outer office from a corridor to his right. She immediately took on an air of interest on seeing Arthur, probably because he didn't fit the profile of a complaining tenant.

"How can I help you, Sir?" she said, pressing up against the counter and emphasising her ample breasts.

Resisting her distraction, he handed his card to her, which she carefully examined.

"Are you interested in accommodation?"

"Not exactly, Miss..."

"Pascoe," she answered.

Arthur felt this was going to be a drawn out conversation.

"Ah... Miss Pascoe. What I mean is, I have a customer, a very large customer, who at this time must remain anonymous, who has asked me to check any development problems from the past and I might add in the future. Can you help me there or do I need higher authority?"

"Oh no," she replied, indicating she was the right person. "I should be able to help you. What type of problems were you thinking of?"

"Apart from a general overview of the future, I would appreciate some clarification and reassurance that a past matter has been settled and won't cause any further problems."

"What might that be?" she asked, glancing at his card again. "Mr Sandhurst," realising by his manner, he had something in mind.

"To be honest, Miss Pascoe, before approaching the management, I did a bit of nosing about with your tenants. I always think opinions from both sides are important and found out that a few years ago the development had problems with the council - can you elaborate on that?"

"I think what you're referring to was the plan to link the service-area with the underground system, hoping commuters on the M1 would leave their cars here and use public transport to the city. Of course we hoped it would generate future business as we intended to expand our entertainment facilities."

"So what happened?"

"Being a public issue, notices had to be advertised, consequently drawing an unusual amount of objection to the scheme. This initially was ignored and the project started until overwhelming public and lobbied opinion pressured the authority to shelve the idea; quite a sad affair actually."

"You say they started... what did that amount to?"

She walked slowly around the counter, giving Arthur the opportunity to see how developed her youthful figure was and walked over to the window. "Can you see the large open green area over to the left, up above the motorway?"

"Oh yes, I see it now, up above all that concrete," he said.

"Well that's where all the trouble took place, thousands of people with placards, protesting against the extension from the existing line."

"Did they actually start?"

"Oh yes. They dug a great big hole into the old workings until they were stopped, then they just filled it in again."

"What... just dumped all the earth back again?"

"Well I didn't actually see it myself but I was told by my boss that they had to go to great expense to finish it off with doors and landscaping."

"That is interesting. What was the objection?"

"I think it was because this monstrosity was only passed out of necessity to service the volume of traffic in and out of London. There was no indication that it would be an out of London entertainment area linked by the underground."

"And that was the end of that?"

"Oh don't press me on that. As I said, they didn't actually fill it in."

"Well, Miss Pascoe, you've been very helpful indeed. I shall note your assistance in my report. I think my client will be most interested in all this."

She became a little coy, overwhelmed by his comment and attention. She led him back to the counter and handed him a few management brochures.

"That's okay, Mr Sandhurst, it was my pleasure. If you want any further information just let me know, I'll do my best to assist your client."

"We're some time away ye, but I'll take note of that."

As Arthur left the building and crossed to the Rolls, which was still standing outside the restaurant, he could feel her eyes watching him. As he opened the door he glanced upwards and saw her framed in the window, she waved. As he drove on around the complex he noticed the taxi hire company that Samuel used, and pulled over thinking his good luck so far might continue.

The man behind the counter obviously didn't see Arthur drive up in his Rolls, his opening remarks referring to whether Arthur wanted a taxi or not.

"No actually, it's some information if you don't mind."

"Fire away, I'll be glad to help if I can," the young man in his company uniform replied. He had a bouncy, jovial personality that put Arthur at ease straight away.

"Well you may think this is an odd question, but do you think you would remember who hired you some two years back?"

The man looked stunned at first until the question sank in.

"It all depends," he answered casually. "Some people you never forget; others you wouldn't remember the next day."

Arthur placed one of the receipts on the counter. The man went over to his computer and typed in the red number at the top right hand corner.

"There you are, Mr Samuel Alluche," he said, and then continued typing.

"What are you doing now?" Arthur asked, curious.

"Well I like to keep a log on all the journeys. You'd be surprised how many times the police come in here. They find a stolen car left in one of the car parks and then wonder how the crooks got home. It's a long walk to the nearest road, and the bus stops after twelve," he continued reading the screen. "It appears he just went out for a run, no particular destination; around the countryside and back."

"Did he stop anywhere?"

"Hang on, I remember this fella; he was one of my rides. Yes, it's all coming back to me now; we went up around Deacon's Hill over there. Making notes he was."

"Did you stop at all?"

"A few times, it was strange now I remember: He would get out of the car, wander off the main route amongst the bushes and trees, then come back and say drive on. On the last occasion I thought I'd lost my fair for the moment, I wasn't worried about him paying mind. I picked him up from his motel you see. Then I heard my car horn go, rushed back, and found him sitting in the back large as life."

"He said nothing about where he'd been?" Arthur asked, really curious by now.

"No... just said drive on back to the motel."

"Would you remember where this was?"

"Oh yes," he pointed to a spot on the large map on the wall behind him.

Arthur pulled one of the maps out of a rack beside him and placed it on the counter in front of the man, along with a ten-pound note. "Mark the position on here for me. Oh and while you're on it, the route you took on the hill."

The man did as Arthur asked, then went to the till for his change.

"Don't bother with the change... you've been a great help."

"Right thanks," he said. "Why the interest?"

153

"Sorry, I'm not at liberty to tell you, but thanks all the same."

As Arthur returned to his car he felt satisfied and he was elated at his successful trip. Up till now this investigating lark had left him cold; but today was different. He sat for a while making notes and checking Samuel's movements on Deacon's Hill. The cab-driver had marked an erratic journey and Arthur wondered if it had anything to do with the extension of the underground to Scratchwood."

CHAPTER 12

It was the middle of the afternoon before Janet and the Vicar arrived at South Kensington underground station ready for their segment of the investigation; at least Janet was–she was not sure about the Vicar.

"Come on, Reverend," Janet called out looking back.

"I hate these places. It can't be healthy down there," he spluttered.

"Stop grumbling, you'll feel better in the daylight, the hotel's only a couple of blocks along here, right opposite the Natural History Museum."

His eyes lit up again as he quickly became interested.

"That's handy, it's been ages since I was in there, I wonder if they've still got the Dinosaur in the main entrance hall?"

"We haven't time for that, Reverend, not if you're to get back for your service."

"Of course, Janet... sorry."

They entered the lobby of the lavish Victorian hotel. It had probably been there since Queen Victoria commissioned the building of the Albert hall just behind the museum. Despite its antiquity, it still appeared to afford a fairly high level of luxury; maybe that's why Samuel's stay was so short.

"Can I help you," a middle-aged man in a grey dress-suit asked.

Janet glanced at the Vicar, who didn't appear to be forthcoming, "Yes I hope you can, this may sound silly but we've lost a relative," she produced the hotel receipt from her bag, and passed it to him. "As you can see he stayed here while in London, and then just disappeared, no one's seen him since."

"Why has it taken so long to look for him, madam?" He questioned.

"This invoice along with other documents has just come to light, enabling us to look for him," she answered, as he lifted a large red ledger from under the counter. He looked at them again suspiciously, especially the Vicar, who was looking very nervous, then wet his finger before running it down the page.

"He didn't stay very long, madam, so I doubt if anyone would remember him. Let me call the Concierge, if anyone can remember him, he can."

Janet and the Vicar didn't have to wait long as they sat on a nearby couch. A boisterous, highly motivated man stepped out of the lift and conferred with the tall man, who turned out to be the manager. The Concierge immediately turned and faced them. The manager hadn't time to brief him and his eyes sparkled, as if he anticipated they were about to become his patrons.

"Madam, Sir... how can I help?"

Janet went through the scenario again, as certainly the aloof gentleman had not, showing him the invoice with room details and time of stay. Peter also described Samuel to him, with an attempt to express his character.

The Concierge looked at the invoice with a puckered expression.

"No need to continue, Madam," he suddenly said. "I remember Mr Alluche quite well, only because he hired me on my day off to take him round the local places of interest, he was very keen on sightseeing."

"Did he discuss his plans with you at all?" Janet asked.

"Not really. He was very talkative about what he was seeing, but not about what he was doing in London."

"So you were aware he wasn't from London then," the Vicar commented.

"Oh yes, he hadn't a clue of how to go on. I'd say this was his first visit."

"So all he did was visit museums and historical sites," Janet continued, desperately trying to squeeze out every last memory.

"That's correct, although I do remember one day, when I said I would take him to the Tower in the afternoon, I couldn't find him anywhere, until the manager told me he was in the main lounge with two gentlemen. I waited for him in the lobby until they finished their business."

"Did you get to see them?"

"Yes... they were very big men I remember. Dark, foreign looking."

"I don't suppose you heard their names?" Janet asked.

"I'm sorry, it didn't register. Except they were Greek, I do know that."

Their eyes opened wide and they looked at each other.

That was wonderful news for both of them. It confirmed the assumption that the two unusual code names were Greek, and most likely, these two men were quite possibly the main characters linking Samuel with the gambling club.

"Well you've really been a good help, thank you," Janet said, shaking his hand.

"Glad I could help, madam, I hope you find him."

The Vicar also shook his hand before he continued on his speedy journey, flitting from customer to customer, seeking out the most profitable.

"Did you hear that, Reverend? The Greek names." Janet prompted.

"I heard, Janet; I was sitting right next to you."

"Well you didn't give that impression, you hardly said anything."

"I didn't need to; you were doing all the talking."

"Is that meant to be a criticism," she said abruptly, turning on the little man before they entered the swing doors on their way out.

The Vicar reflected on his attitude. "No of course not, I'm sorry, Janet."

Jack was sitting in a small open area amidst a row of vinyl seats beside the lift on the third floor, a sort of waiting area for that floor. He was staring at a row of doors opposite, each one neatly inscribed with a name, reminiscent of civil service departments he had frequented.

Even the smell was the same: industrial carbolic with a hint of lavender. At his feet was a mass of grey linoleum, polished so he could see his face in it as he leant forward with his elbows straddled across his knees. A noise behind one of the partition walls made him sit up but it was nothing.

He decided to amuse himself by trying to read the names on the doors opposite without his glasses. It was difficult. Only the name directly across to him was plainly visible, and the further he squinted either side, the more blurred they became. Then his scan stopped on the second door down from his position. He stared at it for a moment until his eyes focused, and then he realised it was the name Brian gave him.

J C Fisher, Assistant Gaming Inspector. The door opened and Jack looked away from the slim man in his mid thirties, as if his wait was of no consequence.

"Superintendent Hammond?" a mild voice called out from the open door.

By the time he looked up the caller had gone and the door

was ajar.

Jack smiled and shook his head, thinking of the time long ago when he sat outside the headmaster's door with five other boys waiting to be caned. He pushed the door open and walked into the sparsely furnished office.

"I'm retired by the way," Jack corrected.

The pasty looking man turned, "I was speaking to an Inspector Binstead earlier and he said you would be visiting me sooner or later. What can I do for you?" he said brusquely as he returned to the leather seat behind his desk.

Jack studied the man while he was talking, a habit he got into in the force that helped him decide what style he should adopt in his questioning. Although the man was slim, he appeared top heavy, and Jack didn't know whether this was due to a large head or narrow shoulders, and his bushy greying hair didn't help any.

"Did Inspector Binstead discuss with you what information I needed?"

"No... we were talking about something else. He mentioned you might call."

"Well I'm privately looking into a matter that I can't give you any details on yet, but it involves an alleged incident at the Fast-Buck gambling club a few years ago, with the names of Mario Camilleris and Arthur Kyriadze."

"I see," he paused; then got up and went to his filling cabinet. "A couple of years ago you say?" he continued flipping through his folders.

"I think so, somewhere in that period."

"Ah," he uttered, sounding surprised to find something. "I have a file here for the Fast-Buck. Apparently an open file going back to that period."

"Would it be possible to see that file?" Jack asked.

He studied Jack from the cabinet with a suspicious expression on his drawn face, then snorted softly and returned to his seat, dropping the file on his desk with a thud. He then cautiously removed the broad elastic band from the thick blue folder and opened it. Jack noticed the spine was held together with tape and the leading edge was curled back and thickened with constant use.

After a few minutes of reading, every now and then brushing his nose and drawing himself further away from the dusty pages, James Fisher closed the file and looked at Jack. "I'm afraid I can't let you see the file, but it appears Arthur Kyriadze called us in to verify the authenticity of the chips that were supplied by a registered manufacturer. The outcome of our investigation proved that some fifteen percent had been substituted with fakes." 'There was that word,' Jack thought. "Of course he had to replace them at considerable cost, and turn the fakes over for further investigation."

"What was the outcome of that investigation?"

"Not much I'm afraid, obviously the reason why the folder is still open. We tracked down the other chips... they were spread across his other establishments in small enough amounts so they wouldn't be noticed. We were not able to trace the fraudulent manufacturer of the chips... they were very good. In fact you might say they were as good as the originals."

"Nothing else?"

"I'm afraid not. According to this we questioned everyone with access to the original dies... with little success, I might add."

"What role did Mario Camilleris play?"

"Mario Camilleris I understand was the Watford manager." He moved the folder to one side, it seemed to irritate him. "Sorry if you expected more."

"That's fine, Mr Fisher, I'm grateful for this information."

James Fisher gave out that little snort again. One of those

things Jack picked up on; not quite a snort of nervousness; the man was too conceited for that, more a sign of satisfaction. Jack had not intimidated him.

As Jack made his way back to Lower Cheedam on the train, he mulled over the reason why Kyriadze needed Samuel's expertise. He concluded it was to redress a wrong, the wrong being the substitution of his gambling chips with fake ones, then selling the genuine chips off in Kyriadze's other clubs.

It was a very clever scheme if the culprit had got away with it, but he didn't. Jack believed his overall concept was right; all he needed now was corroborative evidence. He wondered how the others had got on, whether their information could give him that evidence.

Marjory appeared to be waiting as Jack entered the front door. "Ah there you are Jack," she called out, "How did you get on?"

"Hard to say," he replied, heading for a drink.

"That's not like you, Jack; either you're bursting with enthusiasm because everything's falling into place, or you're in the dumps because you've hit a brick wall."

"I know. It's a case of having too much information and nothing to tie it to. And another thing, like the previous victim, I have this funny feeling things aren't quite right." He glanced back at her as he reached for the whisky.

"Well of course they're not, you're looking for bodies, what do you expect?"

"I know, I know. I said this before. But believe me, Marjory; the more I get into Samuel's alleged killings, the more I don't think he was capable of putting this together…it's far too devious."

"What do you mean… alleged killings?"

Jack poured his drink, "Well we only have the word of a dying man," he took a big gulp and winced. "It's not just that, it's...Oh I don't know what it is," Jack took another gulp, finishing his glass and poured another.

"It's that sixth sense of yours. I told you it would drive you crazy one day."

"Yes... well, things are just not right, and I can't put my finger on it."

"Well I went down to see the girls at Records, you remember, I said I would look into our Greek names," she went to the sideboard for a folded piece of paper.

"Yes I remember," Jack said, not telling her he had found out about them.

"It was very interesting; Kyriadze is the owner of a chain of gambling clubs in London and the suburbs and he started in 1956 after a stint in prison. Did you know he had been in prison?"

"Brian hinted as much."

"You don't already know all this? You're not just letting me go on?"

"No I'm not dear, please continue."

"I couldn't find out who his partners were, it was a holding company. Camilleris was the manager of the Fast-Buck, they appeared to go back a long way, before Kyriadze went into prison, he got a shorter sentence, something to do with his age."

"If he was under eighteen he would have gone to juvenile hall not prison, with a lesser sentence," Jack explained.

"Also, Jack, I noticed something very strange. Camilleris disappeared."

"What do you mean disappeared?"

"Well a few years ago according to his National Insurance, Tax returns and NHS contributions, he ceased to exist, no further payments. In those circumstances, he either became unemployed, in which case he would have claimed assistance, went abroad or died. The funny thing is, there's no passport information that he left the country or death certificate."

"That is strange," Jack commented, "unless Camilleris is our body." Jack's demeanour suddenly changed.

Apart from the fact that he already knew some of the details, Marjory had done well; he didn't expect such important information to come so easily from records the government kept on everyone.

"Anyway, dear, it's all typed out for you; courtesy of Mary in Records."

"Thank you, Marjory, you did well... and thank Mary for me."

"So what happens now?"

"Tomorrow will tell when we all pool our information. In the meantime, I'll get the white board started with what we know already and we'll settle down to a night's television to get our mind off things. I understand there's a good Hitchcock on."

As Jack was about to add Marjory's input to the board, the folded paper containing Mary's typed information reminded him of the folded paper Brian gave him before he hurried off.

He went upstairs to where he hung his suit in the wardrobe, retrieved the single sheet from his inside pocket and opened it. Immediately intrigued by what it said, he flopped down on the end of the bed and continued reading.

It appeared Samuel Alluche's service career was unique to say the least. Although, after reading it Jack felt as if he had read a lot but in fact learnt very little. Starting with his unspectacular training period when he appeared to excel at nothing, spending a good deal of time in the guard house, until his first day on the firing range, when his whole life took on a new meaning.

To his sergeant's delight, he could do nothing wrong. His new found ability with a rifle, or any small-arms come to that;

had pushed him into a celebrity class, confining him to service competition during the early onset of the war.

The next listing mentioned in the report was his secondment to an elite squad referred to as 222 group for special training, and from that point on, only indicating periods of service in the different theatres of war such as Europe, North Africa, Italy and the Far East. It did not of course state what he was doing there or give any personal particulars such as his rank, only the dates he was there.

In 1945 he strangely ended up in Berlin, the only fact to give some credence to his ramblings in death of being used as an assassin. There was no reason for a man of his skill to be policing this war torn city, unless he was working with the subversive element of our occupying military, known in those days as a sweeper.

Unfortunately that did not help either. If Samuel was not the killer, why did he say he was, why did he ask the Vicar to find the hidden ones; and who was capable enough to be an assassin all those years.

Jack checked Brian's report one last time to see if he had missed anything that would indicate what this man did after the last war. There was nothing.

The usual demobilisation details were omitted from the report, either creating a confusing image of that period, or by Brian's source as a measure of confidentiality. Jack folded the paper back into its envelope on hearing Marjory call him from down stairs. Hitchcock was about to start.

CHAPTER 13

Early the following morning, Jack did the rounds on the phone to arrange a get together that afternoon. He explained that the morning was out, as he intended to take a look at the Fast-Buck before it was open to the public; a manoeuvre he used on many occasions as a policeman, which he hoped would work this time.

Janet however, voiced the fact that she and the Reverend had intended visiting Watford at the same time but was quickly dissuaded by Jack. He used Brian's warning about getting too close to the Kyriadze set-up as an excuse.

On setting off, Jack remembered what Londoners said about England finishing at Watford Junction. He never understood why, but always felt the brunt of his London-born colleagues, mocking his midland heritage.

On arriving at St Albans Road around mid-morning, Jack began looking for the club, which, according to Brian, was near Watford Junction station, where he decided to park, away from the thoroughfare of the congested high street. The front doors were open and he could see cleaners busily getting the place ready.

No one appeared to take any notice of his presence; the women in their aprons were too busy listening to each other's gossip as they polished the brass, and two men were busy vacuuming the massive expanse of royal blue carpet.

The only one to actually turn to him and say anything was a thin man in white overalls, on a stepladder, cleaning an enormous chandelier with an extension from the industrial cleaner below.

"Can I help you, Sir, we're not open yet."

"I realise that," Jack said, flashing his old warrant card. "Superintendent Hammond. Is Mr Kyriadze about?"

"No... he won't be in till much later. The manager's about somewhere though, I think he was over by the bar." He climbed back down the ladder, rubbing the cobwebs off his hand and gestured for Jack's card with an annoying click of his fingers.

Jack pulled it out again and flashed it quickly hoping he didn't want a closer look. He shrugged his shoulders and smiled, "Can't be too careful can you?"

Jack said thanks as the man got on with what he was doing and meandered over in the direction of the bar, taking note of all the tables covered with dust sheets, waiting silently for the evening when they would steal the punters money.

The young man at the bar, swivelling a glass round and round hypnotically in a cloth, looked at Jack apprehensively, almost dreading being questioned. Jack knew the look and walked towards him, he enjoyed questioning such people.

"Bar's closed, Sir," he said casually, but he must have heard what the other man said, "and the boss' out if you want him."

"Is the manager about?" Jack asked, with a tone of officialdom in his voice.

"He's down checking the stock, do you want me to get him?" he said.

"Yes if you don't mind, but before you go, were you working here when the previous manager was here?"

"Er... I don't know... um, I'll get the boss for you," he said, and quickly climbed down the open trap behind the counter.

A few minutes later he returned with a stout man in casual clothes following close behind, his face ruddy with exertion, either from moving the barrels about or climbing the stairs, either way he quickly dismissed the barman.

"Can I see your card?" he asked, giving Jack a shock, no one had asked twice before. Jack passed it in front of him, and thankfully his attention was only casual.

"So, Superintendent, what brings you to the Fast-Buck, has one of our patrons been complaining? We run a clean game here."

How many times had Jack heard that one before?

"I already know that, I spent yesterday with the Gaming Authority," the manager's eyes twitched. "As a matter of fact I'm not here about your establishment's activities," Jack replied, returning the card to his pocket as the fat man wiped the sweat from his face and arms with a chequered cloth from the bar. "I'm making enquiries on behalf of a relative regarding the whereabouts of your predecessor, Mr Camilleris."

"Mario? He left some time ago, he doesn't work here anymore."

"I appreciate that Mr...?"

"Bragglia," the man answered.

"Mr Bragglia. As I said, I'm not interested in the club, just what happened to him when he left. No one seems to know."

"Well he did leave under an unpleasant cloud, maybe he's gone back to the old country in shame. It happens."

"Why should he do that?"

"I'm not sure, I wasn't here at the time, but I think he was caught with his hand in the till; a silly thing to do in a gambling club."

"Yes I can see that. So you have no idea where he might have gone?" the young man returned, keeping in the background.

"I can't add any more to what I've already said, Superintendent."

Bragglia turned away and disappeared to his job in the cellar.

Jack sat down at one of the tables and quickly jotted down the new information in the notebook he was carrying. His memory was not as good as it used to be and once that was settled, he headed back to his car.

As Jack pulled into his drive he glanced at the car clock and sighed with relief; his short-cut from Watford had got him back in time for his meeting. Marjory was finishing her pruning and she looked up, "Your cutting it a bit fine, Jack. They'll be here soon," she said, collecting her things.

"Sorry, dear... the traffic was terrible on the motorway."

Before Marjory could chastise him any further he was saved by Arthur's arrival, the others were with him, and they all greeted Marjory and Jack on their way inside, out of the cold chill in the afternoon air.

Marjory came in with hot drinks that she had prepared as everyone settled themselves into their usual places, except for Jack; he was at his white-board quickly adding the new information from the Fast Buck.

He finished scribbling and turned, "Right everyone, I hope you all have some contributions to make to the incident board other than my initial findings," he said, standing poised with his marker, and an eager expression on his face.

"Let everyone get themselves settle first, Jack," Marjory said, sitting down.

"Sorry, dear. I'm hoping we have a lot to get through. Janet, Peter... what did you manage to put together from the papers Marjory sorted out?"

"Shall I, Reverend?" Janet said.

"Please do," he replied, casually.

Janet unfolded the map and began tracing the route they took according to the invoices and transport tickets. She started with Samuel's suspected arrival at Kings Cross Station, pointing out the till-check for the snack he had and the storage stub for something he left in the luggage area."

"I wouldn't be surprised if that was the cricket bag Peter and I found," Jack interrupted. "I see no reason for him to drag it about London with him."

Janet returned to the map. "We then went on to South Kensington underground station, which we linked up with a two day stay at a hotel in Thurloe Place opposite the museum, with invoices and transport tickets to sites around London. It looks like he was filling in time."

"Sounds like it, doesn't it," Jack agreed.

"Yes... we found out from the Concierge that Samuel met two large men one morning with Greek accents."

"The Concierge remembered Samuel then?" Jack said.

"Oh yes... Samuel hired him for site seeing around London."

"I'm sure we can guess who they were," Arthur commented.

"Okay, Arthur," Jack butted in. "We'll come to you in a minute. Anything else Janet," she shook her head. "What about you Peter?"

"No... Janet's covered things quite well."

"There is one thing," Janet said, "At the end of the ten days Samuel just disappeared, no receipts after that date. So he must have had a lift away from Scratchwood by car. I can't think of any other way he could have left."

"Of course it doesn't follow that we have all his receipts," Jack said, scribbling like mad, filling in the appropriate blank places, "he could have misplaced some. Good, now we're getting somewhere. Okay, Arthur... over to you."

Arthur had obviously spent time collating his enquiries.

"Well I arrived at Scratchwood about lunch time, so I thought the restaurant would be as good a place to start as any, and found out from the manager that the service-area had local troubles a few years ago."

He took out the map the cabby gave him and started telling everyone about the proposed underground link, how Samuel hired the cabby to take him around Deacon's Hill and the closure of the work done there.

"What do you mean closure," Jack asked.

"I gather the proposal was almost complete when London Transport backed out, so they closed off the new tunnel with some doors and new landscaping."

"So this tunnel is still accessible?" Jack asked.

"Yes... so I understand."

"Did he find it?" the Vicar finally spoke, after a long disinterested silence.

"The cabby didn't know. Apparently Samuel disappeared on him."

"Disappeared on him... how?" Janet interrupted.

"That's what he said. On the last trip Samuel went for a walk and didn't come back for ages and I gather that was the last he saw of him."

"Very strange," Janet remarked.

"Not if he was looking for that closed up tunnel," Jack said.

Jack went back to the board, rubbed a few things out and corrected them, then after adding more notes he turned back to the group. "Anything else?" he said waiting. "Right... I went to see my Inspector Binstead of the Yard, who gave me a contact to see at the Gaming Authority. Seemingly there was some funny business with chips at the Fast-Buck but he didn't have any details. Apparently someone made some copies and tried to substitute them for good ones in other clubs."

Jack waited for the penny to drop.

"There's that word, Jack," Janet cried out.

"Give that girl first prize," Jack shouted. "Yes... there's that word. The key word as you pointed out, Janet; the link between gambling and our victim and I think I know who that is."

"What already, Jack," the Vicar said.

"Yes... it only took a few questions to find out the club had a new manager, and he told me Mr Cameleris had some trouble, was sacked and disappeared."

"What trouble was that, Jack?" Marjory asked.

"It all fits in neatly with what you found out in the government records."

"What government records?" Janet questioned.

"Marjory did an excellent records check on the two Greeks, maybe you could fill us in on their background dear?"

"All right. From the similarities in their records I deduced that Kyriadze and Camilleris were long time friends, they were both involved in criminal activities in their younger days, until they were caught; Kyriadze getting a longer sentence than Camilleris. When Kyriadze was released in 1956 he started this chain of gambling clubs under the cover of a holding company, making his friend a manager of the Watford club. A few years ago, about the time period we're talking of, Camilleris disappeared, or should I say he ceased making any tax, NHS or insurance payments. Even his passport records showed that he had not left the country."

Jack continued making small notations here and there on the board, it was now beginning to take shape, and the gaps were closing. "Thank you, Marjory, that puts a bit more flesh on the bones."

"It doesn't appear as complicated as it did the other day, Jack," the Vicar said.

"No it doesn't, and that worries me," Jack said.

"Why would you say that, Jack?" Janet said.

Jack turned back to the board, "Don't you see. He's playing with us. He's drawing us away from the object of our investigation. We have all this information about the two Greeks background, the substitution of the fake chips and the possible disappearance of Cameleris; but very little about our victim."

"Your gut tells you he's in that tunnel on Deacon's Hill, Jack," Arthur said.

"Exactly, Arthur. But where are the clues. Only one mention of Deacon's Hill; look it's there in our coded information and no one has mentioned it until Arthur came across it casually. All the other parts of the code were laid out for us."

"I see that now," Janet said.

Jack stabbed his pen at the board, "It's as if Samuel wanted us to know what led up to this assassination and the reason why this victim was chosen."

"He was seeking redemption, Jack," the Vicar said.

"Maybe you're right, Peter... but he's making life difficult."

"Then we need to turn our attention on Deacon's Hill, Jack," Arthur said.

"It looks that way. He spent too much time in the area. First at Scratchwood where he obviously found out about the Deacon's Hill project, then the rest looking for the entrance or whatever they did to block it up."

"We must check that out, Jack," Janet said.

"I agree... and as soon as possible." Jack silently skipped around the board just in case he had forgotten anything. I think our next move is to find that tunnel."

"Well we have the map with some rough directions... let's do it," Arthur said.

While Marjory busied herself making some more hot drinks the others spread the map out on the table, and by the time she returned it was covered in red squares.

She found out they represented the search pattern. She and Jack were to start from Elstree station above Deacon's Hill, down to Barnet Lane covering the left side of the numerous tracks with marked stops. Arthur was to concentrate on the central area, with Janet and the Vicar searching the stops to the right. They had to find and cover something like twelve stopping sites, a tall order which they had to do quickly.

"Any ideas on how we're going to communicate?" Jack asked.

"This may be a silly suggestion," Marjory said, as she slid the cups in around the map, "But has anyone thought of Gary Mitchell, the owner of the radio shop"

They all looked blank for a moment, not appearing to take Marjory's point.

"He's a member of my nature class, and when we had a similar problem looking for rare wild flowers in the countryside, having to communicate with each other, he suggested we used some old 'walky-talky' communicators he had."

"And did you?" Jack asked.

"No... it rained that day, so we didn't go."

"Then let's give him a ring and see if he'll loan them to us," Jack said.

"Would you like me to organise that, dear?"

"Yes please, Marjory, I think that's a brilliant idea."

Once again the group had left full of expectations for tomorrow's adventure. None had given a thought to the difficulty they might encounter looking for the entrance to the tunnel. And more importantly, none had any idea how they would react should they discover Samuel's first victim.

CHAPTER 14

The following day turned out to be a fiasco. Jack realised he was making decisions too quickly, something he would never have done at the yard and he kept missing the obvious. It made him wonder whether or not he had relied too frequently on Brian and forgot about all the little details he looked after.

The fiasco culminated in three hours of trekking along gorse covered animal tracks on Deacon's Hill trying to find what Samuel was looking for, with the added aggravation of the communication devices fading in and out all the time.

Everyone was totally exhausted when they finally managed to meet up again, with nothing to show for their efforts except scratches, torn clothes and most evidently, fragile tempers.

"Okay people," Jack shouted, as they began arguing amongst themselves. "I take full responsibility for today's fiasco, I should have thought it out better, all right?" he dropped down alongside Marjory on the grass. "Let's have a break and see what we've covered so far."

They all followed suit and flopped on the nearest piece of green. Arthur was the first to speak, slightly hesitant at first. He was studying the map, swivelling about on the side of the hill to get his bearings and looking puzzled.

"I was thinking, Jack...while I was hacking my way through

175

the undergrowth back there," he took a drink from his flask, "why didn't we just go to the local Town Planning Office and look at the site plans for this area." The others looked at him. "I mean... they should show all the work that's gone on up here... and they might even indicate where this entrance is."

"Now you tell me," Jack replied, looking more than frustrated. Inwardly he was cursing himself, wondering how much more of his basic investigation techniques he was going to forget. The whole idea of him joining the group was to give them the benefit of his experience, and here he was learning from them.

"I'm sorry, Jack; It didn't strike me when we were talking about it."

"No, Arthur, it's my fault. If this had been London I would have had every authority checking their maps, records, local knowledge, anything, before I stepped a foot into unknown territory. Yet here we are running about like chickens with our heads cut off. It's not good enough."

"You're too hard on yourself, Jack," Marjory said. She knew what he was getting at, even if the others didn't."

"If this is anyone's responsibility, it's mine, Jack," the Vicar chipped in.

"No it isn't, Peter... it's the way things are," Jack assured him. He shook his head and looked back to Arthur. "So, Arthur... what are you like tomorrow morning?"

"Me?"

"Well I don't know what to do... you're supposed to be the expert."

"Okay, I'll call for you at nine."

With that decision behind them, and black clouds racing across the valley in their direction, they voted to call it a day and make their way back to Lower Cheedam. If nothing else it was an interesting excursion.

As soon as they arrived home Marjory was the first to make

Jack a stiff whiskey. She found him in his den scrutinising the white board. He looked worried as he moved his hand through the groups they had established; shaking his head.

"Here's a drink, Jack," she said handing him the glass. "What is it that keeps worrying you?"

He turned and taking the drink, he sank a long gulp, "Thanks, I needed that."

"Forget about today, Jack... it was just one of those things."

"I'm not bothered about today, dear... it's this bloody Samuel."

She pulled Jack away from the board and sat him down. "You've gone on about Samuel all the time, Jack... what is it?"

"I know I told Peter I continued to use Samuel's name as a substitute, but it still grates on me. I'm convinced he's not the killer."

"Well he said he was innocent."

"No, dear... I'm talking about all the other assassinations the governments of Europe are trying to pin on him. I'm certain he's not the man our investigation is targeting. It's someone completely different."

"Then what are you going to do?"

"Do what I should have done in the beginning. I took Peter at his word, I never checked out what he said. He was a man of the cloth... why should I?" Jack gulped back the rest of his whiskey. "Yes... that's what I'll do. I'll put in a check with the prison, see what turns up."

"Good... now can we get on with our life?"

Shortly after breakfast, as Jack collected the information he needed from his den, Marjory shouted that Arthur had arrived. "Will you be back for lunch?" she asked as Jack kissed her cheek and opened the front door.

"I doubt it; we'll probably grab something on the road."

As Jack settled down in the passenger seat he sensed Arthur was not as cordial as he usually was. His greeting was a little short, "Do you know where the Watford Town Planning office is, Arthur?" he asked.

"Yes... I checked it out before I left."

"We're being very succinct this morning," Jack commented.

There was silence for a few seconds as Arthur chose his words, he obviously didn't want to offend Jack. "Sorry, Jack, I just felt a bit embarrassed at the way I pulled out yesterday. I've had enough; this detective work isn't really for me. It's too demanding, too uncertain; I like to know the outcome before I get involved."

"I understand that," Jack replied, as casually as he could, trying to put Arthur at ease, "If this is going to be too arduous for you, we can call it a day now - it makes no difference to me, it's Peter you have to pacify."

"You're right, I don't know how I can face him, you know what he's like," he went silent again; Jack could sense his brain thrashing away. "I don't want to let anyone down. We'll finish this one, but I can't face the next victim."

"That's okay, Arthur. I have a feeling there won't be a criminology group then."

"Don't you be so sure, Peter's a mighty determined man. In any event, I'll certainly help with any research you need, it's just the field work I can't get into any more. I think that's what's bothering the others."

"Yes, I think you're right."

They spent the rest of the journey in silence: Arthur engrossed in what had just taken place, still not happy with the situation, Jack occupying himself with the views from the window, but inwardly miles away, wrapped up in why he ignored his gut.

Jack was almost pleased when Arthur drove into the car park.

When they entered the Town Planning Office through a pair of heavy-leaded swing doors, a thin man with white hair looked up from his position behind the counter. He looked as if he should have retired long ago and asked in a low voice, "Can I help you gentlemen?"

Arthur spoke first, he was more familiar with the procedure, and approached the man with his usual confidence. "Yes... I'd like to see any plans you have relating to the proposed development of an extension to the existing Elstree underground line: The one that would have included the Scratchwood Service Area a few years ago."

"Any particular reason?" the old man asked, dabbing his fingers into a damp sponge and continuing to flick through a mass of documents he was looking at.

"Is that important," Jack interrupted.

"It is, Sir. Only authorised individuals can access the material of certain projects that are under consideration. I'd have to check if the one you're inquiring about falls into that category. If it does you're out of luck."

Jack placed his warrant card on the counter in front of him, hoping the man's diminished eyesight wouldn't notice it had expired. "Does this put us into that category, or do you want to make a telephone call to your superior."

"No, Superintendent, that's fine, I'll get the plans for you if you'll just go into the viewing room on your left.

They entered the long room, with a lofty decorated ceiling and large leaded windows down one wall. At the far end a high red-brick fireplace occupied most of the gable end, from which spread the typical polished parquet floor and four rows of plain wooden benches; but no chairs. They were all around the area next to the swing doors they entered through, alongside small wooden tables. Jack compared the height of the first bench; it came up to his middle, and was raked steeply upwards.

Arthur wasn't as lucky, being a good six inches shorter than Jack. After some ten minutes, the old man shuffled into the room from with a wooden brace, holding a number of large sheets folded in half.

Arthur rushed over to him and took hold of the massive volume. "Here let me give you a hand. You'd think they could think of something better than this."

"They have," he answered, giving out a gasp," Microfilm, that's next door. Unfortunately, as this is a shelved project, it hasn't been converted."

He left them to spread the plans out on the bench. It was difficult to get a bearing on what they were looking at until Arthur found an index page, which for some unusual reason, had been inserted at the back. This smaller version made everything much clearer, with the extended tunnel shown in heavy dotted lines.

It showed the extension was coming from a side branch off the Elstree station section above Deacon's Hill; moving down towards Scratchwood, under the motorway, with an access point marked in the service area.

"This is just the proposed route," Jack commented.

"Here, let me have a look... these plans can be tricky if you're not used to reading them," Arthur said, sliding it across.

He studied it for a moment, tracing all the various lines indicating drainage, telephone and other such conduits. He started at Elstee and examined every notation along the dotted line representing the new tunnel.

"Here we are," he said, nudging Jack's arm.

On closer inspection, right next to the words 'Deacon's Hill', he pointed to a box with the letter 'B' alongside. Arthur immediately associated this with the explanatory legend at the top left-hand corner.

"I'll leave you to sort it out. It's all double-dutch to me," Jack said.

"Look B's here, it says: Closed off unfinished tunnel access. Security door access through County Engineer's Office. Refer plan 0018 - SM."

"Is that it?" Jack commented, still examining the master plan.

"Yes... we won't get in that way, what does this plan reference show us?"

They pulled each large sheet over until they reached 0018 - SM, which was an enlarged section of the area between Barnet Lane and the small tracks they searched on Deacon's Hill. It showed, in greater detail, the tunnel from the direction of Elstree Station, onward to the bottom of the sheet and Scratchwood Service Area.

In one section of scrub, which Arthur said he remembered, was the addition of the construction to seal off the access from above ground to the tunnel below, coming in at an oblique angle with a narrowing to a small entrance in the tunnel wall."

"If we can't get into the tunnel from this point, we need to find another way," Jack said. "No wonder we couldn't find anything... we were looking for a massive hole; not a small access shaft."

"I wonder what 'A' 0017 - ES shows?" Arthur said.

"What does it say?"

"Junction with Elstree Station to link with Scratchwood Service Area."

"Well let's have a look," Jack said, flicking through the top right hand side of the sheets until he found the corresponding plan, then once again he hauled the sheets across with Arthur's assistance. "That's more like it," he said, when they saw the detailed plan of the underground section of Elstree Station, showing the main through line to Mill Hill and onwards into the southern network of London.

A few hundred yards outside the station was clearly shown

181

the extended branch curving off to the right, with a notation of infrastructure such as lines, power-boxes and maintenance service area.

If this was their only way into this branch, Jack suspected Samuel would have hidden the body there, with its work areas and maintenance lockups. Otherwise, it was roughly two or more miles further on to the Deacon's Hill surface shaft.

By the time they had copied the sheets they wanted and paid the old man it was almost lunchtime. Between Watford and Eltree was the spaghetti jungle of the M1 turnpike across from the Scratchwood Service Area, and then another half hour to the station, too far to think of eating on the other side.

"Fancy a pub lunch?" Arthur asked.

"I was wondering when you'd ask...I'm famished.

An hour later and feeling substantially fortified, Jack and Arthur made their way across the busy M1 and up Deacon's Hill to Elstree station. They knew they would need permission to enter and search the closed branch line and immediately sort the assistance of someone in authority.

As Arthur approached a passing porter Jack caught sight of a sign on the other side of the ticket kiosk, it read Stationmaster, and he smiled, 'The very man,' he thought, and turned to catch Arthur's attention.

The porter was already pointing Arthur in the same direction, and he met up with Jack on the other side of the queue outside the kiosk, in front of a flight of concrete stairs leading to the upper floor of offices.

The office windows overlooked the tiled foyer of shops, the entrance to the underground escalator, the ticket kiosk on one side and the rural district platform and lines on the other. Behind them was the door they came through, and on the other side of the counter in front of them was a wall of frosted glass.

"Yes?" a tall anorexic looking woman behind the counter asked.

"Can we see the Stationmaster?" Jack asked.

The woman seemed hesitant at first, then after examining Jack's warrant card she left her seat and disappeared through a door in the frosted glass wall. They watched patiently from behind the counter, as her silhouette appeared to have an extraordinarily long conversation with thin air, until another much taller silhouette appeared.

More words passed between them and she returned to escort Jack and Arthur into the Stationmaster's office. The man was watching a train leave the platform and checking its departure against his watch. He had that bureaucratic look of seniority, dressed in his immaculate black uniform, looking every bit like a Sergeant Major, with shiny brass buttons, gleaming shoes and a rigid back.

Jack was struck with an awful thought, 'What if, after everything, this end was shut off also'; he prayed it wasn't.

The man turned with his arms behind him and stood with his back against the light from the windows, he looked broader than his silhouette; taller even than Jack.

He examined both their faces, "Superintendent Hammond?" he questioned.

"I'm Superintendent Hammond and this is my assistant," Jack answered.

"And how can I help the police?"

"We would like to examine the branch line extension that was going to link up with the Scratchwood Service Area," he put out his open hand towards Arthur, who caught on immediately and handed him the rolled up copies.

"That might be difficult," the Stationmaster said, looking at the plans.

Jack went on to explain the reason why they needed access to the old extension, without actually mentioning the possibility of a body being there, but the man kept shaking his head, informing them that the area was out of bounds.

Jack reminded him that this was an official investigation.

"Oh, Superintendent," the man said, surprised. "That's a whole new ball game."

Arthur looked questionably at Jack, knowing the situation he was putting himself in, should his misuse of his old card become known to the police. "Go steady, Jack, you could be in for trouble with this."

"It's all right, I've used it a number of times already."

The Stationmaster walked back around his desk, picked up the phone and waited, Jack and Arthur crossed over to the window on the pretence they were looking at the train that had just pulled into the platform below.

"That's what I mean, Jack and what's this assistant business?"

"Well you didn't want me using your real name did you? If anyone's going to get into trouble over this, it might as well be me."

"Janice," the Stationmaster called out, "Has George arrived yet?" he waited again and smiled as Jack turned. "Good, don't let him go off until I've spoken to him."

He replaced the phone and gestured for them to follow him.

They returned back down the steps to the foyer, turned to their left and straight through the next door. It was a large changing room, below the Stationmaster's office. Directly in front was a large wooden table with long benches either side. The walls to their left and right were covered with lockers, and a row of washbasins and mirrors decorated the one opposite.

A lean dark-haired man was standing by one of the lockers at the far end of the room changing his clothes, presumably this was George, and he had just come on duty. He looked suspiciously at the two men his boss was introducing as the police when he explained what they wanted, and seemed just as disinterested as the Stationmaster.

He spun the combination dial on his locker, walked over to the table and placed his yellow hard-hat and gloves on one end, then went over to a long metal cabinet in the corner by the washbasins, all the time looking back at Jack and Arthur as he opened the two doors.

"One large and one medium I'd say," he said scrunching up his face.

He took out two white hard-hats, and handed them to Arthur and Jack. Jack noticed his bright yellow hat with the word Engineer across the front, had a lamp on it, while theirs didn't, and wondered why he hadn't given them overalls like his.

"Right gents, follow me," he instructed.

At the bottom of the escalators the only way they could reach the new branch line was from the end of the platform via a set of steps down onto the track. Fortunately they had arrived between peak periods and the station was almost empty.

The engineer glanced at his watch, noting that they had seven minutes before the next train arrived, ample time to cover the hundred yards or so to the branch-off. They became suddenly aware of a low throbbing hum close by. This was the first time Jack or Arthur had been beside live rails and their hearts began pounding.

CHAPTER 15

The engineer switched his lamp on and the shiny rails became even more evident, "Don't get worried gents, that's the one you need to keep clear of," he said, pointing to the rail with the white porcelain conductors and heavy cables leading into nearby concrete conduits amongst the gravel.

In no time at all they arrived at a junction in the lines with a set of tracks branching to the right into a black unlit cavern. "Now mind your step here," the engineer said, grabbing hold of Jack's arm. "This is where we have to cross over. Just put your feet where I do... and be quick about it."

He tipped the light from his helmet onto his watch again; at the same time he grabbed hold of Arthur's arm and yanked him forward. To the second they were caught in a sudden gush of warm air, their ears popped and they couldn't hear themselves shouting what was happening, when a thunder of clattering wheels and flashing lights passed within feet of where they had just crossed the lines.

"He's on time as usual," the man shouted above the screeching breaks and quickly moved off again down the tunnel.

Jack had told him they wanted to check out the service area first, and in no time at all the engineer led them into a wide opening on the left. He moved the beam from the lamp across the wall until he found a large electrical junction box, pulled the red lever down and switched on the lights.

They were dazzled at first and had to sit on a wooden maintenance box for a few moments until their eyes became accustomed. The bemused man switched off the lamp on his helmet and reached for a pack of cigarettes from his breast pocket. He offered them to Arthur and Jack; they shook their heads, rubbed their eyes and blinked.

"What now he said?" drawing on his cigarette.

Jack looked about, "What is this place?"

"It's a maintenance area," he said.

"And what's over there?" Jack asked, trying to get his bearings.

"Over there you've got a signal box, then next to it is the conduits for the junction back there... you're sitting on the toolbox, and at the far end is an access door to the storm drain."

Jack and Arthur searched every conceivable place you could hide a body, but nothing. Jack even examined the walls thinking Samuel might have bricked him up, but they revealed no tell tale signs of fresh mortar.

"Nothing here," Jack called out to Arthur.

The man overheard as he finished his smoke. "What are you looking for?"

Jack didn't answer; instead he threw another question at him.

"How do we get along to the other end? How far is it?"

"Not far... here, help me with this service trolley."

Over to one side was a small trolley used to ride the rails to get from one point to another, the only thing was, they had to man handle it onto the tracks. It looked very heavy until the engineer slotted a wooden platform onto the nearest rail.

"This will get it up to the tracks, we just have to lift it into position," he said.

Surprisingly it was quite light, and was easily moved onto the rails when the engineer locked in the wheel guide and removed the wooden ramp.

"There's no power on at this end to drive the trolley," he said, messing on with a contraption at the front, "So we'll just have to pump it along." He started to move a long bar back and forth. "I'll need both of you to get it going but once the momentum is up one person can handle it quite easily." They did so and within a few moments they were swishing along at a fair rate. "Where is it you want to go now?"

"To the end, there's another service area there I understand," Jack said.

"Oh it's only small, not as big as the last one... just a place for surface access really; in case of emergencies," he replied still pumping.

As the trolley came out of a left hand curve the engineer suddenly applied the brakes; confronting them was a solid wall of clay. Its glistening yellow ochre surface looked alive with slimy rivulets of water seeping through from above, forming a small pool that covered the lines.

Holding back the mass of clay was a reinforced mesh of steel wire anchored to concrete buttresses on either side, red with rust and looking hardly a match for the weight of Deacon's Hill pressing against it. The engineer looked concerned.

On the opposite wall separating the tunnel from the access chamber was a yellow box with a telephone stencilled across it. He quickly inserted his key, opened it, dialled the emergency number and waited impatiently.

Arthur and Jack were still sitting on the trolley, feeling a little claustrophobic. Arthur seemed more affected by the close confines than Jack did, although Jack had to admit his chest was beginning to tighten, and his breathing became laboured; the air smelt like a river bank of rotting vegetation and damp soil.

"Does it feel hot to you, Arthur?" Jack asked, mopping his brow.

Arthur didn't have to answer, he was interrupted.

"It's the lack of fresh air down at this end... it's cut off from the main shaft," the engineer explained as he squelched through the gravel and made his way to a metal door on the left-hand wall.

Releasing the heavy clamps he started tugging at the door. It was stiff, even with both hands, and Jack jumped across the wet gravel to a small concrete platform to help him. When it finally yawned open, a rush of cold fresh air hit their faces, like a gust from a seaside cliff top; filling their lungs as if it were their first breath in ages, reaching over to Arthur and rushing on down the tunnel.

Jack thanked him, Arthur looked much relieved, and the engineer returned to his problem at the end of the new tunnel, lit up another cigarette and stood waiting for the Stationmaster to ring back.

"This must be the service area shown on the map," Arthur said, as they peered into the darkness of the compartment.

Although fresh air was circulating from somewhere, a hint of mustiness caught Jack's nostrils as he brushed his arm across the concrete interior for the light switch; he found it and suddenly they were confronted with four blank grey walls.

There was no equipment or tools, just a few lockers, a large high voltage bus bar, suitably caged and a wooden bench seat. At the far end was a large circular opening in the concrete chamber covered with a metal grill, where the fresh air appeared to be coming from.

Jack was attracted to the gaping four-foot orifice, and immediately grabbed hold of the grill and started to shake it, thinking it would come away in his hands, until Arthur shouted across to him, pointing to the two hinges on a bar across the top.

"Here... I'll give you a hand" he said.

Jack let out a laugh of embarrassment as they lifted the grill up towards the ceiling where he found a bracket to lock it onto. He was curious to know where the access shaft came out, and before Arthur could say anything, he was clambering up the serrated floor of the incline towards the source of the fresh air.

Before long he arrived at another heavy metal grill separating him from what looked like the grassy slope of Deacon's Hill.

Jack cursed as he applied pressure to the rusted framework, but it was no use; it was securely locked with a padlock that had seen better days. It wasn't as if opening the grill served any purpose, they were looking for a body after all – he just wanted to satisfy his curiosity as to where this access really led to.

The inclined passage was so steep Jack had to hang onto the grill to stop himself from sliding back. That convinced him that this was Samuel's point of entry. It would have been simple enough to push the body down the chute towards where Arthur was standing below. But how did he get it up Deacon's Hill?

Jack turned and looked back the way he came, realising everything was so smooth, no side passages, culverts, nowhere to hide a body; so it had to be back in the tunnel; but where? The walls were all reinforced concrete.

Jack made his way back to the other chamber where Arthur confronted him with a questioning look; he was sitting on the bench equally frustrated by his fruitless search, hoping Jack had better news.

"Any luck?" he questioned.

Jack sat in the round opening with his legs on one of the steps, uncomfortably aware of the heavy barred grill suspended above his head by a thin bracket. He didn't answer Arthur straight off; his thoughts were still preoccupied with their problem.

"That was his way in with the body... that's if there is one down here."

He carefully eased himself out of the opening, dropped the

grill back into place, and climbed down the remaining steps onto Arthur's level.

Jack sat down on the bench, "I'm sorry, Arthur, it was a waste of time."

Arthur stood up and started pacing back and forth. "I've been thinking... you don't think he buried him in that wall of clay do you?"

"How did he get past all that steel mesh?" Jack pointed out.

"Well we didn't look at it... did we? He may have cut it back somewhere, dug a hole for the body, and covered it up."

Jack knew Arthur was looking at him for an answer as he continued pacing.

"Look... I'm open to any suggestion," he said.

He couldn't think properly; something was distracting him. At first he couldn't place what it was, until his hearing registered on a clunking sound each time Arthur passed him. Not a sharp bang, more of a dull thud.

"What are you doing, Arthur?" he questioned.

Arthur was surprised. "Thinking," he replied impatiently.

"No I mean what's that noise you're making?"

"I'm not making any noise."

"Yes you are."

"I think the Superintendent means the noise you're making every time you walk over the conduit inspection hatch," the engineer said.

They both looked in the direction of the metal door. The engineer had returned and was standing just outside, leaning inwards with his elbow resting on it, wiping his face with a piece of cloth. He repeated himself as he stepped through the opening onto the floor of the chamber, and stopped just in front of the bench.

He was standing with his legs straddled across the conduit pointing his finger down at the floor between his legs. Below their feet were two large concrete lids set into a metal frame, and one corner was proud of the floor.

"Good gracious," Arthur said. "You can hardly see them."

The concrete had shed its surface and the dust had filled the seams, making the lids almost undetectable. If one of them hadn't been slightly out of align when Arthur paced back and forth across it, they might never have known.

The engineer was now becoming curious. The Stationmaster didn't tell him why they wanted to see this part of the underground, and assumed it was something to do with the access to the surface.

"How do we get them open?" Jack asked.

"Why would you want to do that? I thought you were trying to find out how the vandals got in and out of the tunnel?"

"Just tell us how to get these things open."

The engineer went over to one of the lockers. "Here give me a hand," he said.

When he opened the door they saw two large tee-bars resting up against the back. He pulled one out; it looked heavy, and he passed it over to Jack, who dropped the end back on the concrete with a resounding clunk.

Jack and Arthur took turns feeling the weight of the tee-bar, while the engineer cleaned out the holes at either end of each lid, then gestured to them to place the end of their bar into a hole.

"Well here goes," Jack said to Arthur apprehensively.

The tongue wouldn't drop into the hole; the engineer cursed, then squatted down on his knees, sucked in a deep breath and blew with all his might. "Now try it."

This time the tongue dropped out of sight, "There we go," Jack shouted.

He told them to turn the handle to the left until it clicked into place, and then on the count of three, they lifted the heavy lid up a little and slid it to one side. Arthur was quick to inspect the cavernous hole as the lid slid by enough to let the light in.

"Clean as a whistle," he commented, looking down at the mass of cables below.

The engineer also peered inside. "What are you looking for? Stolen booty?"

"I wish," Jack said and laughed.

They moved the lid back, unhooked the bars, and turned to the next one.

"Has the other service area got conduits like this?" Jack asked, already expecting this one to be just as empty.

"No... it's a different system, they run around the walls slung from posts."

The tongues were inserted and the engineer and Jack hoisted the second lid up on the count of three. They didn't need to wait to slide it back before they knew what was inside; the smell almost knocked them over.

It caused them to drop the lid and lean back against the wall. Jack saw the engineer's face turn ashen, as he let the tee-bar drop.

"I don't know what's down there... and I don't want to know," the engineer cried as he turned and ran outside where he was violently sick.

Jack and Arthur collapsed on the bench for a moment and looked at each other. There was no need for any words; the expression on their faces said it all. They just sat there gulping in massive breaths of fresh air from the grill.

Jack soon composed himself and looked at Arthur, he nodded and began to stand once more, but Jack grabbed his arm. He took out his dusty hanky, shook it until it was almost free of dust, and then wrapped it over his mouth; Arthur did the same.

Reading each other's eyes, they nodded, and then taking hold of the tee-bars once again, they lifted the lid and swung it back onto the concrete floor. Hearing the clunk of the second lid, the engineer returned to the door, he was caught in the blast of putrid air being forced out into the tunnel, and suddenly vomited again.

They stared into the pit; it was like a coffin, although more like an Egyptian sarcophagus, as the partly decomposed body of a man with his arms across his chest was almost mummified.

Jack dropped his hanky slightly and realised the worst was over, the fresh air from the grill in the chamber was vacating the dead man's odour quickly, and all that was left was the remains of a man in an expensive suit.

The skin on his hands and face was grey and leathery and clung to the contours of his skeleton as if the flesh had been sucked-out. The sunglasses he was wearing had dropped into cavernous sockets, his lips had almost disappeared revealing long, well formed teeth, and a chunky gold ring depicting a pair of rolling dice hung loosely on a withered finger.

Jack went through the usual routine of examining the pockets and found nothing, Samuel or whoever was responsible had made sure this body was not going to be identified in a hurry. Even his fingertips had been removed.

Arthur wasn't interested when Jack looked up; he didn't want to see the body. He turned and left to join the engineer as Jack returned to his onerous task of checking the Watford Victim for any signs of evidence.

196

CHAPTER 16

When Jack finally stepped through the door Arthur had returned to the trolley and was doing his best to help the engineer through his shock.

Jack rested his hand on the engineer's shoulder. "Did you arrange for someone to come down and see to this water?"

He was still trying to wipe his mouth, "What was that?"

"Earlier you were making a call on the phone."

"Oh... yes. I mean no, the Stationmaster said he would see to it later."

Jack shook him again, "Is this just an internal line?"

"Yes... but the office can switch you through. Just dial nine."

Although the Stationmaster was curious, pestering him with more questions than he had answers, he gave permission for Jack to have an outside line. As it purred, Jack considered whether he should call Inspector Binstead first or the Vicar.

He decided the Vicar was more important. He wasn't at the church or his cottage and his wife had not seen him for hours.

"I think you'll find him at the school. He's doing choir practise today Jack."

"How do you know that?"

"It's his day for choir practise." Arthur repeated.

Sure enough the Vicar was at the school. It took a little time to track him down but they found him. When he finally answered and Jack told him of their discovery, he was surprised; not quite believing they had actually found him.

"I don't have any time to explain, Peter," Jack started. "Just get over here quickly if you want to give this man his Last Rites before the police pathologists take the body away. I assume you do want to do it here where we found him?"

"Oh yes, Jack... most certainly. Where are you?"

"Take the underground to Elstree Station; I'll be waiting for you there."

Jack waited a few moments before picking up the phone again; he wanted to think about what he was going to say to his friend Brian. When he did get through to the CID he was surprised to find him in.

"What is it now, Jack? You're going to get me in trouble with all these calls. I told you what he said about helping you."

"Just hold on, Brian... it's not help I want this time."

"Oh... then what is it?"

"I've found him."

"You've found who?"

"Cameleris of course... well I think it's him."

"You mean you've found your Watford Victim? Where is it?"

"Elstree Station."

"All right, Jack," he said expectantly without asking any further questions, "I'll be down directly... and Jack..."

"Yes."

"Don't touch any more than you probably have already. I'd like my forensics to have something left to work on."

Jack replaced the receiver, closed the small yellow door and turned back to where Arthur and the engineer were still sitting on the trolley.

"There's little point in you hanging around in the tunnel

Arthur," Jack said.

"Why don't you take the engineer back to the Station?"

"I'm okay now... I feel a lot better," the engineer said.

"Jack's right," Arthur said. "I'll give you a hand. What are you going to do Jack."

"I'm waiting for the police. Oh and... the Vicar is on his way."

"Oh yes, of course. I'll look out for him."

Jack filled in the time waiting for Inspector Binstead and his team to arrive by going over the scenario the assassin played out during his time on Deacon's Hill. He tried not to think this was the work of Samuel. He was convinced he was innocent but how he became allied to the assassin was still a mystery.

"Well, Jack, victim number one then," Brian called out as Jack emerged through the small metal door from the access chamber.

He was sitting on the trolley alongside the small concrete platform staring up at Jack with an expectant look on his face. The three Constables that came with him quickly stepped onto the platform with their bags and tripods waiting for directions.

Jack pointed through the door. "He's in there," they stepped through.

Brian didn't move; he seemed to prefer his seat on the trolley. "Have you got it all solved, Jack? Do you think it's worth me having a look at the crime scene?"

"I doubt it, Brian. You and the DCI are only interested in proving that Samuel is your European assassin. Well we have another victim yet before that happens."

"For the record, Jack... do you know who it is?"

"I suspect he's Cameleris, the missing manager of the Fast-Buck."

"You can leave us to clear up the mess, Jack. You're finished on this one."

"Not so quickly, Brian. Reverend Jay has to say the Last Rites first."

"What down here?"

"No… I thought you might let him have a few minutes up top."

"It's highly irregular, Jack… but, okay."

The Vicar had just stepped onto the platform and was wrestling with scraps of paper picked up by the train as it continued on its journey. He suddenly realised he was all alone apart a solitary policeman guarding a cordoned off area at the end of the platform. He hoped Jack would be waiting for him.

"Only one more Samuel," he said softly, looking up at the curved white tiled surface of the tunnel's ceiling. "Only one more after this one."

The Constable heard his unusual remark and looked across at him. The Vicar realised he had unnerved the young man and smiled, crossing his chest as if he was in prayer. The young man smiled back with an understanding look.

"Reverend."

The Vicar turned in the direction of the voice; it was Arthur.

"Oh, Arthur, am I glad to see you," the Vicar called out.

Arthur walked around the policeman and sat down on the bench. "Jack asked me to look out for you but I couldn't find you upstairs."

"Sorry. As usual I'm causing a commotion."

"No… that's all right, Reverend."

"One minute I was amongst a mass of people, the next I was all alone."

"That's okay, Reverend, I've found you now."

"Where's, Jack?"

"He should be on his way."

"Did you see the body?" the Vicar asked softly.

"Not really… I didn't want to. I just got a glimpse of something in a suit."

200

The Stationmaster had arranged for another trolley to take the pathology and forensic teams to the crime scene, and before long they were pushing Jack and the Inspector out of the small maintenance room while they got on with their business.

Brian was ahead of him with questions of his own.

"What made you think it was Cameleris in there?" he said.

"Well... I managed to account for everyone else in this saga... he's the only one that's missing and there was that ring on his finger."

"What about the ring?"

"It's very distinctive. Something you can easily check. It's a pair of dice... double six's to be exact," he laughed. "What more do you want?"

"I would imagine his associates would recognise a distinctive ring like that."

"That's what I thought."

Their conversation was interrupted by a shrill buzz coming from the yellow box on the wall. Jack opened it and answered the phone. He glanced in Brian's direction.

"It appears my Vicar has arrived to perform the Last Rites."

Brian couldn't help laughing, "Sorry... is this the man that got all this started?" He said. "Giving Samuel's hidden ones their Last Rites."

"Yes... when can he perform his ceremony?"

"Certainly not down here... not until we've finish the forensics."

"I don't think he would want that."

"They'll be bringing the body up shortly, so we can let him do whatever it is he wants to do in the station before they put him in the ambulance... okay?"

"Sounds okay to me, Brian," Jack said. "I'll go up and tell him... I gather he needs to get ready. Is there some way we can screen him off from the general public?"

"Look, I only said that because it can't be down here. If you can arrange somewhere more convenient with the Stationmaster that's all right by me."

"Fine... thanks," Jack said.

The Inspector beckoned to a Constable watching the equipment.

"Help Mr Hammond organise something for the Vicar Constable will you."

"Right, Inspector."

As they approached the main line from the branch tunnel, the Constable had to stop the trolley and wait for a train to pass. They covered their heads with their arms until the maelstrom of rubbish settled, and when it was clear, Jack stepped down from the trolley and crossed over to the lighted platform.

He caught sight of the Vicar sitting alongside Arthur, clutching his small black ceremonial case; they looked less than enthusiastic, until they saw him, then their expressions brightened.

Jack climbed the steps at the far end and waved.

"Oh, Jack... I am pleased to see you, has anything been arrange about the body?"

"They're bringing it up shortly, Peter," Jack said, taking him to one side. "This er... 'Last Rites' thing... do you have to say it over the remains or will it still work through a body bag... it's only plastic."

"Why should you say that, Jack?" he said nervously.

"Well he's not in very good condition and he smells a bit."

Jack looked over towards Arthur and winked. The Vicar was undecided and quite obviously required a little innocent manoeuvring.

"Oh dear... I suppose it would be all right, in fact I'm quite sure it would. I remember a colleague of mine having to say the 'Last Rites' from a boat; he didn't even see the body. It appears it was a sunken vessel and only bones at that."

"Okay then, come with me and I'll try and arrange somewhere away from the public for you, I gather you have to prepare or something."

"Just a small change, Jack... it's more a case of privacy."

Jack turned to Arthur again; he was looking a bit jaded. "Are you okay, Arthur?"

"Yes fine, Jack thanks. I'll be glad when this is all over."

"I think we all will," Jack concurred, then took hold of both their elbows and escorted them through the arch towards the escalator. "What about the engineer?"

"As a matter of fact he came round very well as soon as he got away from the tunnel. You might say he had a miraculous recovery," Arthur said.

The Stationmaster was easy to find standing in the middle of the foyer directing commuters to the trains and apologising for the inconvenience. Jack introduced the Vicar to him and pointed out what was about to take place. He was a bit hesitant at first but once the Vicar explained the necessity to perform this procedure before pathology removed the body for further examination; he soon came round.

He thought for a moment, "Ah... I know just the place. Easy access, plenty of open space to wheel the body around and easily cleaned afterwards." He turned them around and pointed them in the direction of the changing room.

The Vicar wasn't sure but he had to admit it was roomy.

Before he left, the Stationmaster turned back to the Vicar who was lifting his robes and ceremonial paraphernalia from his case.

"Reverend... you don't use any of those smelly things in this procedure?"

The Vicar was puzzled at first and then suddenly understood.

"Oh... good heavens no. This is an Anglican ceremony... I

shall only say a few words over the body."

"That's fine, Reverend, only I have this sensitive sinus."

While the Vicar prepared himself for the event, Jack strolled outside, on the lookout for the men bringing the body-bag up from the branch line. His first hint that something was happening was the commotion from the commuters further down towards the escalator.

"Can we have the body in here for a moment?" Jack questioned the men.

"Are you Mr Hammond or the Vicar?" the man in front asked.

"I'm Hammond, the Vicar's inside."

"That's okay then. Inspector Binstead told us to see you first. Will he be long?"

The man seemed reluctant to break his journey.

"Here he is now, ask him yourself," Jack said, as the Vicar opened the door and stood waiting in his ceremonial vestment.

One man crossed himself as they passed into the room; the other didn't know what to do and nervously removed his cap.

"Can you all wait outside please," the Vicar said.

"We're not allowed to leave the body, Reverend," the first man said.

The Vicar looked undecided and glanced at Jack. "Sorry, Peter, they have to make sure you don't touch the body. Why don't you leave the door open and they can stand there and watch." Jack said looking in the constable's direction.

"The first man looked as if he were about to continue with his official stance, until he saw Jack's face, then thought better of it. "Yes... that'll be fine, as long as we don't lose sight of the body."

Once the Vicar indicated he was finished the police covered the body bag again and continued on their way. He then returned the vestment to his ceremonial case and all three made their way out to the car park. Inspector Binstead was waiting outside. He was leaning against his car with a questionable expression on his face.

"That's the first one out of the way," Jack said. "Do you want a statement?"

Brian gave Jack a wry glance and opened his car door.

"No, Jack, you remember what the DCI said about a low profile. As long as I'm satisfied, we don't want any more paper lying about than is necessary."

"Then what's the look for? I remember that look, when you didn't agree with something I was doing."

"But you still did it anyway."

"So I did... but I was in charge then."

Brian looked at Jack shaking his head as he climbed into his car. He wound down the window and leant out. "You'll think twice if the establishment decide to take over. Just think yourself lucky that they're satisfied in occupying the shadows."

"If they want this thing done properly... it has to be my way."

During the drive back Jack noticed the other two were very quiet, obviously deep in thought. "I gather you've told him, Arthur," Jack said.

"Yes... although I don't think it's sunk in yet."

"That's all right, Arthur," the Vicar jumped in. "As I said earlier, Jack... it's all turned sour. Even Janet's deserted the ship... so it's just Jack and I now."

"I didn't know about, Janet," Jack said. "When did this happen?"

"While you and Arthur were away."

"Well that's it then... we can't proceed without her deciphering the code."

"She's already done it... I've got the papers," the Vicar answered.

Jack glanced in the rear-view mirror to check the Vicar's expression. "It's no good, Peter... you and I can't do this on our own."

"But, Jack; I promised Samuel. We must find the last victim."
"Sorry, Peter... that's the end of it," Jack said.

THE EASTBOURNE VICTIM

CHAPTER 17

The following day was cold and bleak in more ways than one. Marjory had found out how shattered the Vicar was about Jack discontinuing the investigation.

"Why, Jack?" She started. "You know how much it meant to him."

Jack had already cut himself once and looked like doing it again. He flung his razor into the sink and turned on her. "Marjory... as usual you've got the wrong end of the stick. Why don't you talk to me first before listening to gossip?"

"Well... have you shut it down?

"For your information, Marjory, when we found the Watford Victim yesterday Arthur told me he had decided to quit. Then on our way back to Lower Cheedam Peter told me Janet quit also. Now to my reckoning, we already lost Dick a while ago, so that only leaves Peter and me. So... how do you expect me to do this investigation on my own? Peter won't be much help."

Marjory thought for a moment before answering. "You have me."

"Yes you're right, Marjory... I have you."

Before they could continue the phone rang and Marjory rushed downstairs to answer it. When Jack wiped his face and looked over the banister he could see she looked puzzled. "Do you know a Richard Brewer?" she asked.

Jack slowly walked down the stairs, "Brewer?" he questioned. "Oh yes... Warden Brewer; the man who sent Peter the shoebox."

"What does he want with you?" Marjory said, handing him the phone.

"Hello," Jack said, shaking his head.

"Is that Superintendant Hammond?"

"That's retired Superintendent... Jack if you like warden; or would you prefer me to call you Mr Brewer?" Jack answered."

"Richard will do fine; warden is the term used in prison."

"Okay, Richard it is... thanks for getting back to me."

"I understand you want some information on Samuel Alluche?"

"That's correct. I can't go into the reasons why at this stage but anything you can tell me about him would help."

"Oh look, Jack... I don't want to know. I don't really know that much"

They spent the next half hour generally talking about Samuel and his term in prison; how he was an exemplary inmate, how he got on well with those he formed a friendship with, his diminished level of intelligence and the way it affected his thinking. Although interesting, it revealed little more than the Vicar had already told him, except for the intriguing fact regarding his name; something that just slipped out.

"Richard... you referred to Samuel a moment ago as George, was that a slip?"

"No... his recorded name on the file is George Alluche."

"Then where does Samuel come from?"

"Oh that was his given name or chosen name, whichever way you want to look at it," the warden continued.

"I don't follow."

Jack could here papers being shuffled by the phone as if he was checking.

"Most prisoners don't wish to be referred to by their actual name; something to do with old enemies I guess. We either use their number or another name of their choice. In George's case he chose Samuel, I think he picked it from the bible."

"I see... that's very interesting," Jack replied, knowing he was right to be suspicious. So Samuel was not his real name?"

"No... his file plainly states, George Alluche. Not Samuel."

"One last thing Richard... Reverend Jay didn't seem sure why Samuel was being held in Hatchwood indefinitely. Was he actually convicted?"

"No... the judge ordered that he be detained under psychiatric surveillance."

"With no regular appraisals?"

"He had the usual evaluations and they always found him mentally unfit."

Once again Jack felt he was tip-toeing through the establishment's notion of justice. Countless individuals had been locked away because they were unable to defend themselves adequately or those upstairs had not enough proof.

"Well, Richard I'm most grateful for that information."

He seemed surprised, "Really? I didn't think there was much in his file."

As Jack replaced the phone the warden's last words were still occupying his thoughts. He imagined Samuel's file taking little more than a page. He certainly learnt no more than Peter told him. Yet the one omission of Samuel's real name changed everything.

Brian had some explaining to do. If he was thorough in his search into Samuel's background, he would have known his real name and all the relevant information that went with it. Brian's omission was deliberate and Jack wasn't really meant to know.

When Jack sat down for his breakfast Marjory seemed to have

forgotten her defence of continuing the investigation. She was in her persuasive mood.

"Did you remember Mr Brewer, Jack?" she asked.

"Yes... It's been a few days since I contacted him and I forgot."

"That's not like you, Jack."

"Well as you keep telling me, I'm not getting any younger."

"Oh, Jack... I only tease you sometimes. You've still got it... look how you sorted out the Watford Victim. I bet Brian was surprised."

Jack finished his breakfast and got ready to face the onset of winter.

"Are you going out, Jack?"

He glanced back at her on opening the door, "Yes, dear."

"Will you be long?"

"That depends on finding, Peter."

Jack was still not comfortable about cutting across the squire's land and opted for a brisk walk down the hill to the church.

"Peter... are you there?" Jack called out as he walked slowly down the aisle towards the Alter. His voice echoed through the small church with no reply.

"Are you looking for the, Reverend?" a voice said quietly behind Jack.

It was Deacon Threasher, the seventy-year-old parishioner, who could hardly see beyond his nose, let alone know who he was talking to.

"Yes, is he about?"

"He's not here; he's out in the churchyard with Mr Bullen the funeral director."

"Thanks very much, Mr Threasher."

"Oh you know who I am then and who might you be? I don't see too well."

"I'm Jack Hammond."

"The Superintendent... I've heard about you, and I know your wife Marjory."

"I'm reti... oh never mind. In the churchyard you say?"

"That's right, straight down the path and second right."

Jack didn't have to follow his instructions; he could see the Vicar's white vestment billowing amongst the grey stones, alongside the black suits of the funeral men. He seemed quite agitated, with his arms flying about above his head, giving an impression of a white sheet in a stiff breeze.

"I hope I didn't interrupt anything, Peter," Jack said.

The two men left, obviously not satisfied.

"I'm glad you did, we may have come to blows."

Jack had never seen the Vicar so outraged; his face was quite red.

"I doubt that, Peter, you're not a man of violence."

"Those two brothers would try a saint... they would."

"Well from down by the church it certainly looked as if they were."

"I'm hardly that, Jack but they are so difficult. Do you know they had the gall to demand their customer be put under the oak tree. It appears she sat under it when she was a little girl... I doubt if she knew it existed during her lifetime."

"So what's your problem?"

"There's no space for her."

"Then they should realise their request is pointless."

"Oh no they only want me to move one of the old stones for them."

"Well, Peter I'm certainly glad it's you that has to make such decisions."

The Vicar looked at Jack's face intently hoping he could deduce the reason for his visit. It certainly had nothing to do with yesterday's fiasco.

"Was there something you wanted to see me about? Or are

you just browsing?"

"Not out here, Peter... it's freezing."

"Very well, there's little I can do here now anyway."

Back in the warmth of the vestry the Vicar quickly whipped up a hot mug of tea on the single ring he had for such emergencies as he waited patiently for Jack to start. He had a confident look on his face that made Jack suspicious.

Unbeknown to Jack he rang his home only minutes earlier to tell him Janet and Arthur had agreed to continue with the last victim. The news was welling up inside him and he was dying to say something but refrained from the temptation.

Jack shook off his suspicion and sipped his tea. "Peter you know how uneasy I've been about Samuel's involvement in all this. How I always thought there was someone else involved in these assassinations."

"Yes, Jack... it always puzzled me."

"Well I was talking to Warden Brewer this morning and he checked Samuel's file for me and came up with something quite bizarre."

"Why did you ring him?"

"I didn't... he rang me. It was in reply to a call I made last week."

"Why the call?"

"If you remember I had just spoken to Brian and he gave me a breakdown of Samuel's record. It didn't match the profile you gave me. I'm sorry... I just had to establish who was right: Your generous description of a mentally handicapped simpleton or Brian's hardened professional killer."

"And did Warden Brewer settle your problem?"

"He did. Brian has been holding back on us. Samuel's real name was George Alluche. He adopted Samuel as his prison name."

"It seems you might be right, Jack... but how do we prove it?"

"I don't know. I haven't had time to think about it yet."

"Does that mean you're going to continue, Jack?"

Jack suddenly realised he had been caught at his own game. "I knew there was something going on in that head of yours, Peter."

"Sorry, Jack... Marjory told me about your call."

"Well it doesn't change anything, Peter. You and I can't do this on our own."

The Vicar decided now was the right time. "We don't have to, Jack. Janet and Arthur took pity on me and decided to help us until we find the body."

"Well that's all we need. With Marjory's help we have a team again."

The Vicar cupped his cold hands around his drink with satisfaction.

"I know, Jack... isn't it marvellous?"

He took a quick sip from the steaming cup.

"So... when is Janet coming round with the next coded sheet?" Jack asked.

"I expected them here by now."

Before Jack could think of an excuse to leave, there was a loud bang. It sounded like the church door which Peter had begun shutting to keep the warmth in. Then Jack heard Janet dominating the conversation as they entered the vestry.

Jack turned round and said, "So it's not the end for you two after all?"

Seeing their mugs of tea, Arthur made for the kettle, "Well, Jack... we couldn't leave the Reverend alone with you... could we?" he said, nodding to Janet.

Janet joined him, pushing another mug next to his. "Mind you, Jack... we are only taking part in an administrative capacity. Right, Arthur?"

The kettle had boiled and he filled both their mugs. "Quite

right, Janet."

Jack didn't care what they did so long as he had their help. "So... what form does this administrative capacity take?'

Janet stirred her tea and took a sip. "I shall continue decoding the last sheet and discussing things at meetings... but no more field work."

"And I can continue with any research you want, Jack," Arthur said.

The Vicar said nothing, as they all stared at Jack waiting for his response.

Jack put his empty mug back on the table; stretching out their anxiety a little longer in payment for the way they held him at ransom.

"Fine," he said. "We seem to be in your hands again, Janet."

She hesitated, "Oh yes... I've already started."

"Have you got anything to show us?" Jack said.

"Not yet... I didn't know if we were continuing."

Jack stood up from the table and started buttoning his coat again. "That's all right, Janet. Why don't you let me know when you do?"

Janet looked surprised when Jack headed out of the vestry. The Vicar was lost for words and followed him. By the time he caught up to Jack he was opening the front door; bracing his body against the wintery blast.

"You were a bit short back there, Jack," the Vicar called out.

Jack turned and faced him, "If they want to handle this on a business-like basis, that's alright by me, Peter."

"I suppose you're right... they were a bit blunt. I'll speak to them."

"Don't do that, Peter... it won't change the outcome."

"No... I suppose it won't."

Jack shivered and kicked his feet as the red and gold leaves entered the doorway. "I better go Peter before you have to start shovelling me out."

"Winter's almost here, Jack... I can smell it in the air."

"You can see it too," said Jack. "I'm off."

He dashed along the stone path towards the lichgate and paused under the small roof for a moment listening to the rain striking the wooden shingles. Before he braced himself for the next dash up the hill to his cottage, he glanced back to see if the Vicar was still watching. Janet and Arthur had joined him.

By the time Jack was fumbling for his front door keys, the rain had turned into sleet: icy cold lumps, too wet to form snow, yet too solid to run off his overcoat. Marjory heard the noise and dashed to open the door, he was numb and shivering, and felt the beginnings of a sneeze coming on. She brushed the worst off his shoulders, pulled him into the warm hall and helped him out of his coat.

"Oh dear, Jack... you look terrible," she said. "Get those wet things off and I'll run you a hot bath straight away before you catch your death."

Jack laughed, "I think I already did, Marjory."

CHAPTER 18

Jack suspected the Vicar must have had his word with Janet and Arthur; their attitude had improved somewhat since yesterday's fiasco in the vestry. Janet called Jack at a respectable time the following morning to ask if they could come round that afternoon; she had decoded the Eastbourne Victim's sheet.

Aware of what happened, Marjory decided to attend the meeting; if only as a referee to any possible disputes. She knew how Jack responded to being taken for granted, and despite her advice to the contrary, she needed to control him.

Jack remained in his den cleaning the white board, while Marjory did her best to smooth the way for a cordial meeting. As it turned out, she needn't have bothered, they walked through to Jack's den, took their usual places around the table as if nothing had changed and all was well.

Marjory was on tenterhooks when Jack turned and faced them. He looked as if nothing had changed for him also; eager to get started. Once through the usual niceties he turned his attention on Janet and the folder she was clutching.

"Right, Janet... it appears we need your input to start this new investigation but before you do, I think you should be aware of something I've just found out." He glanced at the Vicar. "I have just learnt that Samuel's real name was George."

"What does that mean?" Janet asked.

"It almost corroborates my suspicion that there are two Alluche's."

"What makes you think that, Jack?" the Vicar questioned. "The Warden said it was just a nick-name. Maybe that's all it was."

"I don't think so, Peter. Scotland yard records say their suspect is registered as Samuel Alluche; not George. So we have two official listings: The Criminal Records have Samuel and the Births and Deaths have George. We need to settle this before we go too far into our new victim."

"I can deal with that, Jack," Marjory said.

"Good... then that's settled. Now back to you, Janet."

Janet removed her papers from the folder and handed copies to everyone. "As you can see this code is no different from the other, except there are a few more items to deal with. Some don't make sense at all."

75:28 - BAILEY, 328:25 - ELM, (317:4 /124:14) - EASTBOURNE,

87:2 - BATTERY, 957:9 - SILO, 517:37 - INHERIT, 284:33 - DISAPPEAR,

(7:7 / 39:28) - ACCOUNTANT, 615:26 - MANSION, 418:23 - FUND,

489:12 - HUSBAND, 478:12 - HIRED, 374:21 - FARROW, 333:4 - EMPTY,

810:3 - RANSOM."

"Have you managed to group them at all?" Jack said studying his sheet.

As Janet checked her notepad, Jack went to the white board.

"The names were easy: Bailey and Farrow; although Accountant and Husband must be added if they're not the first two. Then we have location: Eastbourne. The grave site I would say could be one of three places: Silo, Mansion or Elm. Reason for the assassination: Ransom, Fund and Inherit, take your pick. And finally the tale-end items I couldn't fit anywhere: Battery, Disappear, Hired and Empty."

Jack finished adding her suggestions to the board. "Okay, Janet... that looks good. On the face of it I can't argue with that. Any comments anyone?"

"Nothing jumps out, Jack," the Vicar started.

"I know... that's why I want you all to give thought to the words I've underlined. Don't forget... we're looking at Eastbourne here. Janet, I'd like you to check out Fund and Inherit, see if anything jumps out at you. Arthur, you can have a look at maps of the area; see if you can identify any mansions and woods with elms. Peter, why don't you check into the words Battery and Silo. Oh and ring up some of Eastbourne's hire companies and see if they recognise our two names."

"What sort of hire companies, Jack?"

"I don't know, Peter. Think about it... cars, services; look in the Yellow Pages. He certainly won't be hiring baby's things."

"What are you going to do, Jack?" Marjory asked.

"I'm going to check out the local constabulary. See if the names mean anything; any disappearances or ransoms; anything that might fit our victim's profile. If I come up with anything that conflicts with your words I'll let you know."

"Do you think that's possible, Jack?" Marjory questioned.

"To be honest with you... no; I don't think the police will be that helpful... retired Superintendant or not. Although... if I can persuade inspector Binstead to have a word with them, they might prove very useful."

"Why bother, Jack?" Janet said. "You said we couldn't get too many people involved in our investigation."

"You're right... but I can come up with something to satisfy them."

"Jack... what about the names?" Marjory interrupted.

"Names?" Jack answered, checking the board.

"Yes... everyone's looking out for the names in their research, but no one's actually checking the names. I can do that at the same time as I find out about George and Samuel."

"Sorry dear; I thought Samuel's messy paperwork would be enough. And you're right... I did forget. I suppose I was waiting for the names to crop-up."

Jack turned back to the board and underlined each item with a different colour allocated to each person so he wouldn't forget.

"There you are. You each have a colour code."

The Vicar waited for the moment and jumped in, "Jack... this silo I'm looking for, do you imagine it's where the victim is buried?"

"I have no idea, Peter. Initially the whole point of Samuel picking a hiding place was that no one could find the body. So the silo, if that is where it is, will probably no longer exist or it will be covered in some way, just like the underground burial of the last victim. That turned out to be in an unused branch line."

"I just wanted to make sure what I was looking for."

"Peter... at this stage we're just trying to find out what the words mean."

Jack made an early start the following morning; he wanted to see Brian before he visited the local police in Eastbourne. He wanted to get this last case out of the way quickly, and that meant he had to be in full possession of the facts.

Jack was glad he made the decision, when he surfaced from the underground near Scotland Yard the sky had opened and he was a deluge of rain. He decided to phone Brian from Westminster station to arrange a meeting place other than their usually exposed venue by the river, and found out that his boss was out of the country and it was safe to call in at the Yard.

Luckily Brian was looking out of his window, which made it easy for Jack to persuade him to get a passing police car to pick him up. And before long, Jack was shaking his old Sergeant's hand without as much as a drop of rain to mar his new Macintosh.

"You look smart, Jack," Brian said, leading him across to the lift. "You look like Dick Tracy in that new coat."

"Yes... Marjory surprised me with it this morning when she saw the rain. It was supposed to be one of my Christmas presents... thanks for seeing me."

"You know, Jack you're beginning to stretch our friendship a bit thin. You're lucky he's not in or you wouldn't have had a chance," Brian said half-heartedly.

"Then why invite me in at all if that's the case?"

The lift stopped on a floor Jack was not familiar with. He followed Brian down the corridor to a room at the far end. Brian switched on the light and invited Jack to sit down in one of the chairs around a long table. Jack was surprised as he removed his coat and hat; the whole room, except for the small enclave they were sitting in, was floor to ceiling shelving.

"Is this your idea of me not running into anyone?" Jack said.

Brian laughed, "No... I just thought you might be after more information; and what better place than the Records Room."

"Do you think I'd come all this way to pass the time of day?"

"So why have you come?"

Jack hesitated. "We have just completed the code on the Eastbourne Victim, and as with the other, we have to find the meaning of several words before we can start." Jack took a copy of the code out of his inside pocket and slid it across to him.

Brian took a moment to digest the mass of meaningless numbers and words.

"Why now? You didn't need me so early before."

"You'll note I've run a coloured marker through some of the words... I think you might be in a better position to help."

"The names I can check, but what's this Ransom?"

"I thought you might have a file on recent ransom cases."

"You'll have to check with the locals on that... oh I see,"

he cried out. "This is your subtle way of getting me to ring Eastbourne for you."

"Well you must admit, Brian... Scotland Yard carries a lot more weight than an old retired Superintendant."

"And what about the DCI's directive of no outside involvement?"

"I don't have to tell them any more than they need to know... and besides; they're going to find out when we discover the body."

"Oh by the way, I got the forensic report on the body in the tunnel this morning."

"Anything I should know about?"

"Not really... it simply confirmed what we already suspected. Cameleris was shot with the Browning automatic from Samuel's weapon cache."

Brian picked up the paper and disappeared amongst the rows of shelving. It took a while for him to return, giving Jack time to contemplate whether he had been persuasive enough.

"We have no criminal files on these names in Eastbourne."

"But you do have files on Bailey and Farrow."

"Oh yes... but it would take an expert records clerk to separate them."

"Okay... but you will get onto Eastbourne for me?"

"Is that all?"

"Come on, Brian, they won't get that many ransoms."

Brian picked up the phone and dialled another department.

A smart young girl came in carrying a folder, which heartened Jack no end, "There's not much Inspector, Eastbourne mustn't be into ransoms," she reported.

"So what have you got?" Brian asked, taking the folder from her.

"We have three over that time period, Simpson..."

"No, he interrupted we're looking for either Bailey or Farrow."

"No the other's are Preston and Catlow," she replied, checking.

"Damn, that's no good," Jack cursed.

"What's this Constable?" Brian pointed out to the girl.

"Oh this is something I picked up on the open file. I don't know how we got hold of it when it wasn't listed, that's why there's no information attached."

"Where was it from?"

"Eastbourne CID," she said.

"See if you can get any more out of them," Brian asked.

He turned back to Jack, shrugging his shoulders. "What do you make of that?"

"Strange," Jack commented, not really following their new procedure.

"As you may remember, Jack, this is central records for all crimes when they're concluded. So the files I mentioned were cases resolved. The other one, according to the note was still open, no information because the file hadn't been sent through yet, but an indication that it had been requested by someone here; hence the note."

"So at one time the file was here, but returned?" Jack said.

"Exactly."

"Can you get the information from Eastbourne?"

"I doubt if they would appreciate that, since they already gave us the information but I'll give them a ring and see."

"Can we do that now," Jack urged.

Brian smiled at Jack's persistence, nothing had changed.

"Okay Jack... it's a good job the DCI isn't here."

Jack sat back while he listened to him talk to a DI Maitland in Eastbourne CID. He was amused at the banter between them, trying so hard not to ruffle each other's feathers or tread on their respective areas of responsibility.

He had learnt over the years, working from a county CID, how difficult it was dealing with Scotland Yard and its superiority. In this instance, Brian was able to persuade DI Maitland that Jack, a retired Superintendent, was acting in a consultative capacity and needed this information to help him with his inquiry.

"You did quite well there," Jack said, after he finished. "From what I heard they're going to help me; is that right?"

"Yes... provided you give them all the information you get."

"That's fair enough, if you don't mind."

"Mind... Jack I'd be glad not to hear anything more about this case until it's finished. As far as I'm concerned you can deal with DI Maitland from now on and my advice is; if he wants to tag along on this case, you let him."

"Then did he confirm his case was one of our names?"

"No he didn't, Jack."

"Then what were you talking about? Surely he knows the name of the person being ransomed?"

"Jack... you don't seem to appreciate the fact that you've wandered into a live case. He's not going to divulge his name."

"So what are we talking about? This may have nothing to do with me."

"Sorry, it's all they've got. It's the only ransom case that's been reported."

Jack wasn't one hundred percent happy with his trip to London, but he had to be grateful for small mercies. Brian had done his best and a contact in the Eastbourne CID, who was prepared to deal with him; was going to be handy.

Brian looked relieved when Jack stood up and put his new Macintosh on.

Jack took hold of Brian's hand and shook it vigorously, "Thank you, Brian, you helped me enormously. Now I can get things moving... and who knows, we might just have this case sewn up before you know it."

For once Brian seemed happy as he escorted Jack back to the

front lobby.

Jack took one look at the rain outside and turned back to Brian.

"What?" he said. "Have you forgotten something?"

"Could you arrange a lift?"

By the time Jack returned home Marjory was waiting for him with a hot toddy to burn the chill out of his bones before she started the evening meal. It was too late to get the others together for a meeting, and tomorrow he wanted to make an early start to see this DI Maitland in Eastbourne. So he opted for a telephone conference.

"Janet?" he questioned, when she picked up the phone.

"Hello... is that you, Jack?"

"Yes, Janet. Sorry about ringing you so late but I'm off to Eastbourne in the morning and I wondered if you had anything for me?"

"I'm sorry, Jack but I haven't come across anything yet."

"That's okay... just keep looking. I'll check in with you when I get back."

"Why are you going to Eastbourne?"

"I got permission from Scotland Yard today... so we're covered."

"That's good. I look forward to our next meeting."

Jack thought he had better ring Arthur next; he knew Peter would be in the church now preparing for the evening service. Like Janet, Arthur answered straight away; although he did seem a little anxious.

"Yes... who's that?"

"It's Jack... Arthur"

"Oh sorry, Jack. I've had no end of trouble with this phone today."

"What's the problem"

"I don't know... something to do with the new exchange. Anyway, how can I help? I hope you don't want to call a meeting."

"No, Arthur... on the contrary, I'm just letting you know I'm going to see the police in Eastbourne tomorrow so we can't have a meeting."

"That's all right then. This phone has put me back a day."

"I was just ringing to find out if you had anything for me."

"I'm not sure, Jack. I found a title for a large house in the name of Bailey but I would have to dig further to say it was a mansion. As far as the elm forest is concerned, they seem quite popular in Eastbourne."

"That's good, Arthur... you've done well. See you when I get back."

Jack checked his address book again for the church's number.

"Is that you, Peter?"

"No, it's deacon Threasher."

"Oh deacon, it's Jack Hammond... is the reverend about?"

"He can't be disturbed... he's rehearsing a wedding."

"Oh dear... I wouldn't want to interrupt that. Ask the reverend to ring me when he's finished, will you?"

"I'll do that, Superintendant."

It was early days as far as Jack was concerned; tomorrow was going to be a big day. He had the feeling his meeting with DI Maitland was going to set the ball rolling. He already had Arthur's news that he had found a possible link between Bailey and the Mansion and this Eastbourne ransom demand looked promising.

"Finished your calls, Jack?" Marjory said, entering his study.

"Yes, dear," he said, closing his book. "By the way... how did you get on with those names, Bailey and Farrow?"

"I'm seeing my friend tomorrow, dear."

"Good... you might make note that Arthur has just linked the Bailey name with his search for a mansion. We're moving, Marjory."

CHAPTER 19

Jack was surprised with his reception at the Eastbourne CID. He was treated with the courtesy of a ranking officer, placed in a comfortable room with easy chairs and other furniture , unlike the interview room he expected, and served an excellent cup of tea with a plate of assorted biscuits.

While still recovering from this pleasant surprise, the door opened and a well-built man in his late thirties walked in, "Jack Hammond, how are you," he said, not as an introduction, but more like they knew each other from the past.

Jack hurriedly scanned his memories of the old days before Uxbridge, it had to be that time period or he would have remembered him otherwise. His anxiety must have been obvious as the Inspector spoke again.

"You don't remember me, Jack, do you?"

"Well, er..." Jack stuttered. He was caught off guard.

"Of course I've put a bit of weight on since then," he continued, appearing to enjoy Jack's dilemma, rather than being annoyed by it. "Wembley, in the fifties."

That word Wembley brought it all flooding back like a trigger. Bill Maitland, a fellow Constable on the beat. "Bill Maitland," Jack shouted, pleased with himself. "Good lord, that goes back to a time I'd rather forget," he said, surprised.

The greying man's face was a picture, and his memory of their past life together was obviously far clearer than Jack's, and it gave him confidence.

"I thought you would eventually remember, Jack," he said with a satisfied smile on his face. "Superintendent Jack Hammond, I might add... you did well for yourself. I've only managed Inspector," he stated, sitting down opposite.

"Retired Superintendent," Jack corrected. "I suppose you heard how I got it? Almost everyone else has... it's the thing to talk about...I understand."

"We heard the rumours, Jack, I was sorry. We had a good time for as long as it lasted back then... those were the days."

"So I keep... kept, telling my Sergeant, but he wouldn't have any. I suppose everyone's time is the good old days. Remember desk Sergeant Phillips?"

"Do I... he was always on about his good old days."

"Yes... memories; that's all they are now, Bill. By the way what happened with you when you took that transfer? You were here one day and gone the next... Know one had a clue what happened to you."

"Like you, Jack, we all have our crosses to bear. I didn't tell you but I was having trouble with the wife, she didn't like me on the beat all hours, so she gave me an ultimatum; new job or better duties. I had a word with the Guv' and he suggested I transfer to cars, less possibility of danger and better hours."

"And did it work out okay... with the wife I mean?"

"Not really. I think it was just an excuse, she left me shortly after."

"Oh sorry to hear that. So how did you get into CID then?"

"I moved here two years ago, funnily enough about the time your inquiry was on the books. I wasn't actually involved, so I don't know much about it, my predecessor was the one who made a mess of it."

"Mess?" Jack exclaimed; not getting that impression from Brian.

"Sorry I'm jumping the gun, Jack. Probably we'd better start from the beginning, and get things in better order."

"Yes, sounds like you're right, Bill," he agreed, taking the folder out of his briefcase and placing it on the table between them.

"Hold on, Jack, I'll get what we've got," he said, and left the room.

When he returned Jack was expecting him to be carrying a thick folder, instead it was little bigger than his own. "I came here expecting you to be telling me all about this case," Jack said, as Bill sat down again, placing his folder next to the other.

"I don't know who gave you that idea; this is only a missing person file. I was hoping you could help me close it."

"We might not even be talking about the same case."

"Well as I suggested, let's find out first... okay?"

Jack sipped his tea and had a look at the biscuits. "Did Inspector Binstead tell you what my role was in all this?"

"He just said you were a consultant on this case for Scotland Yard, and passed two names through for that period, which activated this file in Missing Person's."

"No other, such as ransom's?" Jack prompted.

"No... although we did discuss that possibility, hence the mess I mentioned."

Jack told him as much of the story he thought necessary, he didn't really have to know any more than the connection between the Vicar and Samuel's hidden bodies.

"So are you hoping the connection with this name might lead to your victim?"

"It's early days yet, Bill. Why don't we share facts and see what happens?"

"That suits me, Jack," Bill said, sliding his file towards Jack.

Jack did the same, opening Bill's first. "Your turn now."

"Okay... two weeks after I started a woman came in asking why she hadn't been contacted about her missing niece. I checked with Missing Persons and they said there was no file under that name..."

"What name was that?" Jack interrupted.

"Bailie, Michelle Bailie. She apparently went missing two months earlier. The aunt only found out six weeks prior, then informed my predecessor, who said he was going to look into it."

"My name is spelt differently," said Jack. "Did he look into it?"

"Who knows, for some reason he left no papers, used no one on his inquiries, and according to the aunt, didn't contact her further on the matter."

"So what happened to him, didn't you contact him?"

"We couldn't, unless we used a medium. He died in a car crash."

"Suspicious?" Jack questioned, sipping his tea again.

"I wouldn't know. It was all over by the time I arrived. If it hadn't been for the aunt contacting me, I wouldn't have known this much."

"Don't you think his sudden death a bit suspicious while he was looking into a woman's disappearance?"

"I hadn't given it a thought till now; I suppose you're right. It does smell a bit."

"Would you accept the possibility that your predecessor was involved in some way, hence the missing documents?"

"I would accept anything, Jack, if I had the proof."

"Jack continued reading Bill's file."

The file had only one sheet inside; a missing person's profile. He had seen many such as this before: Run-of-the-mill documents with little facts to go on, except this had to be his lucky day. Within as many lines he had four of his coded words.

Name: Michelle Bailie; spelt differently here. Address: The Elms, Plantation Grove, Bradley Road, Eastbourne. Age: Thirty-one. Occupation: Accountant. Husband: deceased. Jack just had to read it again.

"This isn't much to go on," Jack said, closing the file. "Although... I must say, there are enough similarities in both files to confirm this is the same case."

"So... where do we go from here, Jack?" Bill asked.

"That I would say depends on you, Bill. Do you let me on your patch to do my thing or simply supply you with information to help your inquiry?"

"For reasons I can't disclose just yet, Jack, I would prefer you to continue with as little police involvement as possible. That doesn't mean we can't meet and confer with each other when necessary, or on occasions I might even come along with you."

"Why is it I'm not surprised by that answer," Jack said, sarcastically.

"Well we have to keep a low profile on this one, Jack."

"Until I solve it that is," Bill said nothing, but his smile said a lot. "What if I turn up anything about your predecessor?"

"We'll come to that when and if it occurs, okay?"

"Very well." Jack said.

After covering the good old days, they had little in common now. Jack had few memories of their time together, despite Bill's enthusiasm, and made no effort to question his motives. Jack wanted this to be a symbiotic relationship; at least until he solved this mystery and discovered where the body is hidden.

CHAPTER 20

Jack was so pumped with discovering the meaning of four of his coded words he felt he should continue, until he realised the only next fact he could investigate was the address he had; an address that sounded like a mansion.

With the possibility of five of the words now, Jack glanced at his watch and decided he had plenty of time to check the address out before he returned to Lower Cheedam and contacted the others.

He suddenly realised he was about to break one of his own rules: Never run faster than you can see ahead. And that was exactly what he was about to do.

Jack had no problem when he handed the address to the taxi driver. Apparently Mrs Baillie was well known to him. She was a regular customer, preferring to do her shopping by taxi, rather than walking through the pleasant streets of Eastbourne like most of its residents. She was a reclusive person he commented.

"Mrs Baillie?" Jack asked the elderly woman behind the half open door.

"Yes... who is it," she said abruptly.

"My name's Jack Hammond, I'm a retired police Superintendent. This is my warrant card," he said, holding it against the gap.

"So, what is it you want?"

"I've just come from Inspector Maitland after discussing the missing person's file on your niece... would you like to check with him?"

She wasn't bothered with his last statement, as soon as he mentioned her niece, she started undoing the chain on the door and opened it.

"Come in quickly; have you any news for me?"

Although not a mansion, her home was quite comfortable. The furniture looked like antiques and the carpet felt expensive. It appeared the money came from the Baillie side of the family, and she was the aunt of Michelle's husband.

She was in her sixties, although she looked younger, probably pampered from birth and never away from the beauty parlour. Jack considered she was expensively dressed with the usual blue rinse of a society hair do. She showed him into one of the front rooms, with the biggest bay window he had ever seen, showing a panoramic view of rolling dunes to the sea on one side, and a continuation of the grand old-style houses leading into town on the other.

"Would you care for any refreshment?" she asked.

"Yes thank you," he hadn't eaten again.

She pressed a buzzer for her housekeeper and arranged a small buffet.

"Now, Superintendent..."

"Retired Superintendent," he corrected.

"Never mind about that, what have you got for me."

"I'm afraid I haven't got anything as yet, that's not the reason I called."

"Oh," she grunted, looking as if she was about to throw him out, without any buffet. "Then what have you called for? Why are you wasting my time?"

"Mrs Baillie."

"Miss," she snapped.

"Sorry... Miss Baillie, I am investigating the confession of an assassin who says he was hired to kill someone here in Eastbourne. One of my clues is the name Bailey." She let out a small gasp. "This doesn't mean this has anything to do with you, Bailey is a fairly common name, although I must admit the spelling could make a difference; but I have to start somewhere and Missing Person's was a good place."

"My god, Michelle's dead," she exclaimed, as the housekeeper entered with the buffet. "Did you hear that, Grace."

"Oh ma'am, don't say it's true," the middle-aged servant said, looking at Jack.

"Now, now ladies, let's not get the wrong end of the stick," Jack called out before they became hysterical. Although he had a feeling the aunt was acting.

"What else could it be, Superintendent, she's been missing for ages."

"We also have the idea she may have left the country. Was she in any financial trouble?" Jack questioned, watching her face very carefully, her reaction to the news differed from what he expected.

She waved the housekeeper off after she poured the tea, then coolly passed Jack his cup saying, "I doubt that very much, according to her housekeeper her passport is still in the draw by the bed. As for money troubles, that's rubbish, Roger left her a wealthy woman."

"Roger?"

"My brother... her husband. He died of a stroke four years ago."

"This housekeeper; is she still at the mansion."

"Of course, she has to keep it up until the estate is sorted out, that's why we must find out what's happened to her."

'There was another connection,' Jack thought.

"Who benefits by her death?" he continued.

"Why I do, but that's ridiculous."

"Why is it? She's been gone long enough."

"Well she hasn't, Superintendent, that's the whole point."

"I see, Miss Baillie, I can understand your dilemma."

She passed the buffet plate of mixed sandwiches to him, distracted by her thoughts. Jack could see her weighing up everything he had said. This woman knew more than she was letting on.

"So, Superintendent, where do we go from here?"

"Is there anything about what happened at that time you can tell me?"

"No... I was abroad. Two weeks had passed before I returned. I got in touch with the police as soon as I realised she had not returned to her house."

"Did the housekeeper not suspect anything?"

"Apparently not. It seems Michelle was prone to dashing off abroad on a whim without telling anyone, until she was returning. Then she wanted everything shipshape quickly, she usually brought someone home with her."

"But you said the housekeeper told you her passport was still in the draw."

"That wasn't until I asked her to look sometime later."

While she was preoccupied with whatever was mulling through her mind, Jack had inadvertently munched his way through most of the sandwiches, they were so little, one disappeared after the other; she didn't seem to notice though.

"Well, Miss Baillie, I shall have to question the housekeeper and whoever looks after her affairs, and I promise I shall keep you informed."

"Thank you, Superintendent. As far as her affairs are concerned, she did that herself; she was an accountant you know.

She managed her husband's affairs."

"He was an older man I gather," Jack commented.

She looked daggers at him, and he had lost her confidence.

"Aren't they all, Superintendent?"

Jack finally made a move, and she walked him to the front door.

They said their goodbyes, with Jack repeating his promise to keep in touch. There was no response, she was too eager to shut and bolt the door behind him.

Facing the esplanade, Jack noticed a taxi rank close by and jumped into the first one in the queue. As it pulled away he turned in his seat by the driver for one last look back up the hill towards the better residences. He pulled out his notebook, jotted down the few pieces of information she allowed him to have and wrote at the bottom of the page: This woman has something to hide.

Back in Lower Cheedam Jack returned to an empty house. Marjory had left a note on the kitchen table stating she would be back in time for the evening meal, and that Inspector Binstead had called. It was important. He rang him immediately.

The call had been to apologise for forgetting to give Jack the answer to his question about Samuel Alluche, the last time they met. He drew Jack's attention to the murder Samuel was convicted of. In the ensuing complexity of Samuel's story to the Vicar and the decoding of his legacy, everyone had forgotten about his victim, even though he actually drew their attention to him by swearing he was innocent.

Jack was struck speechless when Brian read out the name of the victim on the charge sheet... it was Samuel Alluche. Jack's head was in a spin, he had to ask him to repeat what he had just said.

Brian's answer confirmed what Warden Brewer told him about Samuel being a nick-name. He said nothing about having a twin.

Jack was finding it difficult to understand what his friend was actually telling him. He needed to think it out. His broken rule was coming true as it always did. He was becoming engulfed in too much information.

Jack thanked Brian without telling him how he got on with DI Maitland and replaced the phone. He needed to think, and poured himself a stiff whisky. His mind was always clearer when he had a drink inside him, and he sat down in his easy chair and mulled over what the Vicar had told him about Samuel.

Then the Vicar suddenly stood out in his mind like a giant doorstop. He had no idea the man he tended in prison had killed his own brother. He barely came to terms with his real name being George; how would he handle this? and then there was Marjory's work tying up the names; this would change everything.

It was dark when she returned; Jack was still sitting in the lounge, and on his third whisky. At first she thought he had fallen asleep, but soon found he was deep in thought when she switched on the lights and he jumped.

"Are you all right, Jack?" she said, touching the arm supporting his head.

He looked up slowly, "Oh sorry, dear, I was miles away. I didn't realise what time it was," he looked about, still disorientated. "I should have had the meal on."

She stepped back and took another look at him.

She could tell by his expression that something was wrong. "What is it, Jack?" she said, "Something's troubling you. What happened in Eastbourne today?"

"No... actually Eastbourne was good; I found out more than I expected. It was that call from Inspector Binstead."

"What did he have to say that was so troublesome?"

"It's not so much what he said but its implication."

"Sorry, Jack... you're not making sense."

"I had so much luck in Eastbourne. I actually answered five of our code words. I was going to ring everybody and start altering the board; then I rang Brian and he told me something that's going to destroy Peter's faith in human nature."

"What is it? Is it that bad?"

"Bad enough. The man Peter was working with at the prison... Samuel, is the wrong man," Jack said, watching her reaction.

"The wrong man? I don't understand?"

"It never crossed my mind to check into the man Samuel was imprisoned for killing; when Peter kept saying Samuel pleaded innocent, I just shelved it. Then Brian came across a small detail when I asked him to look into Samuel's record. He was so keen to tell me he was a known assassin, he overlooked the fact that he was George's twin brother."

"Twin brother?" Marjory questioned.

"Yes... it's hard to get your mind around, isn't it. Samuel was really called George, and the man he killed was his twin brother Samuel the assassin."

"But surely he didn't have to take his identity to do that," Marjory wisely pointed out, "and why should he kill his own brother; unless it was retribution?"

"I don't know, but I want to find out before I talk to Peter. This new slant on things doesn't alter what we're doing, but if I'm going to tell Peter he's been duped, I need to be able to answer his questions."

"Don't you think he may turn on you for withholding this sort of information?"

"I don't know, he may do. I shall just have to take that chance. It couldn't be any worse than me just telling him outright, without an explanation."

As Marjory began preparing the evening meal, the phone rang.

It was Arthur, returning the message Jack had left on his answering machine, "Hello, Jack, you were trying to get me earlier. Sorry I was out," he said.

"I suppose you were looking into the mansion in Eastbourne?" Jack answered.

"I was, I found out quite a lot,"

"I tried to stop you, Arthur, I was in Eastbourne today myself, and stumbled on the very same information, but you were out."

"Oh that's okay. I had several things to look up at the National Records office. How much did you find out?"

"That the name we're looking for is Bailie, Mrs Michelle Bailie. Living at The Elms, Plantation Grove. Oh... and she's an accountant by the way."

"That's what I got also, except she didn't own the property outright. It appears a few years before her husband died he signed over a power of attorney to a... wait for it Jeffery Farrow."

"Good heavens, you have done well. What's his address?"

"That's it, I don't know. All it said in that area was, 'As above', which means he was either living at the mansion or didn't want his address known."

"Okay, Arthur, thanks for that, that's great," Jack said.

"Have you told the others yet?"

"Give me a chance. We need a meeting... quickly."

"I'll see to that, Jack...At your place?"

"As usual... and can you look into a Miss Baillie?"

"Is that another Baillie?"

"Yes... she's the husband's sister?" Jack gave him the address details.

"Okay I'll do that. I'll get back to you soon."

"Don't forget our meeting; there's a lot to get through."

As Jack put the phone down he spotted Marjory standing in the doorway clutching a tea towel to her chest, intrigued by what she had just overheard. "Good heavens Jack you did do well today, you've certainly come a long way since last night."

"That's not all of it," he said, switching the light off and leading her back into the kitchen where their meal was all but ready. "Come, I'll fill you in while the dinner's cooking; I don't know what information you managed to dig up today, but I have an awful feeling it's going to be out of date."

"That's alright, dear; look upon it as corroborative."

"That's just it, Marjory... everything I set out with this morning has changed. I seem to have hit the right date or something and it all came pouring out. I started with one contact; DI Maitland, and it was as if I stumbled into a hornet's nest."

"Well that's better than you beating your head against a brick wall."

"I suppose so but I've got to get this lot into some order."

"Why don't we have our meal and we can sit down by the fire and sort all your information out before your next meeting?"

"I knew I could rely on you, dear."

After their meal Jack went into the lounge to see if he could stoke some life back into the fire. He was making so much noise he was unaware of the commotion at the back of the house, until Marjory called out to him from the kitchen.

"Jack... the Reverend's here."

He looked up at the clock, it was only eight forty five, and gestured a silent movement of his head as she looked round the door.

"Where is he?" he whispered.

"I left him in the kitchen near the boiler with a hot mug of tea," she answered.

"I'm not ready for him. I wanted to think about what you said."

"He's got to know, Jack... and this is an ideal opportunity."

Jack got the fire roaring again and looked at Marjory hovering over him with the poker. "I hope that's not for me? " he said.

Marjory laughed as she placed it on the hearth, "It should be if you don't tell him. You can't expect him to join your meeting tomorrow, not knowing."

"I suppose your right," Jack said. "Bring him through."

"Peter, what are you doing man, you'll catch your death out there."

"I'm fine, Jack, this hot tea and the boiler thawed me out no end. I tried the front door with no luck, so I came round to the back; I hope you don't mind."

"Of course not... I was making too much noise with this fire."

Jack glanced at the Vicar, who looked more nervous than usual, blowing away the surface heat from his cup and taking short sips.

"Well you've done a good job; it's roaring away now."

"Was there something special?"

Marjory walked in and cut them off. "The fires doing fine now, Jack," she said. "Any more tea anyone, how about something to eat, Reverend?"

"No thanks, Marjory, I ate before I came out."

Marjory gave Jack that prompting. "You wanted to say something, Peter?"

"Oh yes... I couldn't wait any longer. I just had to tell you what I found out."

"Just hold on, Peter for a moment... we can discuss that later. I found something out today that I'm afraid might upset you, and we need to deal with that first."

Jack took his time and slowly edged into the bad news by establishing the Vicar understood Samuel's name was really George; then he explained the detail behind his conviction and the possible reason why he was confused.

The Vicar looked dazed for the moment. "If I understand you right, Jack, you're saying he killed his twin brother George.

That's impossible. Samuel... I mean George would never kill his own brother. He said he was innocent."

Jack glanced towards Marjory sitting on the other side of the fire. "Look, Peter I'm not judging him, I'm only repeating what's down on record."

"Well I'm telling you, Jack... the record's wrong."

"Then why would George take on Samuel's persona and admit to all those killings. You took his confession, Peter... I'm not making this up."

"I know... you're right, Jack."

Jack sighed with relief as he glanced at Marjory.

"So, Peter... what was it you wanted to tell me?"

He looked up at Jack with moist eyes. "Ah yes... I think I've found Farrow."

"I don't believe it," Jack let out. "This has been a fantastic day."

"I'm not absolutely sure, Jack, the man I spoke to didn't employ him."

"What does that mean... oh no, don't bother. We have to follow this through."

"Does that mean you're going to Eastbourne again, Jack?" Marjory asked.

Jack turned and faced her; he had no intention of doing this on the phone.

"It's the only way dear. If we get up early and catch the express we'll be there before we know it."

"We, Jack... is that all three of us?" she said.

"Now, Marjory, you're not going to miss an opportunity like this?"

She thought about it for a moment. "No...I don't think I will."

CHAPTER 21

Whether it was because Marjory had joined them or not, it turned out to be an unusually fine day. The Vicar promised to contact the others first thing and arrange for them to make the meeting at Jack's place at four. That way they had plenty of time to see to their business and get back to Lower Cheedam.

If this was the same express he was on yesterday, there was a restaurant car further along, where they could sit in comfort as long as they had something to eat.

"Why have you brought us to the restaurant car, dear?" Marjory asked.

Jack guided them to one of the booths, "Don't you think it's much nicer here than one of those crowded carriages?"

"Yes but they're all having breakfast."

"That's why I said we'd get something on the train."

The Vicar made no comment; ordering bacon and eggs. Marjory decided to enjoy the trip and try the poached sole, while Jack pondered on the menu until he finally settled on kippers.

"This is nice, Jack," the Vicar said, as the train slowly pulled out of the station.

When they finished their breakfast and ordered some drinks, Jack thought he would take this opportunity to bring the Vicar up to date. Last night was not the right time to fill his head with complex details; not after the truth about Samuel.

As Jack predicted, the run to the south coast was over before they knew it. Marjory's first thoughts were for the weather and she stood for a moment outside the station focused on the sky above.

"What's wrong, dear?" Jack asked.

"Nothing, Jack... I was just comparing the day to back home."

It was still fine; a little grey, but not too cold. If anything, the strong smell of the sea made the difference. It was far better than rotting leaves.

Jack checked the note-paper the Vicar gave him on the train alongside the street-map of Eastbourne. "According to this, the square these legal offices are in is somewhere up here on the right." He turned to Marjory, "Do you want to be in on these discussions dear?"

"I do not... I'm not going to waste my time in some musty old office when I have all these shops to go round."

She had spoken. They soon decided on a place to meet up when Jack and the Vicar had finished. In the meantime they went their own ways.

Forewarned, they arrived at the office of the man who remembered Jeffery Farrow. He turned out to be a middle aged, talkative busybody with tinted hair and he still remembered him because some years earlier a flash-looking young man actually stood where Jack was; asking for a job. He just came in off the street.

"He didn't get it I gather," the Vicar commented.

"Certainly not," the affected man said emphatically. "We run a conservative establishment here; not a gambling house."

His description fascinated Jack; he had to know more. "What does that mean?"

"He showed us references from big investment companies in

the city and his degrees in finance; all false if you ask me," he stated with a hint of envy.

"Why do you say that," the Vicar asked again.

"Well, it stands to reason; a man with those qualifications wouldn't be looking for a job with a small concern such as ours," he realised what he had said. "Of course, in the community we have a high standing."

"I'm sure you have Mr..." Jack started.

"Ian Fraser," the man prompted.

"Mr Fraser. Where did he get a job? Presuming that was what you were about to tell us," Jack said, getting irritated with his small talk.

He walked over to the window overlooking the square and spread the Venetian blinds apart. He then glanced sideways along the row of shops.

"He finally got a job with Peak, Matthews and Timmings, further along, number seventeen. Timmings of course died years ago."

He swung round and let the blinds clatter back.

Jack thanked Mr Fraser for his valuable information and made for the door. He was curious why they wanted Farrow, and looked more towards the Vicar for an answer than Jack. He fobbed him off with a 'need-to-know' reply, and they left.

The offices of Peak, Matthews and Timmings were quite a cut above Mr Fraser's Eastbourne Investments: Wall-to-wall plush carpet, expensive wood panelling and an equally expensive looking receptionist sitting behind a large desk. Only now did Jack understand what Mr Fraser was getting at. Why indeed would Farrow bother with a business as small as his when Peak, Matthews and Timmings were only a few doors away; looking every bit the best prospect.

Jack had already decided it was prudent to use his warrant

card again; even though he had been warned. It opened doors much easier and gave the receptionist something to think about when she inspected them.

At first she stared at the card, and then her expression quickly changed, as if they were expected. She handed it back and hurried off along a corridor, surprising Jack when she returned so quickly; almost catching him checking the papers she had left open on her desk.

"Would you please come this way, Superintendent," she said.

They were escorted down a corridor with glass walls either side, screening off the blurred shapes of clerics frantically typing, to a large mahogany door at the end. She knocked and immediately swung the door open for them to enter.

Directly opposite, across a large Persian carpet on polished boards, stood a smartly dressed man in a business suit and striped shirt. He was on his way around his desk with his hand extended.

"Good morning, Superintendent, I'm Richard Peak one of the partners," he said, enthusiastically shaking Jack's hand first then the Vicar's.

He stepped back and offered them a seat over by the window.

"This is Reverend Peter Jay, a colleague of mine," Jack said, as he sat down.

For some reason the man didn't question the Vicar's presence, he seemed more concerned in why Jack was there.

The confident man with greying hair and a short moustache asked them if they would like a drink. They said a tea would be fine and the man picked up his phone. While he was talking to his secretary Jack couldn't help noticing his hair had been ginger at one time; it was the way the light caught it.

He finished his call, "Now gentlemen, how can I help you."

"I'm led to believe that a Jeffery Farrow works or worked for you."

"Yes, he worked for us for three years," Peak looked

suddenly uncomfortable.

"Do you know where he is now?" the Vicar asked, trying to get involved.

"Afraid not," he said, turning and smiling at the girl when she entered with the tray, "he was noticeably not really interested."

"You don't appear to have had a good experience," Jack stated.

"That's an understatement, Superintendent."

"Would you care to tell me about it?"

"If you tell me what all this is about, it's been some time now... I thought it was all over and done with," he answered.

"I don't know if we're talking about the same issue. We're looking into a woman's disappearance... a Mrs Baillie. Nothing else."

"I see... so she hasn't been found yet?"

"Apparently not," Jack said, hoping that would satisfy him.

"Well now let me see," he mused, turning around in his chair to the small coffee table where the girl had placed the tray, "milk and sugar?"

Jack and the Vicar nodded, they were anxious to continue.

He passed them their cups, took a sip of his and returned it to the saucer.

"Let me see... it all started when Jeffery Farrow came to work for us, I wasn't really keen, too flash for my liking, but the senior partner, James Mathews, was taken in hook, line and sinker. Farrow had all sorts of bright ideas, things he brought from the city, which might have been all right for them, but too risky for my blood. Anyway, I had to hand it to him; he did have a way with people. He soon expanded our clients interests; shutting out any objections I might have had, especially with a hard nose old-timer going back to the days when Mr Timmings was alive."

"Would it be too much to ask his name?" Jack asked.

"I suppose not... he's dead now. He was our wealthiest

client, C. J. Baillie. Problem was he didn't spend much of it on investments, not until he met Farrow."

"He met Farrow first, before his wife?" the Vicar asked.

"Mrs Baillie? Oh she wouldn't have anything to do with him. She was an accountant, damn good one as well. Michelle spotted him straight off but she couldn't prove anything. She only put up with him because CJ was infatuated with the man."

"You knew her?" Jack asked.

"Oh yes, Michelle and I were a mirror of each other, that's probably why we both hated Farrow so much. I know what you might be thinking, we didn't have a sexual relationship, it was purely business."

"Tell us how she fitted into all this," Jack questioned.

"Nothing unusual really; she was the typical attractive employee marrying the much older boss. She worked for CJ as his private accountant for years, they got married, and he died leaving everything to her. That's when it all started."

"What started," the Vicar questioned.

"Well you have to understand that while she was his accountant, he would only let her know what he was doing with his money when and if it suited him. Farrow, on the other hand, had been persuading him to invest heavily in some form of Fund Management but Michelle couldn't find out what, that's when we got to know each other better, she hoped between us we could work out what this man was doing. Eventually the bubble had to burst of course, the old man died of a stroke, and we don't know whether that was through natural causes or from the shock of finding out a good proportion of his fortune had gone."

"What did Mrs Baillie do?" Jack asked.

"At first nothing. Farrow was too clever for her. He managed to hoodwink everyone for some time until CJ's estate was audited, and that's when the discrepancy became apparent."

The Vicar was curious about something and jumped in at the first chance. "Excuse me if I've missed something, but why didn't your company pick this up earlier. Don't you check your client's holdings at the end of each tax year? I mean, with so much money, I would have thought the tax man would have known."

"No... you're quite right to question it. I'm afraid our procedures failed and it wasn't addressed until our founder died. You see he always allowed our Fund Managers to have their own portfolios of investments; the customer's privacy was sacrosanct. The only figures that entered our ledgers were the profit and loss, so that we could address the legal and tax matters, hence he was able to manage CJ's affairs privately until the end. Ultimately, when the Executor took over he began demanding these funds be made available. It was then, when Michelle went to Newcastle to look into another of CJ's investments that she disappeared or didn't return to Eastbourne. Know one has seen her since.

"What about Farrow," Jack asked.

"Farrow was here right up to the week before the Executor came to audit our accounts for Mrs Baillie, he appeared to know everything the Executor was doing. I think he had inside information from someone close to what was happening. You might say Farrow disappeared also, although he did make it look like a legitimate trip to France, he had a client there who confirmed his visit. He just didn't return."

"What was the outcome of the Executor's search?" the Vicar asked.

"Terrible. He found that the fund was empty."

Jack glanced at the Vicar; it was another of their words.

"The entire investment, if there ever was one, had been mysteriously siphoned off. We tried to trace share movements, but it seems he did that under his own name, which of course was wrong. Now, legitimately it's all his."

"How much are we talking about?"

Richard Peak took his time answering Jack.

"That's just it, Superintendent, we have no idea. The only people who have any idea of what took place are either dead or missing and another thing... CJ's file is back where it was before Farrow joined the company."

Jack looked frustrated. Although he had miraculously put a meaning to most of the key words, he was no nearer the truth of how they fitted together.

"Just before we leave, a different question," Jack said. "Has a Miss Baillie contacted you recently?"

"You mean the sister... Michelle's aunt?"

"Yes."

"She was the Executor," Peak said.

"I thought you referred to the Executor as a man?" the Vicar questioned, now becoming more alert to the plot's twisting intricacies.

"That's true. She didn't actually do anything herself; she hired professionals.

"I thought the Executor wasn't allowed to be a beneficiary?" Jack asked.

"That's true also, Superintendent, she isn't. But in answer to what I think you're getting at, she would benefit greatly if the estate was intact. Her brother left her a legacy on his death amounting to a pension, plus living free in his luxury home. Of course now the estate has to pay off a number of debts, including the property which was re-mortgaged to support the Fund investment."

"Why did you say 'You thought it was all over and done with'?"

"Because when Miss Baillie came back from holiday, a week or so after her niece was expected back from her trip north, she came in to see me wanting to know what was going on. Knowing our closeness, she expected me to know Michelle's every movement, which I didn't. When I couldn't give her a satisfactory explanation, and made it clear I hadn't notified the police, she went crazy, saying she'd take things into her own hands."

"Is that when she called in the police?"

"I'm not sure. If you ask me, the truth of the matter was not so much her concern about Michelle, but the deadline imposed by the bank to clear the estate."

"But you said that was some time ago," Jack reminded him. "She's still living in her house. It is the same house I presume?"

"Oh yes... luckily her brother left the house to her before he died. Unfortunately I can't say as much for her pension. That and the mansion were gobbled up by the deficit, although to the annoyance of the bank they cannot dispose of them until the Executor has finalised the estate."

"What's holding that up?" the Vicar asked.

"There's a waiting period before Michelle's officially declared dead, and the Coroner won't do that in a hurry. Because everything was left to her, the bank can only utilise the premises for accommodation, that's why they continue to maintain it."

"And a housekeeper, I understand?" Jack commented.

"Yes... the same one that's been with the Baillie's for years."

There was little more of value they could draw from this source, they had done quite well, and luck was still with them. In the last two days Jack had gathered most of the information they wanted, knew who the main players were, what had gone down to cause such a catastrophe and the probable reason behind Samuel being hired.

Jack thanked Richard Peak for his time, with the proviso that he might need to question him again, but would most certainly advise him if that was the case.

The attractive receptionist escorted them to the door. As she said good bye, she pressed a card into Jack's palm. It was one of

Richard Peak's cards and as they left the building Jack turned it over. Scribbled on the back in a hurried scrawl was a short message: 'The housekeeper knows.' Below was an address; it was different to the house Jack visited when he saw the Aunt.

Jack put the card to his nose and smiled. "Well, Peter... there's nothing sweeter than a good lead." He showed the Vicar. "We'll have to visit this housekeeper."

"What about Marjory?" The Vicar questioned.

Jack laughed as he hurried towards their meeting place. "Don't worry, Peter, I wouldn't dare forget Marjory; especially when we're about to visit a mansion."

CHAPTER 22

Overlooking the city from an elevated position on the outskirts of Eastbourne, Jack was pondering on how their luck was still with them as they turned off the coast road towards Mrs Baillie's Mansion. He could feel Marjory's excitement sitting next to him, gazing out across the open sea; and even more as the edifice came into view. This was the Mansion they were looking for.

As the taxi swept round the broad arc of the gravel driveway in front of the white building, Jack was already opening the car door. The Vicar gasped and sucked in a deep breath as the blast of crisp air rushed passed him, bringing with it the familiar hint of a salty freshness from the port below.

Leaving him sitting in the taxi, Jack jumped out and climbed the half dozen steps to the front porch, and was about to ring the bell when he noticed the door was ajar. He could see someone standing in the shadows, and stepped closer.

"I'm looking for Mrs Baillie's housekeeper," he said.

"Who are you?

Jack reached into his inside pocket and took out his warrant card. "My name's Superintendent Hammond," he said thrusting it into the small gap, and for the first time he saw the ruddy complexion of a woman's face.

As she studied his card Jack beckoned to Marjory and the

Vicar. He paid off the taxi and they followed Jack up the steps to the double-doors and stood to his side. The woman seemed to take ages studying the card, and was about to hand it back when she saw the Vicar; she hesitated and opened the door a little more.

"What's wrong," she cried. "Has someone died... is it Miss Baillie?"

"No... Miss Baillie is fine."

"Then it must be Mrs Baillie... you've found her... is she dead."

Jack took the card from her podgy fingers before she dropped it. "No... no one has died. Please let us in and I will explain."

She slowly opened the door, shuffling back with it and standing aside to let them through. They were standing in a marbled entrance hall, almost as big as Jack's house, although at the moment it resembled a mausoleum: cold and lifeless, with everything covered in dustsheets, and heavy curtains draped across the windows.

The place hadn't been lived in for some time, it smelt stale and there was dampness in the air. Jack quickly scanned the hundred and eighty degrees from where he stood; it was palatial, white marble and ivory silk wallpaper, with the relief of polished mahogany rails on the curving staircase. It was wide, inlaid with black treads and a white balustrade that separated at the top and ran around three walls.

On the floor to one side of the staircase stood a large cardboard box; the lid was still open and Jack could see the top part of a magnificent chandelier covered in polystyrene chips.

The White panelled doors either side were closed but Jack imagined the rooms behind them were just as empty. The only light he could see was coming from an open door in the far corner to the left of the staircase.

During Jack's assessment the housekeeper's eyes never left him.

"I'm sorry it's so cold," she said, manoeuvring her way around them. "The house has been shut down until Mrs Baillie returns. Would you like to follow me?"

She led them over to the door, pushed it fully open against the wall stop, and asked them to enter. The first room looked like it was the servant's quarters, and was warm and bright, with comfortable furnishings for several people. As they entered Jack noticed a panel on the wall next to the door, covered in small lights with numbers underneath going up to twenty.

Directly opposite was another door that was open and it was the source of the heat they could feel. Jack continued, even though the housekeeper was showing Marjory and the Vicar to easy chairs; he wanted to know what lay beyond. As he guessed it was the kitchen, and the source of the heat was a large black range, and she was cooking something.

"Superintendent," she called out. "Would you all care for a hot drink?" she asked, "I was just about to make myself one."

Jack could see a tray on the large kitchen table, with one cup and saucer, a jug of milk, sugar and a plate of biscuits. On the range a teapot was warming.

He walked back to where the Vicar and Marjory were sitting and joined them.

They both nodded, "yes... that would be nice." He answered.

The housekeeper disappeared into the kitchen for a moment and Jack continued inspecting the room. Marjory said nothing; she was too engrossed in the size of the place. The Vicar was preoccupied with a newspaper lying across the arm of his chair. He was about to draw Jack's attention to an advertisement that had been outlined in red ink, offering Mrs Baillie's mansion for sale, when the housekeeper returned with the tray. She set it down on a coffee table and started pouring out their drinks.

Between them first entering and her making the tea, her manner had changed.

"So, Superintendent, without sounding theatrical, what brings you out on a day like this?" She asked, sitting down beside them.

"We're investigating Mrs Baillie's disappearance," Jack started, and then he realised the others had not been introduced. "This is my assistant Marjory and a colleague, Reverend Peter Jay."

"You're a bit late aren't you?" she replied.

"This is a separate inquiry to the one at the time," he continued.

"What inquiry, there wasn't one."

Jack was surprised. Even though DI Maitland had no information on file, he intimated that his predecessor had started an inquiry."

"How can you say that when Mrs Baillie's aunt went to the police to report she was missing?" Jack rebutted, watching for a reaction.

"I don't know where you got your information from, but she did everything she could to keep the police out of this, especially when we got the ransom note."

"Ransom?" the Vicar let out, unable to hold his silence.

"I think you'd better tell us what happened from the beginning," Jack said.

The housekeeper went silent for a moment. Jack studied her closely, as he usually did with suspects when he had the opportunity, and at this time she was just as much a suspect as the aunt.

"I don't know whether or not I can remember it all as it happened," she said.

"Why don't you try, and let us put it in order," Jack coaxed.

"Very well... I suppose you know all about what happened when Mr Baillie died, they say it was natural causes, but I don't believe them."

"Why would you say that?" Jack questioned. He was interested in her version. He had little input from the others he questioned.

"Well he'd begun to drink a lot in the evening, and became very irritable. It was unlike him until he started seeing Mr Farrow. He had become a regular visitor; much to Mrs Baillie's annoyance... they didn't get on at all well you see. He would arrive whenever he liked and go straight upstairs to see Mr Baillie.

"I don't know what it was but every time Mr Farrow arrived they argued and Mr Baillie was always in a terrible state afterwards. Mrs Baillie tried desperately to find out what was wrong; she even had Mr Farrow's boss round a few times. I didn't hear what they said mind you, but I knew it was about Mr Farrow."

"You didn't hear anything?" the Vicar asked.

"Not really... except I know it was to do with the fund. I heard that word a lot."

"Was that all?" Jack asked.

"Yes... after that last visit Mr Baillie was found dead later that night."

"Wasn't there a Coroners Inquest into his death?" Jack said,

"I don't think so... his doctor signed a death certificate."

"You would have known if there was, you would have had to go to court and testify in front of the Coroner," Marjory said, for the first time.

"I didn't do that, so there wasn't one," she jumped up to fill her cup.

The Vicar showed Jack the advertisement.

She returned with the teapot, refreshed everyone's drinks and started again.

"Things got worse after that; Mrs Baillie told Mr Farrow to leave, and then she spent ages in the house going through her husband's papers. She was like a crazy woman; I couldn't understand it and then she packed a bag and left."

"Did she say where she was going?" Jack asked.

"She just said she was going up north for a while. Her husband had an interest in a mine in Newcastle and she had to sort it out."

"What did she do when she came back?" Marjory asked.

"She didn't... I never saw her again."

Jack had been overtly making notes, but he felt there was more to this, "When did the aunt come in?"

"She was away when it happened. I didn't see her until this Inspector Buck met her here one day and they discussed her missing niece and Mr Farrow. I don't know any more because she took him into the lounge and shut the door."

"That is strange," Jack commented. Knowing Inspector Maitland had no knowledge of his predecessor's meeting with Miss Baillie. Just as he had no idea of any ransom note sent to the aunt.

"You said you knew about the ransom note." The Vicar interrupted.

"Yes... well I assumed that was what it was, I could only hear when I brought the food in and served it. He was looking at a sheet of paper with letters crudely stuck on it, you know... cut out of a magazine."

"Did you see what it said?" Jack asked.

"No... except I did see five hundred thousand pounds. I suppose that's what made me think it was a ransom note."

"What happened then?"

"Nothing, as far as I know. I never saw the Inspector again or heard any more about a ransom and when I kept asking about Mrs Baillie's return, the aunt said the police were looking into it; but I knew they weren't."

"By the way, I didn't get your name" Jack said.

"Mrs Irene Gaynor. Widow, my husband died some years ago. He worked for Mr Baillie and was killed in an accident, that's why he promised me a job for life. Doesn't look like he'll be able to keep his promise now... does it?"

Before they left, Jack made a phone call to order a taxi to take them back to the station. Meanwhile the Vicar questioned the housekeeper about the advertisement in the paper, which she was obviously looking at when they arrived.

"Yes, Vicar, that's the second time it's been in."

"What does it mean?"

"The bank is trying to find a buyer, even though they can't sell it yet... that must be illegal... don't you think?"

"I'm sorry, I wouldn't know."

"What's that?" Jack said as he returned.

"Mrs Gaynor was asking if this advertisement is illegal."

Jack took the newspaper off him and read it. "Of course it is."

Jack's answer made little difference to Mrs Gaynor's disposition; she had far more serious problems to worry about, but she did manage to raise a smile when they excused themselves on hearing the hoot of the taxi's horn.

On their journey back to the station all three were noticeably quiet. Jack was sure they were all mulling over the same thing. There were two missing people now: Michelle Bailie, and Jeffery Farrow. Any one of them could be Samuel's victim, but which one they still had to discover. On top of that, they still have to solve the riddle of where the body is buried.

Back on the train Jack had too many pieces running round his head to be drawn by either Marjory or the Vicar's questions. Today had been one of the best days so far when answers were found to Samuel's coded words. But those words still had to be placed in their proper order; only then will this last case make sense.

"Let's just wait until we get this lot down on the board," he said.

Marjory checked her watch, "We're making good time, Jack; we should get back in plenty of time for Janet and Arthur. You'll have a lot to tell them."

"I will, dear," he replied. "I wonder what they've got on in the

Restaurant car?"

The Vicar glanced at his watch also, "Is it lunch-time already?"

When Marjory opened the door to Janet and Arthur, Jack was in his study putting the finishing touches to the white board. The Vicar was helping Jack by reading from his notes; mumbling all the time about his bad handwriting. As soon as they entered the room their eyes went straight to the board and they both let out a gasp.

"Good heavens, Jack," Janet uttered first. "It's totally different."

All Arthur could say was, "You've been busy."

Jack turned round as they were taking their seats. "I don't know what happened. Two visits to Eastbourne was all it took; and we found all these code words."

"I don't know about Arthur but after my dismal input, I was prepared to get stuck in today. It seems I needn't have worried."

"Believe me, Janet, once I found the ransom case, it all fell in place," Jack said.

"...and I found the Fund Manager," the Vicar said.

"Don't forget my input on the Mansion," Arthur added.

"Okay... this is not a competition; we're a team. It doesn't matter who did what as long as the code is broken," Jack commented. "This only gives us the why and who... it doesn't give us the where; and that's what we have to concentrate on next."

"I notice you're spelling Bailie differently, Jack," Janet pointed out.

"Yes... I imagine the code's spelling was the nearest Samuel could find," Jack said, then was prompted to mention Samuel's twin brother and the mix-up of their names.

"You've lost me on this one, Jack," Arthur said.

"I'm sorry you two. A lot has happened in the last two days and it's taken me all my time explaining it to Marjory and Peter.

I still have to keep checking my notes to see if I understand."

"Have you got everything in order now, Jack?" The Vicar asked.

Jack turned back to the board just as Marjory brought the tea and biscuits in. They all helped themselves and Jack started to explain what it all meant.

"I'm not going into any great detail, so feel free to ask any questions." They all nodded as they sipped their tea. "Knowing I had to deal with the local police sooner or later I contacted my source in Scotland Yard. After shocking me with the latest information about the Alluche brothers, he arranged a meeting with Inspector Maitland in Eastbourne the following day. Apparently they had a suspicious ransom incident. I didn't expect much, but was surprised when he mentioned a missing person in connection with the case. Her name was Michelle Bailie."

"Good gracious, Jack... what luck," Janet let out.

"Oh that's nothing... just listen to the rest," Jack replied as he continued. "From what DI Maitland told me and a subsequent visit to Michelle's aunt, before her disappearance, Michelle's husband died of a stroke after he was involved in a fraudulent fund transaction, organised by a Mr Farrow."

"That's where I came in," the Vicar said.

"Yes... with Peter's discovery of the Fund Manager, we just had to go back to Eastbourne the next day, where we found the company that employed Farrow. That in turn led us to more code-words such as Michelle hiring a detective, her being an accountant and consequently discovering the fund was empty."

"That's almost everything, Jack," Arthur commented.

"Except we now have two missing people."

"I thought you said Michelle Bailie was the only missing person?" Janet said.

"I did at first... but by the end of the day we also had Jeffery Farrow and the policeman who died suspiciously, Inspector Buck."

"That name wasn't part of our code," Janet said.

"It wasn't... but it means, despite all we have decoded, we're still no nearer discovering who Samuel killed and where he buried his victim."

Jack sat down with the others and finishing his tea he checked the biscuits.

No one appeared to have anything to say, so Marjory glanced at the small clock on Jack's bookcase, "My... it's only six-thirty... we've done well today."

"Yes, I promised my wife I'd be back early. She promised her sister she'd call in to see how she was getting on," the Vicar said.

"Is there a problem reverend?" Marjory asked.

"Not really. She's eight months pregnant and she's getting nervous."

"That's understandable, Peter," Jack said, "Why don't you get off... it's been a long day. Your wife must be getting anxious."

"Me too, Jack," Janet said. "I've got a lot of home-work to correct."

Marjory had laid the seed and before long everyone was bundling into Arthur's Rolls Royce and they were alone again at last. Marjory had plans for a special evening meal to celebrate. It was going to be Sunday's meal but she could get something else. Jack had another look at his board before disappearing into the lounge to prepare the fire. It was the first time he suddenly felt cold.

"I hope that's a sign of satisfaction on your face Jack Hammond," Marjory said, sitting down beside him among the cushions in front of the fire. "And not just that whisky you have in your hand."

She reached over to the mulled drink he had just prepared for her.

"Sorry it's not mulled wine," he said, "whiskey is just as good and it's that beautiful meal I've just had and your company that's making me look satisfied."

"Go on you old fraud," she said, cuddling into him. "Do you want to talk about today or is it something you would rather forget?"

"No… I don't really want to talk about it, and yes, it was a successful day."

"Oh what's wrong with you, usually if you've had a successful day I can't shut you up," she replied, not really wanting to talk. There was something about Jack's voice that comforted her. Not the abrupt voice, when he was frustrated, but the soft melodious voice, when he had so much to say he couldn't stop; not even to breathe.

"It's not that, dear. It's the fact that we finally know what all the key words mean but still don't know how to connect them together or who's buried and where."

"Oh dear," Marjory sighed, jumping up, almost spilling her drink on Jack, "Coming out with you today made me forget."

"What are you going on about woman, sit down."

"No, Jack it's important," she said, and left the room.

He shook his head; he was too comfortable to wonder what she was up to. He felt a warm fullness in his tummy and the hot whiskey was just beginning to dull his senses. The warmth from the fire had just started to creep into his bones.

Marjory returned with a folder and snuggled down beside him again.

"Oh, Marjory… not more, can't it wait till tomorrow?" Jack said.

"So you're not interested in the definition of the word silo," she said, sitting with her legs crossed looking down at him.

"Good heavens, I forgot all about that," he said, sitting up and resting his back against the chair. "Marjory… you have my undivided attention, fire away."

"It's funny you should say that," she started quizzically. She opened her folder and took out a single sheet of paper. "On my first inquiry all I could find out was, silo's were for storing grain or animal fodder and the other ridiculous use was," she checked her notes. "An underground launching place for ballistic missiles,"

"That's not that ridiculous," said Jack. "It reminds me of something, what was it?" he banged his forehead with his clenched fist.

"I know it struck me also," she said excitedly, already knowing the answer. "You remember, Jack, when we went to Dover on holiday." His eyes suddenly light up with recognition. "The old gun batteries along the front from world-war-two?"

"That's right... I remember now," he exclaimed. "Well done, Marjory, we have our Silo and now our word Battery, what else did you find out?"

He was alive again, so excited he wanted to see the paper she was reading from.

"Easy, Jack... this is my find, let me tell it."

"Sorry, dear... please continue."

"Once I convinced myself I was on the right track, I did as you said and went to the library; the man there was very good. He was in our age group and knew what I was talking about. We soon found some information on the gun batteries that were erected along the south coast," she reached back into the folder on the floor. "Here's a photocopy of a drawing showing the underground silo where the shells were kept."

As soon as Jack saw it he remembered, "of course."

"Now you remember. I thought it would come back to you."

"My God those days. I used to play in one of these things when we went on holiday after the war. It was all dark and damp, and smelly, if you know what I mean. No one seemed bothered about the danger, not in those days," he paused, took another drink and pondered, "Isn't it funny, we had more reason to be frightened back then."

"Well they do now, Jack," she emphasised. "All these war relics and military areas are controlled by the War Office through the local council. Mr Connery, that's the librarian, says they're all either fenced off or locked up now."

"How does he know?"

"He belongs to the local Conservation Society, and they've been chasing the Council for years to do something about these sites. Some are quite dangerous even though they're locked up, with eroding concrete, bits of barbed wire and only recently they found a live shell in the sand beside one; not to mention an odd mine or two."

"Did he say he knew where all these sites were?" Jack questioned, now very interested in the possibilities of this new evidence.

"Yes… he said he has a map of the Eastbourne coastline with all the batteries, old mined areas, now cleared of course, wrecks, caves and so on. All identified at his society's office. He said he would make a copy tonight and have it ready for me to collect in the morning," she said, looking pleased.

"How did you get him to do that, he doesn't fancy you does he?"

"Oh, Jack," she said, slapping his arm, "don't be silly."

"Well if he's got all these sites marked for us, our job is easy."

She returned the papers to the folder as she continued.

"I wouldn't be so eager until you see where some of them are."

"Do you think you could persuade him to bring his map here and show me where the good ones and bad ones are?"

"I can only try," she replied, putting the folder to one side and snuggling back into Jack's side," she raised herself up again and looked into his eyes. "We can't have you falling into any holes, can we?"

CHAPTER 23

It was the weekend and Jack had no intentions of doing anything until Monday. He looked out of the window and thought it had been snowing, but on closer inspection it was only a deep frost. It had to be very cold out there to do that, so his first duty of the day was to get a roaring fire going in the lounge.

Since the onset of winter he decided not to go to bed until he had filled the coal scuttle, chopped a few sticks and rolled up several sausages of paper to get the fire started. As he reached for the poker to clear the previous night's ashes he noticed a manila envelope wedge behind the clock on the mantelpiece.

"Marjory... when did this envelope arrive?"

"What, dear," she said as she entered the room.

"That envelope behind the clock, it looks official."

"Oh dear," she gasped. "I forgot all about it, it came yesterday."

Jack took it out from its hiding place and held it at arm's length trying to see what it was without his glasses. He could make out the Royal seal in the corner, and his first thought was a letter from the Inland Revenue.

Marjory handed him his glasses and he saw immediately that it was a letter from the Metropolitan Police as he slipped his thumb under the flap.

"What is it, Jack?" Marjory asked.

"I don't know... it's from Scotland Yard."

Inside was a single sheet of thin copying paper with a card clipped to the left hand corner. It was from Brian and he had written a short note across it.

'Sorry Jack, I'm so busy these days; I forgot this. Hope it helps. Brian.'

Jack threw the clipped note into the fire and examined the sheet. It was a copy of Samuel Alluche's pathology report. Not the Vicar's Samuel, but the brother he was alleged to have murdered.

The gist of the report was quite simple: one brother placed a gun at the other's head and pulled the trigger, for what reason they will probably never know; but one fact Jack couldn't ignore stood out above all others. To him it was the most significant fact detailed on the sheet. A single line of only a few words, yet it proved to him who the killer really was.

It read, 'Distinguishing Marks: Twelve-millimetre scar on second joint of left forefinger knuckle.' This was what Dick had seen with his inner eye when he clasped the brass cartridge. A man sitting on the edge of the bed with a weapon and bullets, this could only have been the assassin preparing for his next kill.

Marjory was looking quite anxious by now, with Jack's arm still outstretched, motionless. "I'll be damned," he finally exclaimed.

"What, Jack?" Marjory couldn't bear his holding back any more.

"Did I tell you what Dick saw when he held the brass cartridge in his hand?"

"What do you mean, saw?"

"You did know he was a clairvoyant?"

"Well I knew he dabbled a bit in astrology and someone said he was a medium at the spiritualist church," she pointed out.

"Okay, well when we had our first meeting and Peter told me of this gift, and suggested he may play a role as a profiler, I felt like laughing. I asked him if he could see things when he touched them, like some profilers do. He said he hadn't given it any thought, most of the time he did his thing through a channel, although for years he had these strange feelings, but didn't attribute anything particular to them. But as soon as he was asked to focus his attention on what each object said to him, he panicked. Those feelings had taken shape."

"What happened?"

"I gave him the cartridge to hold, telling him to concentrate on its vibes. He did, and immediately dropped it as if it was red hot. He said he saw a man sitting on a bed with a gun and many bullets."

"Good heavens," Marjory gasped.

"That's not all; he was most emphatic about a scar on the knuckle of the man's left forefinger. This man you have to realise was obviously the assassin."

Jack handed Marjory the typed copy of the pathology report before she could ask any further questions. She read the single sheet, as Jack leant back watching the expression on her face suddenly turn to amazement.

"My God," she gasped, as the full significance of what Dick had seen, struck her, "What was Dick's reaction to this new ability," she asked.

"Well you know. Actions speak louder than words. It was all too much for him to take in, that's why he resigned."

"I wondered why at the time, but no one was forthcoming."

"Well now you know."

"Of course," she remembered. "Now you mention it, we haven't seen him in the shop for some time... poor man. Now he realises he has this ability, he's going to be aware of everything he touches. What have you done, Jack?"

"Me? Why am I responsible?"

"Well you told him what to do."

"No… I don't take any responsibility for that."

She could see by his expression that she was treading on shaky ground, and let the Inspector's letter drop to the floor alongside its envelope.

The following morning Jack was struggling to rouse himself and rationalise what was happening. It was Marjory, she was shaking him with an offering of breakfast in bed, and she was reminding him of the magnificent evening it had been.

"Is it Saturday?" he questioned as she moved the tray onto his lap.

As he rubbed his eyes he could see she was dressed to go out.

"I'm off to see the man at the library and I'll see if he can come round this afternoon when it closes. Oh and Peter rang, he'll be round later this morning."

"What was that?" he asked, holding the orange juice still while he turned to look at the clock. Too late she had gone. When his eyes focused he saw it was only eight thirty and turned back to his bacon and eggs.

Showered and shaved Jack spent the next hour studying the white-board. He remembered telling himself he was going to have a rest over the weekend, but here he was; making little changes and trying to narrow down his victims. He also had to add the final word, silo and an explanation.

Once finished, Jack felt he needed some fresh air and wandered into the back garden. The paddock behind the cottage almost blinded him. The temperature was low enough to keep the countryside covered in a blanket of frost, with only the fine dark filigree of the treetops to break the white starkness.

He spoke too soon; a bright red anorak appeared around the trees, standing out like a bloodstain on a white sheet. He watched the awkward figure slip and slide across the shiny surface until he spotted Jack. He waved enthusiastically.

When Jack was sure it was the Vicar, that little tell tale square of white on black under his chin, he cried out for him to be careful.

The Vicar raised his hand up to his ear, and cupped it as if he couldn't hear. "What was that, Jack," he shouted.

When the Vicar finally climbed over the stile, Jack took hold of his arm to steady him. "I said watch your step. You must stop coming this way; it's too dangerous. What are you going to do when it snows?"

"I thought of getting myself some snow-shoes, Jack."

Jack laughed and led him into the warm kitchen. As he removed his boots and anorak, Jack put the kettle on and set up the mugs for a hot drink.

"Okay, Peter?" Jack asked, placing the drinks on the kitchen table.

"Yes... oh you mean why am I bothering you at the weekend?"

"Something like that."

"When I got home yesterday and checked my notes, I suddenly realised we missed two code names; *Battery* and *Silo*. So I thought I might pop over and discuss it with you. It could be something for me to do on Monday."

"I'm sorry to disappoint you, Peter, I had forgotten I gave that job to Marjory, until she reminded me last night. Apparently our two words belong to the Second World War period. Battery being a gun emplacement and Silo the arsenal."

"Dear me," he exclaimed. "She did do well."

"Better than that, Peter; she found a local enthusiast who has information on all these things along the south coast and hopefully, he's coming round here with a map this afternoon. Would you like to be present?"

"Oh yes please."

"Right... Marjory should be back soon. Bring your tea into the study."

Studying the white board, the Vicar was unable to shake the prospect of the silo being the burial place. "How can we find out what happened in the end between Michelle and Mr Farrow, knowing that they're both missing?" the Vicar questioned.

"With difficulty... but I'd put my money on Michelle being the victim and Farrow sunning himself on some beach somewhere."

"On what?" the Vicar questioned again. "Didn't he lose all the money?"

"That's what we're led to believe, Peter. If you remember, I said he might have siphoned it off. Then there's the ransom money of course, five hundred thousand, if you can believe the housekeeper's story."

"Is it worth us digging further to find out?"

"Certainly not," Jack exclaimed emphatically. "I'm not doing all of Maitland's work for him, let him decide that. I'll make my recommendations and that's it."

"Don't tell me you're not the least bit curious, Jack."

"Peter... after the last case, I just want to find your hidden body."

"I know what you mean, Jack but sometimes I do get curious."

The Vicar sighed, "They're all so plausible, Jack," then looked at the board for a moment in silence holding his breath, then let it out with a gasp, looking as if he had an idea, "Of course, Jack... have you considered Michelle or Farrow aren't the victim's after all, but the killer's and that we have some other victim?"

"It had crossed my mind."

Before they were able to continue, the front door made its usual sound for this time of the year: an initial jolt as it stuck on the threshold.

"That'll be Marjory," Jack said.

"Hello, Reverend," she said. "Are you stopping for lunch?"

"Thank you, Marjory... my wife is still with her sister."

"Is this man from the library coming?" Jack asked.

"Yes, about four thirty, when he gets off work."

"Oh dear" the Vicar said. "I won't be able to stay that long. I have a choir rehearsal to conduct."

"Okay then, Peter, so you won't be able to meet this man about the silos?"

"No I can't, and I did so want to be in on that."

Jack left the Vicar studying the board and joined Marjory in the kitchen as she began preparing their lunch. "So how did you get on?" he said.

"All right, he seemed very interested. I didn't tell him about the body of course, only that something was hidden in one of the silos, and you would give him more information. I also told him you were a retired Superintendent, helping the police."

"Sounds good... the least he knows the better," Jack said.

"As it turned out I didn't need to; he knows all about you. You're quite famous Jack; everywhere I go people want to know how the Superintendent is doing. They know about your involvement with the Reverend's criminology group."

"Then he'll want to know why I want to see a silo."

"Well he didn't say as much, even if that is the case."

"Oh God, I can imagine what this afternoon's going to be like."

"Never mind, dear, I'm sure you'll cope like you usually do."

"Cope is the right word," Jack snorted, laying out the knives and forks. "I've dealt with all sorts in my time, but country folk are beyond me."

The afternoon turned out to be quite pleasant. The sky had suddenly cleared like it had the day they went to Eastbourne, leaving the sky a mass of brilliant blue.

Jack had decided to brush the last of the frost off the patio when Marjory appeared at the French windows. Beside her was a bald-headed man with a ruddy complexion in his mid-forty's, clutching a large cardboard roll.

She opened one of the doors and called out, "Jack... Mr Connery's here."

Jack propped his brush up against the wall and made his way to the open door. Mr Connery's eyes were shining moistly, either from the cold or his excitement in meeting the infallible Superintendent of Lower Cheedam.

Jack's first impression of people didn't let him down. As he removed his Wellingtons by the French windows he could hear the man going on about something with Marjory, his voice was hard and demanding; not easy to miss.

Marjory shouted out as she saw Jack pass the open hatch between the kitchen and dining room, "We're in here, Jack, where it's warm."

The sunburnt man greeted him with a firm handshake as he entered the kitchen and Jack took the opportunity to way him up. He looked as though he spent a lot of time in the open, and by the look of his hands; in a windy location.

He judged by Marjory's brief description when she returned from the library that his interest in conservation would account for that; being out on the moors and open beaches most of the time. He had already laid out the contents of the cardboard roll, a large survey map, on the kitchen table.

"Thought I'd get things all ship shape for when you came in Mr Hammond," he bristled, his eyes still sparkling, obviously not from the cold."

"Look we can't go on calling each other Mr all afternoon. My name's Jack and of course you know Marjory."

"Oh fine... they call me Greg," he said, followed by a forced laugh.

"Okay, Greg, it's very good of you to spare your time like this..."

"Excuse me, dear," Marjory interrupted. "I have to go out... I won't be long."

Jack followed her to the door. "I thought you wanted to be in on this?"

"He's insufferable, Jack... he's not the man I spoke to at the library."

"Okay, dear, that's fine," Jack answered.

"Goodbye, Greg," she said. "See you soon, at the library maybe."

"Yes, Marjory, I look forward to that."

Jack looked at the bald-headed man, thinking he would have to control him; otherwise they would be here all night. He had to resort to subterfuge to divert Greg's enthusiasm to his own ends.

"Greg, have I your confidence?"

"In what way, Jack?"

He fiddled nervously with the edge of his map, listening intently.

"Well can I confide in you and trust that it stays between us?"

"Oh yes, Jack, most definitely," he confirmed, taking on a new look of responsibility. Jack had won his first move.

"Right... first of all, Greg I cannot emphasise enough how grateful I am for your support in this, everything depends on your input. All the work we've done to date could be for nothing without your guidance in this last phase."

"Only glad to help."

His eyes seemed to sparkle more than ever, if that were possible, as he gradually became putty in Jack's hands. He knew his type; he had met enough in his investigations. They were insignificant people who had become fixed in a mundane existence, and usually resorted to exaggeration and constant reference to their expertise in a particular field to impress people.

"Now what I'm about to tell you is in strictest confidence, known only to Reverend Peter Jay, Scotland Yard and myself."

"I understand, Superintendent... I mean, Jack."

"Yes well I hope you do. I don't mean that in any derogatory sense," Jack pointed out. "I meant I hope you understand how serious it is to maintain secrecy."

"You can rely on my absolute silence, Jack."

Jack pushed him down in the nearest chair.

"Very well. The Reverends involvement in this will become apparent in time, all you need to know is that I am acting in this matter in the capacity of a Superintendent, working closely with Scotland Yard."

"I see."

"Good, I think we understand each other now."

"Oh we do, Jack, we do."

"I can't tell you the details leading up to your involvement, it's a need to know situation, but suffice to say we are looking for a body."

Shock suddenly crossed his face, "a body?"

"Yes... although we're not sure where."

"And you think it's buried in one of the Eastbourne silos?"

Jack mustered his best impersonation of an officer of the police.

"All the evidence points in that direction," Jack stated. "That's why I need you to help me check them out. You see... we can't progress in this case until we've eliminated these silos or discovered our body."

"What led you to think it was in a silo?"

"I can only say at this stage that we have reliable information."

"But I don't know how? They're all either locked up or sealed."

"Well let's hope it's not in one of the sealed ones... show me."

Greg pondered over the survey map where he had already marked the sites along the coastline looking over the channel. He took a red pen from his inside pocket.

"What are you doing?" Jack asked, looking over his shoulder.

"The sites with crosses are collapsed silos, taken over by concrete cancer. The circled ones are still complete but locked up to protect the public."

"What about the ones you haven't marked?"

"They're still in reasonable condition although under supervision."

"What exactly does that mean?"

"Well if you look at the map you'll see they're all in developed areas... like this one for instance on the main front opposite the Fun-Fare. This one has been turned into a museum, open to the public, so I doubt if anyone could get in during the open period; at least not to dump a body."

"So we've got three possibilities?"

"That depends on what this person wanted to do with the body."

"Good question," Jack said, remembering Samuel followed a particular way of dealing with the other bodies to ensure they weren't found.

The body in the unfinished underground tunnel came to mind.

"I suppose for the moment we should forget those, you're right, too much exposure, unless he found a way in without anyone knowing. No, let's concentrate on the locked ones that might still be okay but closed to the public."

He studied the notations on the map.

"It has to be a place where he can easily hide a body: a disused tunnel, a drain pipe... anything that would not be readily visited or checked." Jack continued.

"Well that rules out all these." He began changing circles to crosses on a good many sites, leaving a lot less than they started with."

"Wait a minute, why cross out all those?" Jack protested.

"Not suitable - they're only one chamber for a single gun emplacement."

"So... what difference does that make?"

"Well these others are cluster batteries."

"Explain," Jack said.

"They use one ammunition silo in a crescent arrangement: three guns usually. Between each gun runs a series of passageways, with offshoots to the common silo, which at one time had hoists rigged inside."

"And the others wouldn't offer the same opportunity?"

"No... they're totally featureless inside; a concrete box with holes in it. The gun was mounted on top, with steps down to this chamber where the shells were stored. The holes were for small arms should there be the need for close combat."

Jack looked at the survey map with the town of Eastbourne in the middle, where two of the gun batteries were open to the public. Greg's marked positions spread out either side, below the winding coast road as far as Beachy Head to the left and Langney Point to the right.

When Jack saw Greg slashing away the possible sites he was infuriated, but now it looked more orderly, he had rendered them down to no more than a few. This meant they could give more time to their initial search.

Luckily, in the ensuing conversation, it turned out that the following day was Greg's roster day off; Jack's cue to let him know he had been seconded to the ranks of head silo searcher. Jack wouldn't take no for an answer.

CHAPTER 24

Jack's first call the following morning was to collect the Vicar from the church, then on to the centre of town where he arranged to meet Greg by the pond. He was sitting in the local tea shop looking out of the window and when he saw Jack, he waved. Jack had already established with the Vicar that no introductions were necessary; he knew Greg from his many library visits. Jack pulled up alongside; then opened his boot for Greg to drop in the large back-pack he was carrying. He looked cheerful enough when he climbed in beside the Vicar, despite how cold it was.

Jack's earlier hopes for an uneventful journey had been realised. The motorway down to the south coast was dry and almost free of traffic; even the secondary roads on the outskirts of Eastbourne were good.

A brisk southerly kept the coast road clear and within the hour they were pulling off the road onto a small inclined side road to a picnic area above Beachy Head; looking out across the grey angry waves of a winter Channel.

The warmth of the car did not prepare them for the icy blast they faced when they stepped out into the open. Greg warned them what it could be like at Beachy Head; advising them to wear plenty of jumpers underneath their Parka's.

As they slung their backpacks over their shoulders the Vicar crossed himself and made a remark that was surely uppermost in their minds.

"Let's hope we're successful quickly Lord."

Jack laughed, "I'll say Amen to that, Peter."

Rather than take the easy route, Greg led them slightly upwards along a small natural path winding amongst the sand dunes and course grasses until they reached a small cliff with an outcrop of rock leading off to one side, which suddenly changed into a man-made slab of chipped concrete and rusting reinforcement.

"Here we are," Greg called out; pointing to the first of the marked batteries on the folded survey map he had hanging from his neck. They stood looking over the expanse of concrete that ran off below them and to their left. It was pitted with rusty holes where an iron cleat or other holding device had been embedded to retain the mechanism of the great coastal guns.

The salty fret kept the whole area free from sand, making it easy to see most of the foundation, except an area at the far end that disappeared under the eroding cliff. Greg had already moved on, he was beckoning them to a locked metal plate looking very much like a manhole cover.

"This is the way in," he pointed out, as he straddled the metal cover.

Jack thought it looked exposed as he jumped down alongside him, leaving the Vicar sheltering under the overhang.

"If this was where the guns were, why didn't they have any protection?" the Vicar shouted, shivering in the background.

"They did," Greg answered, pointing down to the jagged scar running around the leading edge of the platform. There was a two foot wide area of chisel marks on the flat concrete, along with molten stubs of metal reinforcing.

"It was removed long ago," Greg said. The council thought

these concrete pillboxes along the front were an eyesore."

He began unlocking the two large padlocks on the metal cover.

"How come you have a key?" Jack commented.

"This is a master key. As I said earlier, my group have to monitor these structures regularly from an environmental point of view."

He had difficulty lifting the heavy iron plate and needed Jack's help.

"This isn't original, is it?" Jack said.

"Good heavens no. Most of the wartime metal rusted long ago."

By now the Vicar had become curious enough to venture down onto the concrete platform and stood alongside Jack staring into the gaping black hole. Greg had already taken the torch out of his pack and was shining it into the pit. First on the iron ladder that was set into the wall nearest to them, then further down where they could see their reflection in the water below.

"It's got water in the bottom," the Vicar called out. "How deep is it?"

"That's why I told you to bring Wellingtons with you," Greg answered, starting to climb down. "It's usually no more than six inches or so."

"I hope not," the Vicar continued.

Jack turned to him before he followed Greg. "You can stay up here if you like, Peter, we don't all need to go. He paused a second with his hand on the top rung.

"It's hard to tell what's worse... standing up here in an icy wet gale or down in a damp watery hole." Jack didn't wait and carried on.

Once Jack's head disappeared below the surface and the Vicar realised he was alone, he quickly followed, trying to keep as close to Jack as possible. The water only came up to their ankles, and the ceiling was almost touching Jack's head.

"Is this all the light we have?" Jack questioned.

"Sorry," Greg apologised. "I'm so used to rummaging around in these places I forgot to use the main beam." He flicked a switch and the torch suddenly became a floodlight. "Is that better?"

"That's fantastic, Greg," Jack remarked. "I'll have to get one of those."

The first small room was suddenly filled with the bright light showing little of interest other than the graffiti that appeared to decorate every wall. It was the names and dates of those who occupied these defences from 1940 to 1944.

They stood silent for a moment, staring at the names of each soldier; they were as important to England's wartime history as the batteries themselves. In the far corner there was a dark opening, and as Greg described, it led to two more such rooms linked by a corridor with an individual shoot to supply ammunition to each gun.

The internal mechanism had been dismantled long ago, leaving only a gaping hole about a foot in diameter, and deep gouges in the concrete wall with traces of green paint, where a trolley had been dragged along carrying a shell.

With the aid of Greg's torch Jack stuck his head into each tube one by one, and other than a mass of roots invading the cavity through cracks, they were all empty, just as every other nook and cranny they found. There were no bodies here.

"Well that was a waste of time," he said, with the Vicar nodding in agreement. "Those were the shoots they used to bring up the shells weren't they?"

"That's right, Jack," Greg said.

"It's just that I don't remember seeing any covers up top where the guns were."

"Oh they're there," he said, leading them back to the ladder. "When they were working, the mechanism inside was like a small lift with a flap on top to stop people from falling in. When the gun was removed they just concreted the flap over."

On the platform again Jack soon found the tell tale circles Greg was referring to when he brushed the sand away from where the guns had been mounted. It was then that he appreciated Greg saying it would be impossible to hide a body down there.

Despite Greg saying he visited these sites regularly and had no difficulty using his master key, Jack could not understand why Samuel had used the word silo in his code; unless he had buried the body in one of the collapsed batteries.

By the end of the morning they had to get back to the car and have some hot tea from their flasks to warm them up, and a sandwich or two to stem their hunger. They were disappointed and beginning to think the whole exercise had been a waste of time.

As they rubbed the warmth back into their aching limbs, Jack started looking at some of the crosses Greg placed on his map; the less inviting sites, the majority on this side, and some over by Langney Point.

Greg reminded them that most had been filled in due to their dangerous condition, but bowed to Jack's determination not to give up on this, convinced the body was in this location somewhere.

There was just one more site at Beachy Head before heading around Eastbourne on the coast-road towards Langney Point. Greg was quick to point out that this one was exactly the same, but Jack was still determined.

The weather improved as they moved around the point. The sky was blue and cloudless, the sea was still breaking in a white foamy cascade across the foreshore, but not as menacing as it was above, and the air was crisp and salty. They scrambled down the soft sandy bank to the only intact site on this side, half buried amongst the sand dunes, with the same familiar concrete platform as the others.

Again, Greg was able to unlock the metal cover. Jack almost wished he hadn't; as this silo proved to be little different than the others. The three underground chambers left nothing for the imagination, except they were dryer with a better flow of air, but just as stark with nowhere to hide anything let alone a body.

"That's it," Jack cried. "They're all exactly the same."

The light from the open hatch up ahead seemed sufficient. But as the Vicar followed them down the narrow corridor he stumbled on something. It was soft, yet firm enough to unbalance him and he fell to the ground. Greg shone the torch down to the floor passed Jack's feet.

"Careful, Peter, we don't want any casualties this late in the game," Jack said, grabbing his arm, and helping him up.

"It's sand," the Vicar said, taking a handful and letting it slip through his fingers.

"Turn the light in this direction, Greg," Jack asked.

Sure enough, piled up against the wall was a mound of sand, which they must have passed the first time when they were in single file. Jack took the lamp and traced its path from the pile on the floor against the wall to the ceiling, where they discovered an air vent in the junction of the wall and the ceiling.

Jack was so concerned with all the water under foot, and the possibility of bumping into something, he omitted to look upwards.

"What's this," he said, looking in Greg's direction.

"It's a vent to draw the fumes out of the silo."

"Why didn't you tell us about this before?" Jack snapped.

Greg suddenly looked offended.

"I didn't know, Jack! I'm not an expert on these places, I'm just as surprised as you," he replied unapologetically.

"But you said it was to vent the fumes," Jack continued, a little upset that they missed this in the other silos.

"That's just a guess, Jack; it stands to reason this place would need to vent the fumes from the guns when they went off."

"Of course... you're right, sorry," Jack apologised.

"Never mind about that," the Vicar said. "Let's get out, you couldn't stuff a body up there anyway," he grabbed the torch from Jack's hand and waved it about in the vent, "See... nothing.

"All right, Peter, since you have the torch, you lead the way."

Outside, Jack immediately started to pace off the concrete slab from the hatch, unknown to them he did the same in the chamber below and was looking for the exit. They were puzzled as he paced out one coordinate and made a mark, and then paced out another, which led him into the encroaching dunes.

He frantically began brushing the sand down to the concrete, then stood up looking bewildered, scratched his head as he surveyed the steep bank in front of him, then walked back to the open hatch, and examined the area where the iron ladder was fixed into the concrete.

"What on earth are you doing, Jack?" the Vicar questioned.

Jack was going over the sums again in his head.

"I'm trying to find out where the vent comes out," he said. "When I didn't find it back there it threw me, until I saw how deep it is between the top of the slab and the underside of the ceiling. The other two also examined the slab; they hadn't noticed the two foot difference before.

"So you're suggesting the vent goes through this two foot of concrete?" Greg said, scraping the hardened sand away for a better look.

"Of course it would have to be this thick to carry the weight of the guns," Jack pointed out. "I reckon the opening is up there somewhere, "trouble is it's covered in a mountain of sand," he said climbing the dune.

"Be careful, Jack," the Vicar shouted. "It doesn't look very secure to me."

"Go over to where I was digging, Peter, so I can get a line on the vent."

"That's supposing the vent goes straight out at right angles," Greg chipped in.

Jack took a few minutes to reach the top after slipping back several times, forcing him to grab at nearby course grass to steady himself, then sat down and rested a moment to catch his breath.

He sat there looking down at the Vicar examining the surface in a line from his position, while Greg remained at the junction of the other coordinate. It wasn't easy with all the high grass blocking his view, until he spotted an indentation; much like the smooth crater left when the sand is running into a cavity of some kind.

The surface was steep and Jack decided to slide down the slope on his backside, digging in his heels to stop him from overbalancing. Finally he arrived at the piece of gorse next to the spot, and wedged his heels in firmly.

Once there he suddenly realised he couldn't see the indentation anymore and shouted down to the Vicar. "Peter... can you see an indentation by my feet?"

"An indentation?"

"You know... a crater in the sand."

The Vicar instinctively did as Jack had done earlier; he got down on his stomach and looked along the surface of the sand. "I'm sorry, Jack, I can't see a thing."

"Are you sure? When I looked down it was so obvious."

"There's too much grass in the way... can you clear some of it?"

"I don't know, Peter... it's taking me all my strength to keep my balance."

His back was now vertical, although at an angle to his legs, and as he leant forward to bring the grass within his reach, he began to overbalance and started sliding forward. Shifting his weight seemed to slow his decent until he was forced to open his legs; and that action stopped him dead.

As Jack maintained his position, for fear of starting his slide again, he noticed the sand suddenly began to pit in front of him. It started with a large circular impression that rapidly began to form an inverted cone in the middle. The slope was giving away under him as his weight pressed on the area, and the whole top surface started to slide further forward, prompting Greg to try and scale the dune.

Jack's foot suddenly became wedged on something hard, giving him the opportunity to use his hands to scoop away the surface around the object. A rusty shape about two feet square with sloping sides began to emerge. The more he removed the sand from its perimeter the more it began to resemble the roof of a house, and below that, the beginnings of a meshed grill.

"Come up here you two, I've found it," Jack shouted.

It took a little time as the Vicar had to take the long way round, but both were amazed at the sight of the metal housing he had uncovered. Jack had already removed the mesh and was anxiously looking into a dark shaft easily capable of holding a body. He looked up at Greg, grabbed the torch from his hand and pointed it down the shaft.

Good luck now was too much to expect, the shaft was empty.

"Bad luck Jack," Greg said.

"Well at least, Jack, you've established there is a place for a body, we just have to find the right one," the Vicar concluded.

"I knew it had to be something like this. Will I never learn? Every time this man has given us the impression he's buried the body in a specific place, when all the time, he's slipped it in through the back door."

"I don't follow you, Jack," the Vicar said.

"Don't you get it? – each time he's found a way to get the body into the chosen burial place from another entry point. I should have realised as soon as Greg had to use a key to get in... Samuel chose this place as an obvious subterfuge."

"Does this mean we have to dig up every site?" Greg asked.

"Ultimately we may have to, but let's hope we don't," Jack answered him.

"Oh, Jack," the Vicar exclaimed looking tired. "I earnestly hope we don't."

"Did he know this area?" Greg asked.

"I don't know, but he hasn't done anything yet without research."

"That's why I asked if he knew this area. Only someone who frequented these sites regularly would have known about this shaft."

The Vicar suddenly remembered something they found out earlier. "What if he went sightseeing when he was in Eastbourne, like he did in London?" he suggests.

"Go on," Jack said.

"Well I just remembered Samuel's taxi rides around Deacon's Hill, and thought what if he did the same in Eastbourne, and it brought to mind what Greg told you about the pillbox that was refurbished for the tourists."

"But I thought we agreed it was too public?" Greg interrupted.

"Wait on... I like the sound of this," Jack said. "Carry on, Peter."

"I didn't mean he actually decided to put his body there, of course he would need somewhere quiet. But he could have made inquiries about the possibilities in others."

"I like it," Jack exclaimed. "Let's get down there and see."

CHAPTER 25

It was lunchtime when Jack turned into the parking area near the pillbox and immediately a certain smell caught his nostrils: it was the irresistible aroma of fish and chips. The thought of a hot meal on the front was too tempting to miss and they all agreed, and followed their noses.

If it hadn't been for Jack noticing the long queue of day-trippers eager to experience what it was like to man one of the south coast guns trained on the open expanse of the English Channel, waiting for the imminent invasion of German barges, they may well have sat enjoying their fish and chips all afternoon.

"These were not to be confused with the smaller versions used to defend the coast from enemy aircraft," a middle-aged man vocalised, telling his captive audience about the history of the gun emplacement they were now occupying.

"You don't 'ave to tell me young man, I was in the 'ome guard on guns like these at Dover. We 'ad a lot of responsibility in those days," an old man spoke up.

"So you did, Sir, and I take my hat off to you," the guide said, removing his hat while everyone clapped; although it was obvious most were off the same coach.

This particular gun battery had been lovingly restored down to the camouflaged concrete, except for the addition of railings in dangerous areas. The tour included a demonstration of the artillery gun, which was still operational, at least as far as its movement was concerned, and culminated in a recorded blast. The interesting part came when the man lit a small tin of powder following the salvo, its fumes gave off an acrid smell of cordite, and Jack immediately reminded the other two of the reason they were here. As part of the show, Samuel would have experienced this also, and the following announcement that the fumes would soon be vacated through the silo's ventilation system, would not have gone unnoticed.

It was difficult in the confined space, with the number of people about, to get passed to investigate the silo below for themselves, so they had no option but to tag along and enjoy the tour.

The hatchway had obviously been adapted slightly to accommodate a safer stepladder; nonetheless only one at a time was able to descend into the well lit chamber below. Once gathered together they were shown the main shell store with the adjoining small detonator room, where the shells were primed before making their last journey on the trolley.

Jack pointed out the marks on the wall leading to the lift shaft where it was hoisted to the surface ready for loading into the breach of the gun; they were the same as the ones they saw earlier.

While the guide was explaining all this to the trippers, Jack and the others took the opportunity to examine the rest of the chambers, especially the vent to the surface, which in this case had been fitted with a modern fan to keep the air fresh for the tourists, and vent off any excess from the abnormal number of occupants.

Even so, some of the older folk were beginning to feel claustrophobic, and asked to be escorted back to the surface, tending to encourage those who were not really interested in large shells and things, to volunteer.

Jack took the opportunity while the guide stood to one side

to make sure no one was left behind, to ask him about the air vent; before it had been modified. He showed him his warrant card before he asked why they were interested.

"You appear to have a good memory," Jack started.

"You have to in my job," he replied, appearing to be proud of the fact. "I don't just look after the guns you know, I do several different guide jobs."

He started giving Jack his full itinerary until Jack prompted him.

"That would really stretch your memory," Jack continued. "Can you cast your mind back a few years ago?"

"Depends," he said, "on whether or not it's a regular thing."

"This isn't I'm afraid," Jack answered.

"Then have a go, see if it rings a bell."

"It would be a man on his own, probably tagged onto a group, so there's no reason for you to remember him. But sooner or later, like I did, he would have found a way of asking you about any other passages or side tunnels, even that vent up there."

"Mm," the man mumbled, "gazing studiously into space.

His eyes darted back and forth as he regressed back in time, until a glimmer of recognition crossed his face when he glanced back at the air-vent, and he anxiously clicked his fingers as if something was on the tip of his tongue.

"There... there was someone, I can't quite place his face. I see so many people each day, but I remember he was very interested in the build up of fumes from the gun blast. He didn't ask about any passages or vents, just what happened when the gun went off. Said something about studying respiratory diseases."

"Is that so?" Jack interrupted.

"Yes... I remember now. He was interested in where it came out."

"Can we go and see?" Jack asked.

"Of course, Sir. I've got to go and see what's happened to that lot anyway."

They followed him back up the ladder to the gun-deck above where another party was waiting for his tour behind a sign. He apologised, telling them he would only be a few moments, nodding his head to one side questionably at Jack.

"We shan't keep you long," Jack reciprocated.

The guide then stepped over the circle of railings and headed across the landscaping towards a group of shrubs on the right. He took one step onto the border, reached forward, and parted two small bushes, revealing a large square duct with the same roof like lid on top as the one Jack found earlier.

"There you are, that's what I showed him. He got really excited and asked if there were any more sites about. Which I thought was strange."

"Is this tour starting mate," a man called out gruffly from the entrance.

"Sorry... on my way," he shouted back. "I must go."

"That's fine thanks," Jack said, then grabbed his sleeve before he left.

"Sorry, one more thing... where did you send him?"

"Langney Point," he replied on his way back, and then turning said. "Oh, I just remembered, he wasn't alone, there was a young man in the car he went to... just opposite where you're standing."

Jack stood by the shaft trying to get his bearings; it was difficult with the shrubs almost covering it, even though it came up to his shoulders. The other two had moved off, Greg had returned to the entrance, interested in what the guide had to say, and the Vicar looked conspicuous, as he paced off the distance between the shaft and the opening to the silo.

"I don't think you'll find a body inside that one, Jack," the Vicar said.

"There's no harm in looking... actually I was trying to find out how it opened," he continued looking, "By the way... why were you pacing out the lawn?"

"I was curious to know if these things are all the same size, and if the shaft was in the same place as the one on the other side," he pulled out a small spiral bound notebook and pencil. "They are," he said, checking the measurements.

"I didn't see you write that down," Jack said.

"You don't see everything, Jack... you're not the only one who takes notes you know," he returned the pencil to the metal spine and put the book back in his pocket.

"Very good, Peter. I'm glad someone else is taking an interest."

It was ironical that Jack's car was standing in the same parking zone that Samuel used on that day, according to the guide. As the others got in Jack stood for a moment looking at the road sign, contemplating what Samuel was thinking that day. 'He would have turned round and followed the coast road out of Eastbourne on to Langney Point. But which silo did he choose: one that was almost intact, or one of the collapsed structures they hadn't bothered to consider?'

"You want to be to the right, Jack," Greg said.

"I was just wondering what Samuel was thinking," he said as he shut the door. "Okay, let's try and think this out as if we were Samuel. He was in the same position; he wouldn't just go off blindly."

"That guide said there was a young man waiting in Samuel's car," the Vicar reminded him, "which means our theory must be correct. Farrow must have hired him. More than likely Michelle Bailie was in the boot then, and they were looking for a place to hide her body."

"I don't think so, Peter... he would find his spot first."

"I suppose you're right."

"He was a professional, Peter... he would choose his killing place very carefully; not too far away from the hiding place, and certainly away from any prying eyes. He would need his own transport and something to wrap the body in; so there would be no trace of blood or other evidence."

"And the wrapping would have to be handy; not something he had to buy. And he would leave it with the body... if it was wrapped up tight enough it would easily fit inside one of those shafts. What do you think, Jack?"

Jack was surprised, "I couldn't have put it better myself."

Greg looked totally bemused. He hadn't been brought into anything like this before, and it was suddenly becoming interesting.

"I wish someone would tell me what's going on?" he said.

Jack suddenly realised he had overlooked Greg's presence. He had allowed him to hear too much already and it had to stop. "I'm sorry, Greg, but as I told you at the beginning, this was a 'need to know' situation. You just have to remember that your part in this is as an advisor on the silos and their locality. Okay?"

"I suppose."

"Are you still prepared to help us?" Jack asked.

"Yes of course I am."

"Good... now let's do what Samuel would; let's find the first site."

"Hold on, Jack," Greg said, how did he know? I had to show you on a map, and the guide didn't say he gave him directions."

"That's a good point, Greg," Jack agreed, "Would they be marked on a tourist map, like a relic or historic site?"

"I doubt it," Greg said.

"We can't afford to go off blind, Jack," the Vicar interrupted, "I'll ask the guide if you like. He may well remember something else."

"I agree, Peter... okay, if you want to chase him again, be my guest."

The Vicar made his way back to the pillbox as they watched

him from the car. There was another group of tourists gathering by the small gate, and he stood to one side knowing he wouldn't have to wait long, apologetically explaining to the people in front that he wasn't a tourist and didn't wish to jump the queue.

His pleas weren't necessary, one sight of his clerical collar and they were eating out of his hand, pushing him to the front, and offering him money, thinking he was collecting for charity. Jack and Greg couldn't help laughing, although they knew they shouldn't. The Vicar looked so embarrassed.

When the guide came back the Vicar asked, "Did you give the man directions."

"No I didn't... I didn't need to," he replied curtly.

"Why was that?"

"He bought one of our guide books," he answered, and reached over to a metal-framed turnstile carrying small paperbacks about Eastbourne and the gun battery. He picked out a red and blue book with a photo of the battery on the front titled, 'Eastbourne World-War-Two Artillery Defences', and handed it to him.

As the guide continued selling his tickets the Vicar quickly scanned the book, it looked just like what they wanted, and bought one. He then thanked the man and the patient tourists, and returned to the car waving it in the air.

"What's he doing now?" Greg exclaimed.

"He's obviously bought a guide book," Jack replied, laughing. "Why didn't I think of that, we probably didn't need you after all?"

Greg looked indignant, "I doubt it," he said.

When the Vicar arrived at the car he was excited, and passed the book to Jack as soon as he climbed into the front seat. Jack's sarcastic remark to shut Greg up was suddenly truer than he expected, he looked at it with utter exasperation.

After going to all this trouble with Greg and his survey map, here was a small book with all the sites marked on tiny maps, old photographs showing the original pillboxes and the men who manned them, accompanied with a detailed narrative on where the silos were, even down to the nick names they were given, such as 'Piccadilly', as shown on the photograph he was looking at.

Greg looked over his shoulder amazed.

"You obviously didn't know about this little gem," Jack questioned.

"Obviously not," Greg answered. "By the looks of it I wish I had, it has far more detail than I'm aware of."

"Well done, Peter," Jack complimented. "Now that we're armed with the same information Samuel had, let's follow the trail as he would have."

He started the car and the Vicar turned to the double-page spread showing a plan of the batteries on both beaches, ready to give directions once Jack rejoined the Coast-road outside Eastbourne.

Greg was still smarting from the discovery and sat in the back with his survey map spread out across his legs following the Vicar's remarks with his pen. He was surprised when he called Jack's attention to a small dirt track running off to the right, although it was marked, there was no battery in this vicinity.

"According to my map there's nothing down here," said Greg.

"Are you sure this is the way, Peter," Jack asked, getting worried when the hard surface turned into a sandy track.

"Well it is as far as this is concerned."

"That's odd, I don't have anything on my map," Greg commented again, trying to recoup some of his lost pride.

"Well I suggest you look again, Greg," the Vicar prompted, "because this guide definitely shows a site at the end of this track."

"But does it say the track is fit for motor vehicles?" Jack asked.

The wheels of the car were beginning to spin in the soft sand.

"Ah," came an exclamation from the back of the car. "I see... there appears to be a small path running down to the beach area with a site tucked into the hillside," Greg said, "I must have missed it."

"It doesn't matter now," Jack stated. "We're here... and by all accounts it's as far as we're going to go."

They got out of the car and Jack began checking the track. He dragged his foot around the front wheel and uncovered a hard surface about six inches below. "It's all right," he said, sighing with relief. "It's just a covering of sand."

There was no answer, and he looked around to see where they had gone. They had continued walking on down the track, and were standing on a curve frantically waving their arms above their head. They started shouting but Jack couldn't hear them above the whine of the wind coursing through the tall grass.

He jumped back into the car, started the engine, put it into third gear as if he was on ice, and slowly moved forward. They stood waiting for him, both giving him directions to turn right, and Jack pulled the car into what looked like a hard area cut into a copse of sea blown trees, and stopped alongside a concrete rubbish box.

As he stepped out of the car Jack noticed there was no wind here, the gnarled trees and the sandy cliff on the bend was protecting this small area that was obviously set aside as a car park.

"This is handy," Greg called out, as Jack walked over to him. "I thought for a moment there you were going to get bogged down."

"So did I," Jack said.

"I'm sorry, Jack, I missed this place altogether," Greg continued.

Jack wasn't really taking any notice; he was looking for the Vicar.

"That's all right, we're here now...where's the Vicar?"

Jack continued walking around the curve in the track, and beyond the blind spot of the cliff he saw the Vicar standing a short distance away looking towards the west. Greg joined Jack and they walked over to where the Vicar was standing, he was occupied by the sight of a large concrete structure backing into the cliff of sand.

"So you've found it, Peter?" Jack said.

The Vicar didn't answer straight away; he looked frozen, although he didn't complain. They were back in the wind again, a harsh, chilling wind that swept up the slope towards them from the open shore below, where the waves could be heard crashing ominously onto the shallow beach on the other side of the trees.

The sky was still bright blue as Jack assessed the time they might have left to search on the site, it wouldn't be long and they had to work fast. He didn't bother with the exposed area of the platform which once carried the pillbox, although parts of that structure could still be seen embedded in the cliff wall of hard sand. Instead he made his way up the incline directly above the hatch.

As Greg had explained earlier, this gun battery had long-since caved in on itself, evident by the filled in crack across the slab and the rakish angle at the other end. This explained the welded seams running around the hatch cover that Jack glanced at and quickly moved on. Greg's master key would be no use to them here.

"Where are you going, Jack?" the Vicar asked.

"Up top, like I did this morning, to find the metal air shaft," he said, trying to visualise the whole pillbox as it was in Eastbourne.

Although most of the platform was below the cliff, the fact that it still had part of its superstructure enabled them to work out how much of the hard sand was left lying on top, and how much of the battery had been destroyed.

As the Vicar climbed up to help Jack, Greg started to draw a floor plan of the battery in his notebook, remembering the paces Jack took to the shaft's entrance.

He then went over to the hatch by the sandy wall and waited for Jack's signal. Jack was on a steep exposed part of the hard sand escarpment, and it was slowly breaking away and slipping over the edge.

"Now, Greg, how far am I away from the hatch?" he shouted.

Greg leant up against the face and looked up at Jack, "I'd say about a pace to the cliff and another to where you are."

"Fair enough," Jack said, "That leaves me three paces to the junction."

"Shouldn't you be going the other way, towards the vent?" Greg said.

"How can I... it would mean climbing along the edge... it's not very safe up here. I'll be lucky if I can make the three paces before this lot collapses," he reached out for the next bush and took his first step. "You get on working out how much sand is on top of this thing."

"Okay."

Jack quickly stepped out his three paces as he had done earlier and stuck a marker in the sandy ground. It wasn't as hard as he thought. The surface he expected to break away under his feet turned out to be no more than a small slide of powdery sand pouring over the edge and down onto the concrete slab below.

"I'm coming, Jack," the Vicar called out.

The Vicar arrived from his longer route further over and supported Jack as he tried to steady himself, then they sat down for a breather.

"Is everything all right down there," Jack called out to Greg.

After a moment's silence they heard some coughing and spluttering.

"I'm all right... just."

Jack smiled at the Vicar, jumped up, and started pacing off the next co-ordinate towards where he guessed the shaft was located. He stuck a stick in the ground and with another started drawing a large circle around it.

"What are you doing, Jack?"

"I'm trying to locate the shaft."

"By drawing a big circle on the ground?" the Vicar questioned.

"Well it must be in this region," Jack said, pulling out the grass in his immediate vicinity. "Come on... give me a hand to clear this area... and keep a look out for an indentation... you remember."

The Vicar looked at the amount of grass in the circle, then got down on his hands and knees like Jack and started pulling, "I hope we're not wasting our time."

"Greg," Jack shouted, "how deep would you say it was?"

"I've already worked it out, Jack... about two feet."

Jack was now lying face down on the sand examining the surface in front of him, with no success; the previous tell-tale dimple in the sand signifying a cavity below was not there. There was nothing; he had to start pacing out the area again.

The Vicar sat back exhausted watching Jack pace out the coordinates over and over, each time with the same result, until he finally dropped down beside him. He reached over for a stick and started to draw a plan on the flattened surface between his legs, then studied it carefully, drawing diagonal lines from one coordinate to another.

"I wish I was good at geometry," Jack said.

"What good would that do?"

"It might help me find a path that would dissect the line of the ventilation duct. If I could find where the duct was I could work my way back until I found the shaft."

Greg had arrived by this time, and was standing silently looking down at them. He had something to say, but when he looked at Jack's disappointed expression he hesitated and pondered on the best way to tell them it was all for nothing.

"This one's different, Jack," he finally said.

CHAPTER 26

Jack was reaching the point when he would happily admit defeat and make his call to Maitland; the police could take it from here. But he remembered the smug look on Maitland's face when he, rightly or wrongly, looked back on their time together as green constables and came up with the idea he was top dog.

"What do you mean different?" he shouted.

"Well... when I started pacing the slab off it didn't add up. When I saw you standing there, and I was on the other side of the platform, I realised you were too far forward... so I did some sums. I think this one only had two guns. I'm sorry, Jack, I should have realised by the size of the slab."

"How much difference would that make?" the Vicar asked.

"At least another chamber."

"That means we could be at least ten feet out," Jack shouted.

The Vicar stood up and walked over to where he could look down on the slab.

"There you go again, I thought you were going to think like Samuel, but you're following your policeman instincts again," he said.

"You're right, Peter... thanks for reminding me," Jack agreed. "So why don't you give it a shot for a change; pretend you're Samuel.

"I can't think like Samuel, Jack, at least not the one that's an assassin."

"What do you mean assassin?" Greg questioned, becoming more confused with each new revelation: although he had given no thought to how they died.

Jack struggled to his feet and started brushing the sand off his clothes. From above the dune he could see across to the point and the dark clouds that were racing towards them, warning him that their time was running out, and there was no time to explain or come up with a new plan.

"That's not important, Greg, what is, is that we do something quickly before we lose the light. I don't want to come back here tomorrow," Jack called out. Then looking at him, a silly idea crossed his mind. "You've listened to what we've said about Samuel, so why don't you have a try?"

Greg looked surprised, yet he felt flattered that Jack should ask him.

"Okay... I'll give it a go," he said, scanning the site. "Since we have no co-ordinates for a two gun site let's look at the problem in reverse, let's imagine he found the shaft, and dumped the body; what would his first priority be?"

"Fill the hole back in?" the Vicar answered.

"Yes, but look around you, the battery was built into the side of an outcrop of sandstone amongst some dunes. So it's a pretty good bet that the shaft was brought up on the other side of the rock face, which at the time was probably a hill of sand."

"Sounds good, Greg," Jack said, starting to get his drift.

They studied the terrain surrounding the remains of the pillbox, towards the demolished side where the hatch entrance was, and could see there was nothing to hold the sand, instead it drifted over the slab as it probably had done since it was built, forming a mound in front and a constant cascade of loose material above.

On the other side, where the structure was positioned up against the rocky outcrop that protected the upper level of the pillbox from erosion, a very hard layer of sand had developed, and was being held together by a dense cover of gorse.

"We need to test the ground above the cliff," Greg said.

Greg pulled out one of Jack's markers and began testing the area between where Jack thought the shaft was and the defined line of gorse bushes to their left. At first the stick entered the sand without any effort, and was so loose he almost overbalanced.

Then the next jab was different; so abrupt that the stick snapped in his hand.

Jack and the Vicar looked on in interest as Greg scraped away the sand until he came across the edge of the sandstone supporting the remains of the concrete pillbox. This meant they now had the confines of the two-gun battery, and the air-shaft had to be somewhere between where he stood and the edge of the overhang.

He looked over at the other two, supposedly enjoying their break, with an exhilarated expression on his face. He hadn't found anything yet, but it looked a much more promising place to start. Jack groaned and grabbed his back, then reached down to help the Vicar to his feet, and they carefully made their way to the edge of the gorse where Greg had started prodding again. Amongst the gorse shrubs, he came across an unnatural cluster of boulders.

"There!" Greg shouted, pointing to the rocks. "Look how neatly they're all piled up under the shrubs."

"They could have rolled there," Jack said.

"What on top of each other?" Greg emphasised.

As all three crawled down to the edge of the undergrowth it became more evident how a few years of invading vegetation could totally wipe out any sign of human intervention; or deliberate camouflage.

"This hasn't been disturbed in ages, Jack, we must have the wrong spot," the Vicar commented, trying to brush aside the prickly spines that kept catching his Parka.

"That's exactly what Greg's talking about, keep going."

They pulled at the vegetation that was binding the boulders to the hard compact sand, even clearing a few gorse branches in the process.

"My environmental colleagues would go crazy if they saw this," Greg said.

Finally they dug around a group of boulders close by. They were big but manageable, and they found they were easier to slide than lift. As they did so, the largest suddenly began to slide away from their grasp, gathering speed quickly, as the sand below started to break up.

Rivulets of shifting grains cascaded down between the gorse bushes and poured over the edge of the mound, taking them by surprise, forcing them to seek a more secure footing and wait until everything had settled.

It didn't; they had started an avalanche. The drier sand continued to break away between the smaller rocks supporting the boulders, and once they were loose the whole structure collapsed.

They moved to higher ground and waited. Jack looked skyward, he was more concerned with the weather and the dark, threatening clouds that had now moved out to sea, and he thought they might make it yet; unless storm clouds turned back on them.

By now the river of sand and rocks had almost stopped, and the deafening explosions of boulders impacting on the concrete slab below had ceased, until all they could hear was the gentle clatter of pebbles on metal.

"What's that?" Jack said.

He was the nearest and heard the sound distinctly.

"Metal, Jack," the Vicar followed. "It was metal."

They all sat back and waited, their feet embedded into firm ground, their hands grasping tufts of course grass, listening to the last of the loose pebbles chattering as if they were passing over a tin roof.

Jack moved forward not realising that a wedge of hard sand had moved in behind the shifting boulders, and a trench opened up in front of him as the loose section slipped away over the edge.

Again they waited, until to their amazement, a square rusted lid was exposed. The Vicar was the first to speak, "It doesn't look very natural, does it?"

"That's just what I was thinking," Greg said.

"Don't move anyone," Jack said. "Let it all settle down."

The pitched lid of the shaft stood about a foot out of the sand, enough to expose the meshed panels on all four sides. Satisfied the worst was over, Jack eased his way down slowly to the front face, resting his feet up against it. He stopped, as if waiting for something else to happen.

While Greg moved closer to the other side the Vicar was satisfied to wait where he felt safe for those dreaded words: The body's here.

Greg was the first to speak, after rubbing away the sand that was clinging to the mesh on his side. "It's only sand... it's full of sand."

Jack wasn't jumping to any sudden conclusions; he reached over to one of the gorse bushes, tore off a branch and stripped it of its leaves, then began poking the end through the mesh to dislodge the packed sand inside.

As he worked his way diagonally down the mesh, he suddenly became interested in a specific area and started digging deeper; twisting the branch back and forth. As he did so, he caught Greg's interest, and in turn, the Vicar's curiosity.

"What have you found?" Greg asked.

"It's a piece of green carpet," Jack reported, reaching into his pocket for his trusty Swiss multi-bladed knife.

"I've got some too," Greg said.

Jack undid the screws holding down the lid on his side, and then passed the knife over to Greg to do the same on the other, until they were all removed. But still Jack couldn't lift the lid, even with Greg tugging on his side, so he started kicking the shaft with his foot to loosen the rust.

After a short rest they tried again, first pulling one way then the other, until it gradually started to give way. When it finally broke free they realised it was too heavy for them to hold and they let it slip down one side of the shaft wall towards the slope. They feared it would start another avalanche, but it didn't, it had lodged against a gorse shrub and they breathed easy again.

"At last," Jack shouted, as he rested his weight against the metal casing and peered inside. "It's caked solid with sand. I wonder if it was placed there deliberately or did it just drift in over the years."

"Sand is terrible stuff, Jack," Greg said. "It gets in everywhere."

They both reached into the two-foot square chamber and began scooping out the compacted sand with their hands while the Vicar watched from above. He was standing up trying to see what they were doing, even though he didn't really want to see the body. They were up to their elbows and were so preoccupied they didn't notice the sand had started to run away from their feet again.

"Hold on, Greg... I don't know about you, but either this shaft is getting higher or I'm sinking," Jack said, grabbing hold of the top and pulling himself back up to the front face. Greg did the same and they clung there waiting for it to stop.

The Vicar slid down the slope on his bottom and stopped

when he hit the mesh front between Jack and Greg. "It's the loose sand around the bottom of the shaft," he called out, trying to steady them. "Let's see what it's like down here."

He leant forward to where Jack's right foot was still sinking precariously into the shifting sand, and started to dig into it to see how deep the loose sand went. Two or three inches below he discovered it was quite hard and guided Jack's foot onto it.

Jack swivelled his left foot over to give him room to shift his balance, as the Vicar waited for him to transfer his full weight. It was okay, but Jack was a little lower. He had lost his reach advantage and was clinging onto the top rim of the shaft by his elbows. Greg had managed to wedge his feet onto the rocky outcrop.

"Peter... can you make your way back up to where you were?"

"Yes I think so, Jack... why?"

"I can't reach any further into the shaft from here so I'll just have to work my way around to the front. What about you, Greg?"

"I don't seem too bad on this side, it's rocky here. You climb round."

The Vicar moved back to the nearest bush and anchored himself there as Jack took the weight on his right foot and moved his left nearer the middle of the front face of the shaft. By now he was spread eagled on the corner of a two-foot square metal frame and he was running out of breath.

He rested a moment then lifted his right foot and swung himself around to the front. He was a lot higher now and was able to reach further into the shaft than Greg, so he told him to hang back and support him so that he could use both of his hands.

With more stability the going became a lot easier and the green pile of a good quality carpet slowly began to appear. It was a plain carpet with a short, plush pile and as Jack carefully scraped away the packed sand and forced it out through the open mesh he began to reveal an area about the size of a football. It was the top of the carpet, with two leather-bound edges folded over each other.

"It's a car carpet," Jack exclaimed. "The type you have in the boot."

He turned and looked at Greg and the Vicar; they were too concerned with who might be inside the carpet to see the anticipation on his face. Jack took hold of a leather bound edge and gradually started to peel back the stiff corner.

A strange musty smell emanated from the wrapping, it was damp and clammy. It was a smell he knew well, and it made him sick to his stomach. Not because he was squeamish, he had seen too many corpses for that, but because he felt saddened at finding another of Samuel's victims.

Greg turned away with a shudder, not realising the full impact of the short dark hair Jack had uncovered. It was his first corpse and he was suddenly sick. Turning his head away from Jack for fear he would catch it in the wind.

"Man or woman," the Vicar shouted.

"It's a man," Jack said.

The dark clouds Jack saw earlier did turn inland and were now upon them. It was difficult to see what was taking place on the small parking area at Langney Point.

Jack's car was no longer alone; there was an ambulance, a small rescue Land Rover and two police cars, all casting their lights towards where a group of helmeted absailers were operating their hoist.

Inspector Maitland was standing beside his car talking to Jack, Greg was enthusiastically watching the police lower the carpet-wrapped body to the medics below and in the light from the open back of the ambulance stood a solitary figure preparing himself for the 'Last Rites'.

"Well Jack you appear to have accomplished what you came here to do, maybe you can tell me who it is we have wrapped up in that carpet?"

"At this moment I don't know, Inspector," he replied. "I expected to find Michelle Bailie in there; everything pointed to her being the victim."

"So who do you think it is?"

"At a guess I'd say Jeffery Farrow, the Fund Manager, but our investigations indicated he went abroad, unless someone else used his passport."

Jack's thoughts passed over the possibility of Samuel using the passport somehow to situate Farrow out of the country and give the impression that Michelle was the victim. "Very clever," Jack said.

"Pardon... who's clever?" the Inspector asked, still watching his men.

"Michelle... here we were thinking she was the victim taken in by Farrow, when all the time it had to be her scheme and he was the victim. She must have hired Samuel to get rid of him after he gathered all her husband's money together. Probably they were conspirators all the time; until she had access to the funds."

"Nasty woman by all accounts," he commented, not taking his eye off his men. "They've got the body out; shall we go and see?"

The Inspector introduced Jack to the doctor who had been waiting to inspect the body; he was a young man and didn't look particularly interested in the proceedings. For some reason forensic pathology didn't appeal to him, he revealed to Jack in passing, he was more interested in the living.

Jack didn't question the Inspector's choice of personnel as they walked over to the ambulance. The Vicar was sitting to one side, not able to watch the unwrapping, and far enough away to avoid the smell.

"Are you ready for me now, Jack?" he said.

"Wait until he's bagged, Peter, then you can do your thing,"

Jack said, as he passed with the Inspector, taking out a hanky and covering his nose and mouth.

"What's he all about?" the Inspector asked.

"That man, or should I say Vicar, is what all this is about. Without him we would never have known about these bodies. He needs to read this man his Last Rites; when you're finished of course."

Inspector Maitland glanced over towards the Vicar with little interest.

"I don't have any problem with that."

They watched as the doctor began opening the carpet that wrapped the body. It had acted as a preservative, keeping out the air, and contributing to the mummified state the corpse was in; in any event it was still a nasty sight.

Greg took the long way round the back of the ambulance to sit by the Vicar, he had had enough, and they both sat quietly while the specialists got on with their gruesome procedure. Forensics came up with a damp flaky looking wallet; surprisingly Samuel had left it behind, indicating how confident he must have been.

The Inspector examined the contents through the plastic bag it had been placed in. It definitely belonged to Jeffery Farrow, little had been touched: the usual driving licence, photographs, credit cards and money were still intact.

"Just a minute," Jack said, watching what he was doing. He reached across to the photograph of a woman. Smoothed out the plastic, and muttered that it looked very much like the photo he saw at Michelle Bailie's house. "It's Michelle."

"Well your guess was spot on, Jack... it's Farrow all right. Of course we'll run the usual checks but it looks a formality. All that's left now is your statement on what all this is about, just to clean up the record you understand."

"Of course... although I shall have to contact Scotland Yard first."

"Why the Yard?" he said.

"I didn't want to scare you off, so I kept it until the end."

Maitland looked suspicious," I suspected something wasn't quite right when that Inspector Binstead introduced us. So what's the problem?"

"Samuel Alluche, the killer, was in fact a known assassin. He's been causing havoc in Europe and to be honest, he's an embarrassment."

"You don't have to say any more, Jack. If MI6 is involved in this I don't want to know. You make your report to them."

The remains were carefully separated from the carpet, which was left on the blue tarpaulin for further examination, and placed into the body-bag that was already laid out on a stretcher, before the medics carried it to the ambulance. Jack looked across to the Vicar for a sign that he was ready and he nodded his head.

"At your leisure, Jack," Inspector Maitland said, as he climbed into his car. "But don't leave it too long, the Chief Super likes things all neat and tidy."

"I heard that," said Greg, standing close by, "They don't look as if they're going to leave the site neat and tidy, have you seen the mess they've made?"

Jack looked up to where the shaft was still exposed, standing further out of the sand now, with police still tramping through the gorse, and the men who had erected the hoist, scaling up and down the steep overhang above the slab as if they were enjoying a spot of abseiling.

"Well at least they had the good sense to put the lid back on," Jack said.

"I suppose so," Greg commented, following Jack back to the car.

"Look, Greg... a few good storms and you'll never know anyone was here," Jack assured him, noticing the Vicar sitting in the car with his legs outside, looking terrible.

The ordeal had taken a lot out of him, especially this last one, and Jack thought he probably wouldn't get over it for a long time; if he ever did.

"I think it's time we left," Greg said.

"Yes you're right, there's nothing here for us now. How about you, Peter? Shall we go home?" Jack questioned getting into the car beside him.

"What's that, Jack?" he replied; miles away.

"Just pull your legs in, Peter, we're off."

It was dark by the time they got back to Lower Cheedam, and Jack was the first to speak. No one had uttered a word all the way back, Greg had closed his eyes almost immediately and was breathing heavily, and the Vicar was still staring out of the window as he had done for the past hour.

On entering the village Jack stopped by Greg's car. He looked apprehensive as he shook their hands, "Jack I've been thinking about this all the way back... will these MI6 people want to speak to me?"

"No, Greg... as I said earlier, it's all on a need to know basis. I shouldn't have told you the little I did; so I won't be telling them about you. The only way they will find out is if you blab your mouth off."

"Oh I won't tell a soul, Jack... I promise."

"I hope not. If you do it will get you in a lot of trouble."

Greg nodded his head, smiled at the Vicar and made for his car.

"Don't you think you were a bit had on him, Jack?" The Vicar said.

"The fear of MI6 should keep him quiet."

Jack was interested to know if his wife was still away and when the reply was a muted yes, he asked him to stay for dinner; he knew Marjory would be pleased.

They both laughed as they watched Greg turn off in the opposite direction, as Jack pulled away from the circle around the pond and headed up the hill.

"What's up with the Reverend," Marjory asked Jack after they dumped him in front of the fire in the lounge.

"He's suffering jet lag," he replied taking his Parka off.

"Jet lag?" she called back at him, clearing all the scattered Wellingtons and things to one side, and placing the Vicar's black satchel on the hall stand.

"You know what I mean. Now it's all over, the stress of it all has hit him. That's why I asked him back here... this last one was the worst."

"Was it? You poor things. Of course he can have dinner here."

"I was thinking of getting him drunk and tucking him up in the spare room."

"I don't mind him staying, Jack, but getting him drunk, isn't that a sin?"

"I can see you don't know much about the clergy."

"Oh dear," Marjory said, rushing into the lounge. "We've left him sitting in front of the fire with his Parker on."

By the time Marjory was putting the dinner on the table, the Vicar had recovered sufficiently to be cognisant with what was going on around him; supported by two glasses of Jack's best port. He could not be tempted to take a whisky, even for its medicinal value, but port was different. He didn't look upon it in the same light as an alcoholic beverage; more a drink of sustenance. Jack was silently amused, while Marjory looked on with frowns of uncertainty.

"What have you been doing, Jack, he's positively tipsy."

"Merry I think is a better word, and I didn't do anything, he

317

was the one who chose the port... remember?"

"I apologise, Marjory, that was a marvellous dinner and here I am spoiling it. I think I'd better go to my room and sleep it off." the Vicar said.

"You haven't done any such thing, Reverend."

He started to stand up unsteadily until Jack pushed him back into his seat.

"No you don't," Jack interrupted. "That was an expensive port I gave you to cheer you up, and you're damn well going to enjoy it."

"Jack, that's uncalled for," Marjory said.

"No, Marjory Jack's right, but I don't know how to shake all these doubts out of my mind, I keep wondering if I did the right thing."

"You need a nice cup of tea," Marjory said, getting up and yanking her head to one side for Jack to follow.

"I'll give you a hand, dear," he said, getting up.

In the kitchen Marjory turned to Jack and asked if he had talked to the Reverend about the real Samuel yet and if not... why not?

"You know I have... you were there."

"But you didn't tell him everything."

"He's suffered enough... I'm not putting him through it again."

"He needs a conclusion to this jack."

"Marjory... he has one. He's fulfilled his promise."

CHAPTER 27

Two weeks later Jack decided it was time to set things straight with the Vicar. He was still unsure how to, or whether he was wise in doing so, nevertheless the Vicar could not go on without knowing the truth about the man he had spent so much time with during his prison visits.

On his way from the lichgate down to the church Jack's attention was drawn to a movement on his right, which he instinctively investigated. It was the Vicar and his trusty deacon, Mr Threasher. They were in deep conversation, evident by the swirls of gaseous vapour drifting from their mouths.

"Don't tell me," Jack called out as he reached them, their arms gesturing this way and that. "You're not counting stones again?"

The Vicar turned to see who it was while the deaf deacon continued unaware of Jack's presence. "Oh, Jack, what a nice surprise," he said, removing a glove to shake his hand. "I was beginning to think we weren't going to see you again."

"We?"

"Yes... Janet, myself and the others. We're still meeting as a church committee, even if not as the criminology society any longer."

"I wondered if you got back together."

"Oh yes, Jack... we're still good friends."

Mr Threasher now realised Jack was with them and was trying

so hard to pick up their conversation.

"You continue here Mr Threasher, I need to talk to Jack," he told him loudly, passing his note book over to him. Then taking Jack's arm he directed him towards the path leading back to the church.

"This is not a casual visit... is it, Jack?" he questioned.

"I'm afraid not, Peter. Although I had second thoughts on whether I should upset you after all this time, I can't close this until you're aware of the truth."

"Don't be fooled by outward appearances, I still have some way to go," he replied quickening his pace. "Let's get into the warmth and you can tell me what it is that's kept you away from us all this time."

"How did you know?"

"I may not be as good as you at solving crimes, Jack Hammond, but I think I know a little more about human nature, especially when someone is struggling with something unpleasant they have to tell another."

In the comfort of the vestry Jack sensed the Vicar was still hiding behind the protection of his own well-ordered, acceptable account of what they had been through these past weeks.

"Peter?" Jack faced him eye to eye, his reaction to this question was vital. "I've told you things that I thought you could handle, and I've also held things back. How much did you pick up along the way?"

"To be honest, Jack, I must admit I shut myself off most of the time."

"I thought as much," Jack said, contemplating where he should start and how much he should tell him about Samuel's past.

"Jack... I've learned the wisdom of your decisions, even if I didn't agree with the way you executed them. Now you've made me aware of this untruth, as you say, do you think I could live with that any better than the truth itself?"

Jack had struggled so long with this, giving Marjory the excuse that the Reverend wasn't ready, when all the time it was him that wasn't ready.

"I don't know what the truth is any more, Peter. Do you remember when I told you Samuel was only a nick-name?"

"Yes... you said it was to protect him in prison."

"That's right... and do you recall me telling you Samuel's real name was George? and that he had a twin brother... and his name was Samuel?"

Jack could see the recognition on his face; along with confusion.

"I recall something about George being Samuel's brother."

"Peter... I need you to understand this. It was George you visited in the prison. It was George who told you about the bodies and it was George you promised to find them and say the Last Rites over."

"Yes, Jack... it's all right, I remember all that."

"Then do you remember me telling you and the others it was Samuel who was the assassin... not George."

"He was innocent after all."

"I'm afraid not, Peter."

"What does that mean. You just said..."

"You're not listening to me, Peter. Do you remember Dick telling us he saw a man sitting on a bed with a gun... loading it with bullets?"

"Yes... of course."

"Well I think that man was Samuel and George was in the room with him."

"Dick didn't see anyone else."

"I know he didn't... but Inspector Bridger found the gun that killed Samuel and it had George's fingerprints on it. That's why he was sent to prison."

"They didn't convict him, Jack... he was sent away for psychiatric observation."

For some reason Jack could not get through to the Vicar. He preferred to think it was Samuel he knew and he was wrongly accused of killing that man.

"All right, Peter. The evidence is debateable anyway but the facts show George held the gun that killed Samuel. Now I would prefer to think Samuel told his brother about his life as an assassin. About the open killings and the hidden killings, and George couldn't stand it anymore. So when he saw Samuel was about to kill again, he picked up the gun and fired."

"But what about the shoebox... and all the clues?"

"I think that was George's way of putting things right. At least the ones he knew about. For some reason his confused mind placed the burden on him, and so that he would not incriminate himself, he chose you to do it for him."

"And the clues?"

"I don't know, Peter. I think his brother had a need to absolve his deeds by creating a code to show where the latest victims were buried; and at the same time incriminate the ones who hired him."

The Vicar's expression changed to one of contemplation. "Do you think we'll ever get over this experience, Jack?" he asked.

"I can't speak for you, Peter. As far as I'm concerned it will join the queue along with all my other experiences."

"Yes... I was forgetting this was nothing new to you."

"It was certainly stimulating."

"That's an unusual thing to say, Jack."

Jack laughed, "Not really... this last eighteen months since I retired have been a bit of a drag. Marjory was beginning to call me an old slouch... and she was right. But these last few weeks have stirred the old grey matter. I feel alive now... and do you know, I'm sorry it's all over. What about you?"

"Well I suppose I'm glad I saved those peoples soul's and was able to give them their Last Rites so they can enter the Kingdom of Heaven," he paused waiting for Jack to say something, he didn't. "By the way, how do we really know which twin was which? I presume after all this someone has taken the trouble to find out?"

"Oh that's easy," Jack said. "Samuel, the assassin that is, had a scar on his forefinger. It was on his service record and his autopsy report. And I might add, for the record, that's what Dick saw when he touched the cartridge, if you remember."

"I do, Jack... I think it was that vision, more than anything else that turned him against the investigation."

"Dick had other problems too; he just couldn't sort one from the other."

"True, Jack," he agreed. "I felt sorry for him, I must try and help."

"Sometimes, Peter people don't really want any help, they want someone to listen, maybe even pass a comment, but not help. I think that was the case with George. We will never know whether or not he knew what he was saying, or frankly whether he knew he killed his brother."

The Vicar decided it was time he made a drink and turned to Jack as the kettle was boiling. "I was thinking about Michelle the other night when I was finally trying to explain to my wife what I had been doing all these weeks.

"What were you thinking about her?" Jack said.

"Oh... just where she was, wondering what she was doing right now."

"Sitting in a cell in Vienna no doubt... waiting for her extradition."

The Vicar looked surprised as he set the mugs of tea down on the table.

"I beg your pardon?" he said. "In Vienna you say?"

"Yes... Inspector Maitland rang me. He said they found her and he went across to see her. Apparently she made a full confession once she knew we had uncovered the body. She said she found the burden too much."

"And?" the Vicar questioned, not allowing Jack to take a breath.

"And what?" Jack cracked back.

"You know... the confession of course."

"Oh you want all the gory details do you?" Jack jested with him.

"Well the details, you can leave the gory bits out."

"All right, Peter," Jack said, trying his tea. "It appears her husband found her intelligence stimulating to say the least. He was jealous; marrying her more to control her than to make use of her ability. It was as if he wanted to own her, lock her up and show everyone how an old man was able to attract a beautiful young girl. Being an accountant she had big ideas about increasing his already substantial fortune, but he rejected her suggestions, relegating her to a lesser role than she was used to.

"After a few years she grew tired of his game and decided to teach him a lesson. She hunted amongst her many financial contacts in the city until she found Jeffery Farrow, a junior Fund Manager: a glossy character with little potential. She schooled him under the guise that she was infatuated by his charms, until she was ready to set her plan in motion. He was to apply for the job she had arrange with Peak, Matthews and Timmings, knowing he would ultimately draw attention to himself, and her husband would become interested in his investment ability."

"I've heard about that type of woman," the Vicar commented.

"That sounds like the voice of experience, Peter."

"I meet all sorts in my vocation, Jack."

Jack smiled, and then continued. "Of course she was the

324

brains behind his ability, capturing her husband's greedy instinct at first, little knowing Farrow was only a mouthpiece, and slowly siphoning off the funds into a Swiss bank account."

"Wasn't Farrow aware of what she was doing?" the Vicar asked, sounding as though he was beginning to feel sorry for the man.

"Evidently not, at least there's no evidence to prove that, unless he became part of the charade. Anyway, eventually she orchestrated her husband's stress, by causing tension between him and Farrow: dropping innuendoes regarding the security of his investments. You know the outcome, her plan was working perfectly: he had a stroke that ultimately killed him."

"What happened then?"

"She hired Samuel, through a source she would not divulge, to set up a trail of suspicion that she might be the victim and Farrow the guilty party. She persuaded him to believe things had gone wrong and he had to get out of the country immediately and she would join him later. Samuel had already obtained his passport with the excuse he was getting the name changed, but instead he kept it for himself and substituted his own picture."

"That's what fooled us, Jack," the Vicar interrupted.

"It did, she was very clever. She would have got away with it if George hadn't killed Samuel, setting off the chain reaction that prompted us to look for his victims."

"What about the ransom?"

"Oh yes, I asked Maitland that question myself. It appears Michelle became greedier than she should, nearly up-staging her whole plan."

"How so?"

"Well she found out there was a considerable amount in assets that could easily be converted to cash in an emergency as collateral. Her husband had set them up that way. Of course

Michelle needed an accomplice for this to work..."

"The aunt," he jumped in.

"How did you guess?" Jack laughed. "She would be in dead strife if what Michelle was doing came off, so she had no option but to agree. They arranged for this to happen when she came back off holiday."

"So did they do it?"

"No... that's why we didn't hear any more. They had to set this up with the police, the bank insisted. Then Inspector Buck had his accident. Yes it was an accident, and it was too hot by then to continue. The bank got suspicious when there were no further ransom notes, so that was it. That's why the aunt made such a fuss when she came back; she wanted to divert attention away from herself."

"What will happen to the aunt now?" the Vicar asked.

"I don't know, Peter... her age will be taken into account. Michelle's the one they'll lock up and throw away the key. Now Samuel's been identified as the killer, the fact that he's dead makes no difference as far as her part in this is concerned."

"Isn't it amazing what lengths people will go to?"

"What does that mean?"

"Well... if he hadn't treated her so badly, and made better use of her talents, she wouldn't have needed to do what she did."

"Yes, I suppose you could be right. It just goes to show, if you go back far enough you can always find the root cause to any situation," Jack reflected. "Although Peter... if you're born to be a criminal, it will always surface."

"You're so right, Jack; I can see it all now."

"That's good. I'm pleased you feel that way."

It was time to go. Jack had accomplished his goal and made his way out into the body of the church. He said goodbye to the Vicar and continued on up the aisle until he reached the open doors and the cold winter blast from outside.

Pulling his collar up around his neck, Jack turned and looked back towards the Vicar standing in front of the Alter. The ordeal had not changed him as Jack thought it might; he was himself again: hassling Mr Threasher as they returned to the routine of getting the church ready for the next service.

Jack noticed the curtain move as he opened the front door. He was sure Marjory must have been checking for his return; anxious to know how the Vicar responded to the awful events surrounding the Alluche brother's activities.

"How did the Reverend take it?" she said, helping him off with his coat.

"Let me get in the house first, Marjory."

"Sorry," she said, following him through to the lounge.

Jack went straight over to the drinks cabinet and poured himself two-fingers of whiskey. He took it neat. Marjory refrained from her usual scolding and waited for Jack to compose himself.

He looked at her and a warm smile began to light up his expression. "You have no need to worry about Reverend Peter Jay any more, Marjory. He was a little confused at the beginning, but when I took him through what happened slowly he soon got the picture. In fact he seemed relieved. I left him as cheerful as ever, busying himself, laying out the hymn books for the next service."

"Oh that is a relief. I was dreading him turning into a recluse."

"I can't see that happening, dear."

Marjory moved into the kitchen where she had started to prepare the lunch. Jack followed her and she noticed he had a fresh drink in his hand.

"And that's got to stop now, Jack. I put up with it while you were involved in that case, but now it's all finished I want you getting fit again."

"I just had to have a drink, dear. You don't know what it's like dealing with that man. And just think about it; no more criminology group."

Marjory stopped what she was doing and turned him to face her so that she could look into his eyes. "Is it all finished, Jack?"

"I don't know dear... we'll just have to see."

"Oh, Jack."

Melton Writers Festival - August 2016

About the Author

As a child in the London blitz, Charles Beagley distracted himself from the horror of his family's situation by making up stories or drawing. His eventual training was at Art School, which equipped him for the many years he spent working in advertising and design. He lived in London initially, did two years National Services in the RAF, worked in Ireland and Belgium and then set up a Design Consultancy back in England for twenty years.

He married and had two sons whose futures concerned him as things were grim economically in 1982 England. He jumped at the opportunity to move his family to Australia when he was offered a managerial position in design. During his years in England, his writing developed as he wrote promotional text and an occasional short story.

Since coming to Australia he has honed his skills, writing many fictional stories, mainly mysteries.

Last Rites is one such novel that mixes fact with fiction and unites a village to solve a dead man's promise.

OTHER TITLES BY CHARLES BEAGLEY

Blood Brothers
It takes a plane crash to bring two cultures together.

Who Goes There?
The "Troubles" in Ulster is a place where only villans and heroes survive.

The Sherwood Forest Man
The skeleton that revealed more than its ancient origin.

Cult Wars

In war, man reverts to his beliefs and they can prove far worse than imagined.

An Eye for an Eye?

The sequel to Who Goes There? When vengeance is all that's left.

The Blue Pen

Six individuals come in contact with a magical blue pen that changes their lives forever.

Carter's Boys

An assassin is determined to track down and kill everyone involved